The Light

Book:

Awakening

Christina L. Barr

Aciana
Hope ya enjoy!

Christ

2

To my family,

Whatever blessings I expect to have in this life born from God's will and my sheer determination, will never compare to the blessings he gave when he put me in such a loving family.

Thank you for your love and for investing in my future whether it was time, labor, or finances. I won't disappoint you, because you'll never stop believing.

Table of Contents

Prologue..5
Chapter One 6
Chapter Two 25
Chapter Three 35
Chapter Four 39
Chapter Five...61
Chapter Six 71
Chapter Seven...88
Chapter Eight..101
Chapter Nine...117
Chapter Ten 132
Chapter Eleven...140
Chapter Twelve...156
Chapter Thirteen 170
Chapter Fourteen 181
Chapter Fifteen 198
Chapter Sixteen..213
Chapter Seventeen 225
Chapter Eighteen 241
Chapter Nineteen 251
Chapter Twenty 269
About the Author 280

Prologue

Ever since the beginning, the world has been living in darkness. The people have forgotten how to hope, but some of the children still remember how to dream.

Chapter One

She had never known such joy and wonders. Many days she had looked up at the sky and wished that she would be able to touch its emptiness and taste its air. She would ask herself many questions as she matched their shapes to animals, familiar objects, and friendly faces. Did the clouds feel like cotton? Could she bounce and laugh the day away on their comfort? Could she hold one, press her face against it, and smother herself like it was a pillow, or would it wisp through her fingers until it was gone?

The answers were now hers. She could soar in the sky like a bird with nothing beneath her but the wind. She could run her fingers through the clouds as if there were nothing there at all. It was bittersweet to imagine something so vividly and have it be something completely different. It did not dampen her mood though. The sight was much too grand for that!

Below her was the earth arranged in patches of green and brown. From where she was, everything was small.

"Tice."

She heard a voice call out. It was so faint that she ignored it.

"Tice."

This time the voice was louder. She searched for it, but there was nothing in the sky with her but the clouds. Not even a bird could have been speaking her name—if it were even possible.

"Tice!"

Then a force grabbed her foot. It was as weightless as the clouds, but it felt like the hand of any human being. She clawed up at the sky and fought against gravity or whatever it was flinging her back to the ground.

She looked below her and saw the earth growing at an enormous pace—faster than what she should have been able to see. When she looked above her, she was no longer in the sky. Frightened and desperate, she looked back down below to a patch of land that had become a forest. Within that forest, there was a large stone house overrun and eroding away.

She fell within the roof like a ghost and inside a room where a young girl who mirrored her body from the tip of her nose to the tiniest toe was sleeping. She fell inside of her, and when they collided, they became one.

"Tice!"

Her shock was the only thing that kept her from screaming. She rose off of the floor and threw her blanket off of her. She observed her tiny fingers to make sure they were her own. They were just as pale and tiny as ever. There was no way that they belonged to anyone else. She felt her face next. It was still a chubby baby face stuck on a thin little body. Then she pulled her hair to her eyes. It was still colorless.

Everything was in perfect order!

"Are you alright, Tice?" The voice that had called to the young girl belonged to her friend. She was just as small as she was, but she was full of colors.

Tice was going to speak out a response, but decided to nod instead.

Her friend smiled. "Good. Your brother and the rest of the older kids are back with food."

A smile wrapped around her entire face. "Finally!" She jumped up in excitement, paying no mind to her sore back from a cold night on the hard floor. She missed her brother and wanted to tell him of the things she had done while she was asleep.

She joined a rush of children as she left her bedroom and ran down the stairs. Tice grabbed a hold of the rail and let the bigger kids pass. She was clumsy and didn't want to take the risk of being knocked over.

As she held on, she stuck her head through the wooden beams to see the children crowding around two boys who were beginning to fight. One of them was her brother.

She gasped and let out the biggest scream she could. "Riss!" She let the last kid pass her and ran down the stairs while lifting up her white dress, being extra careful not to fall.

All of the kids were screaming and chanting for the other boy named Mal. Not even Tice's roommates cheered for her brother.

She paid them no mind and wove her way through the crowd to the front to see. The boys were simply wrestling. Mal was smiling most of the time. It was no wonder why. He was stronger and bigger than Riss, and could throw him around without trying much.

When Mal threw Riss over his back and on the ground, Tice puffed up her cheeks in anger. "Get 'em, Riss!"

Riss blinked hard from hitting his head, but got back up quickly. He charged at Mal, and the two of them were at a stalemate with their hands pressed up and pushing against each other. It was the first time the two of them looked even, so Tice began jumping up and down. Her voice was higher and louder than everyone else so her brother could hear her over the cheers for Mal.

Mal smiled harder. "I'm glad you at least have one fan."

"I'll have more once I win," Riss teased.

"Maybe another day." Mal stopped pushing and pulled Riss forward into him. Riss lost his grip and balance and gave way to Mal's force. Riss was flipped over Mal's back once again. This time, Mal jumped on Riss before he could get up. He grabbed Riss's arm and twisted it to end the fight.

"Riss, get up!" Tice whined.

Riss tried, but when he did, his arm hurt too much to continue.

"Give?" Mal asked in his ear.

Riss raised his head to rest on his chin. He thought about his twisting arm and moaned. "Give," he said quietly.

Mal jumped off of him and helped Riss to his feet before he could protest. "Maybe next time, Brother."

Tice was still pouting with her arms folded.

"Don't be mad, Little One." Mal bent down and rubbed her head roughly, messing up her hair as much as possible. "You'll all be big and strong like me one day."

Tice didn't like when people touched her hair, but she did like Mal. When he smiled in her face, she couldn't help but eventually do the same to him.

"That's my girl." He gave her one final nick on the chin before joining all of the other kids in a corner of the room where brown sacks of food awaited all of them.

Riss didn't seem upset, but he was pulling and tugging on his arm.

"Are you okay?" Tice asked.

"Of course I am," he said. "We were just playing a game."

Tice stared at her brother questionably. "But he tossed you around a lot."

Riss rolled his eyes. "I'm very strong, Tice. I could have won if I wanted to."

She didn't mean to, but she let a giggle escape her. "If you say so…"

He glared back down at her. "Let's get you something to eat." Riss took his sister by the hand and led her to the line of crowded children waiting patiently for food.

Tice's stomach was rumbling from the moment she woke up. It had been a full day since the last time she had eaten. The day before that, she only had a loaf of bread, a slice of cheese, and a warm cup of milk. She hoped it was something worth the wait. She hadn't had meat in a few days. She hoped it was something sweet enough to pinch her cheeks like a pineapple. What if it were cake? She hadn't had cake since her last birthday. It was stale, but it tasted like sweet potatoes and the glaze on top was delicious.

Tice's stomach began to rumble louder. "What did you bring us?"

Riss felt guilty when he looked down at her beaming eyes. When she was excited, it was the only time it looked like there was any color to her face. "It's not much."

Tice's stomach rumbled again loud enough for her brother to hear. She blushed and held it with her tiny hand. "Not so loud, Tummy."

"I'm sorry," Riss said.

"At least we're together." Tice didn't have any memories of her mother or father. Her earliest memory was of Riss holding her and singing. He didn't have much to give her. The only toy that she ever had was a doll that died last week when her head fell off. He helped her bury her in the backyard. There were other graves around the orphanage. Riss and Mal didn't like to talk about them, but Tice remembered other children who were smaller than her getting sick and never getting better. She didn't realize what had happened until she cried over her doll's grave.

Riss was very afraid that Tice would be like all of those other children. Tice seemed the most fragile out of everyone. She couldn't play

10

outside with the older kids when the sun was very bright and hot. Her skin would turn red, and she'd cry if you'd touch her. If she looked into the sun, her head would ache. It was hard to keep her from harm, but he did his best. His earliest memory was taking care of Tice. His whole life, that's all he had ever done.

"Tell me what's the best thing you've ever eaten, and I promise I'll find it for you."

"The best thing?" It was a hard question for her. Once she had a glass bottle of honey in the shape of bear that she kept hidden under her pillow. She would pretend it was a doll when she was bored, and when she was hungry she would put it in a cup of water or on her bread. It seemed like a clear choice until she remembered what happened while she was asleep.

Tice smiled as wide as she could and said, "I want to eat a cloud!"

"A cloud?" he asked. "I think a cloud would taste like cotton."

"I'm joking," she said. "Clouds don't taste like anything."

He shook his head. "But they're solid. They have to taste like something."

"But I've tried to eat one!"

"Oh?" he laughed, thinking it was all a game. "Have you flown up to the sky?"

"Yes." She smiled and swayed her hips to watch her dress swing. "I did it last night!"

Riss envied her imagination. She didn't know anything outside of the orphanage, so she couldn't know what the real world was like. He wished he didn't know. "I saw birds in the sky. I didn't realize that one of them was you."

She laughed. "It didn't really happen, Silly. I saw myself doing it while I was asleep."

Then something familiar yet odd happened to Tice. Everyone stopped what they were doing to turn around and stare at her. She was used to it. When a new child would come to the orphanage, they would point and stare at her. Some were even too afraid to play with her. She had a vivid memory of an older girl who had left after calling her a monster because of her red eyes. Mal made her leave, but not before all of the other children became uncomfortable.

Tice was very used to being seen as strange. The odd thing was that she didn't know for the first time in her life why people were staring. Even Mal and her brother were looking at her oddly. The other children were shocked, but Mal and Riss seemed afraid.

Riss pulled on her hand and yanked her body across the floor until the two of them were outside. Tice nearly tripped up on her feet. She did her best to keep up with her brother, but she wanted to know why the children were still looking at her as if it were the first time they had seen her.

"What did I do?" Tice looked up at the sky and whined from the brightness. She closed her eyes, but the image of the sun was still burning in her eyes.

He let go of her hand and then knelt down beside her. He felt bad for making her come out into the sun on a warm day, but it was a cloudy morning. He was confident that the sun would be covered long enough for her not to be burned. "You can't say things like that."

"What are you talking about?" She opened her eyes and saw how worried he looked. She didn't understand, but it made her afraid. Her big brother had never been scared of anything. "What's the matter?"

"You said that you saw things while you were asleep."

She nodded slowly. He was making it sound like it was a bad thing. She had never talked about it before, but it happened every night. Some days she could fly, some days she was in very deep water, but she

12

could move and breathe freely. She saw things that she had never seen before—beautiful things that she wished she could share with her brother. How could something like that be bad?

"I've heard of it before." Riss looked back inside to make sure no one was around. All of the children were trying not to look, but their eyes did find them every few seconds. They all turned away once Riss saw them staring. Then he leaned in closer to his sister and spoke quietly. "It's called a dream."

"A dream?" she asked. It even sounded beautiful! "What's wrong with having a dream?"

"I don't know, but bad things happen when people have them."

Tice became too frightened to raise her voice above a whisper. "Bad like what?"

He didn't know for sure. They were merely rumors that he heard when he went out searching for food with the rest of the older kids. Riss was going to answer, but Mal was coming up to them with a sack in his hands. Riss trusted Mal, but he didn't know what he would say or do if he found out how strange Tice truly was.

"I think you two should leave," Mal said.

Tice gasped. She knew that he heard her talk about her dream, but he had never done anything to make her feel out of place.

The two boys stared each other down. Tice couldn't tell what either one was thinking. They were both like stone.

Finally, Riss broke the silence. "I think that's probably best."

"But why?" Tice whined, and her eyes welled up with tears.

Mal smiled at her sadly. "I love you like you're my little sister, Tice. I don't mind that you have white skin or red eyes. I want you to stay here until you grow up, but I'm the oldest. Riss is responsible for you, but I'm responsible for everyone else."

He came over to Tice and placed his hand on her head. She looked up at him with a frowned face. It was hard for him to tell her what he needed to, but he had to do it. "They're afraid. They've…We've never had a dream before."

Mal sat the sack on the ground and got on his knees to grab her shoulders. He tried to be as careful as possible with her. "I've heard stories about what happens to people up north if they have them. If someone from up there comes here, one of the other kids might tell. Believe me when I say that you can't be here if that happens."

Tice understood that Mal still liked her. She understood that she couldn't stay there. What she didn't understand was what was going to happen next. "But where will we go?"

"South," he said. "I don't know much about the rest of the world. All I know is that it's worth taking a chance if you two can be safe."

"But I don't want to leave. I'm scared." She hugged onto him. Deep down inside, she hoped that if she held onto him tight enough, everything could go back to the way it was.

He wrapped his arms around her and squeezed. "Don't tell anyone I ever said this, but I'm scared too."

"Really?" She found that hard to believe. No one else she had ever seen was bigger and stronger than Mal.

"Yeah, so you'll just have to be brave enough for the both of us."

Tice opened her eyes and saw Mal's arms around her body. He was so different from her. His skin was the color of the earth while she was as white as the clouds. Even her thin white hair differed from his dark brown spikes.

She let go of Mal, and he stood up on his feet. Mal and Riss said their goodbyes by playfully meeting knuckle to knuckle. They looked more alike than Riss and Tice. They had the same green eyes. No one believed that Tice and Riss had the same mother when she had red eyes.

"You'll always be my best friend," Riss said.

"And you'll always be my brother."

Tice was sad that they had to go. Riss had already given her so much. She didn't want to take away his best friend too.

Mal handed Riss the sack that was halfway full. Tice hoped there was something tasty inside. She nearly licked her lips thinking about it.

Riss grabbed Tice's hand and pulled her until her feet started to move along with his. She waved her hand to Mal until her arm began to get tired. He smiled and waved at her. Her feet stumbled on the dirt, but she couldn't turn her head just yet. She watched Mal until he left to rejoin the other children.

"Come on, Tice."

"But that's our home," she spoke sadly.

"It was a stop on the way home." Riss looked at Tice with her sad eyes and pouted cheeks. He could barely stand it. "Don't worry, Tice. We'll find where we belong."

The yard of the orphanage was barren, flat land a few miles all around. There were a few trees and a small garden, but all the fruit and vegetables had been picked clean. Tice would often look outside her window and out toward the jungle, but she was never allowed to go. Her brother didn't want to take the chance of her skin burning or her getting lost. She never played outside if he weren't there to watch her.

Tice couldn't wait to go into the jungle. The thought of what kind of animals waited for them was exciting. She only knew of birds that would fly over the orphanage or small creatures that might pass by the yard every so often. She would want to play with what looked friendly, but the older kids would always catch and cook them. It would be nice to see new things for a change.

All of that lush green called out to her. The orphanage was dusty and dull. She wanted to see a burst of colors. One of the older girls picked flowers for her once. They were pink and bloomed out in every direction. Her favorite part was the white at the very tips of the pedals. She wanted to find that flower to put in her hair.

She began to walk in front of Riss and tug on him to walk faster. He pulled on her hand to stop her from running in front of him. She looked up at him and pouted, but he scolded her with his eyes. "We need to be careful," he told her.

"But I've wanted to go to the jungle for so long! You never let me go anywhere. Now I want to see!"

"We'll see, but there are all sorts of dangerous animals, bugs, and even plants."

"Plants?" she almost laughed.

"Yes, like plants that like to eat people."

"People?" Tice planted her feet into the ground. She pulled on her brother's hand to stop him from moving as well.

Riss smiled at her fearful expression. "I'm joking. People are much too big." He waited for her to smile with him, but she did no such thing. "But there are a lot of dangerous things out here. That's why we don't come into the jungle looking for food."

Tice did want to go into the jungle, but not at the cost of being eaten alive by a giant and angry plant! "Then maybe we should go back."

"I wish we could," Riss said.

Tice bit her lip as she thought. She had friends at the orphanage. Would anyone actually tell on her? Why would anyone really care? It was normal for her. What could be worse than going through a dangerous jungle? What did northerners do to people like her? "Are having dreams really that bad?"

Riss bent down beside her and gently grabbed her arms. "I don't think so."

"Then why will bad things happen if people up north find out?"

It was difficult for him to explain. "Sometimes people can't understand people who are different. Maybe they try. Maybe they don't. It's like your red eyes and white skin. I know you don't like it, but that doesn't change how spectacular you are."

She frowned as she looked into her brother's dark green eyes. "I don't even look like your sister."

"But you are my sister," he said quickly. He remembered holding her as a baby. He remembered taking care of her when no one else would. He remembered defending her when his mother cried. He carried her in his tiny arms to the orphanage while she was wrapped up in a blanket so she wouldn't get burned from the sun or freeze when it got cold.

"There's more to us than color." He grabbed her nose and squeezed it. She scrunched up her face at the brief pain, but laughed when he let go. "We have the same nose, mouth, and everyone says we look the same when we smile. You're pretty just like how I remember Mom."

She smiled pleased and embarrassed by his compliment. "I wish I could remember what she was like."

"You were just a baby." Riss didn't talk about her much. He had many good memories of their parents, but they didn't compare to when they left home.

"I know," Tice said, "but I wonder sometimes. You know?"

"I'll tell you plenty of stories once we're safe." He opened up the sack and pulled out a glass bottle full of milk. The bottle was warm, but it wasn't spoiled. He handed it to her and patted her on the head.

Her eyes lit up. She gulped it down until it was halfway full. It was tastier than the rain water she had last night before bed. It warmed her throat and soothed her belly.

Riss put the milk back in the sack and they began walking hand-in-hand again. He wanted some milk for himself, but she needed it more.

17

The orphanage began to look like a faded speck. It was the only building Tice had ever been in. It always loomed over her like a shadow. She was sad to be leaving, but the jungle held so many curious wonders that could only be explored if she went in.

Still, the closer the two of them got to it, the closer she leaned into her brother. An hour and a half later, the barren land had become a grassy hill with trees stretching high into the sky. Tice was afraid to reach her neck back to see the top of the trees because the bright sky was waiting for her red eyes. She instead imagined that if she could climb the trees, she could touch the clouds.

"Are you afraid?" Riss asked.

"No!" She puffed up her cheeks and held onto her brother's hand tighter. She was close enough to have her body pressed against his legs. "May we sit and rest?"

"Is it because you're tired or is it because you're afraid?"

"I'm not scared!" she said stubbornly.

He eyed her carefully then smirked. "In that case, I think I should carry you on my back if you're too tired to walk."

From that point, she knew he was onto her. There was nothing left to do but whine about it. "Why can't we rest?"

"It's going to be noon soon. Your skin is doing fine, but I don't want you to get burned. The jungle will give you the shade that you need."

She moaned and pulled on his arm. "Please. I just want to sit."

He sighed. "Okay."

Tice wasted no time in falling off her feet and on her butt. It was true that she wanted to stop because she was scared, but her feet did ache and her legs itched. She scratched them, but nothing made it feel better. The feeling came from the inside.

"I guess you're out of shape, Little One." Riss was a bit slower as he eased off his feet and onto a boulder a couple of steps away. His feet ached from the search for food that lasted two days. A rest would be good for the both of them.

He reached inside the sack and pulled out a long loaf of baked bread. Tice clapped her hands excitedly. There was another loaf, what was left of her milk, a few apples, and a small jug of water. It wouldn't last them long. He needed to give her a small piece, but he couldn't leave her hungry when he could fix the problem.

He broke it apart unevenly, giving the bigger piece to her. He took a big bite out of his before she had the chance to judge. He was a growing boy, but she was a little girl. If he didn't take care of her, no one else would.

Tice wasted no time eating. The bread was fresh and soft. She didn't wait to finish the first bite before taking another. When it was gone, she licked her fingers and picked the bread crumbs off her dress and ate those too!

"Is it good?" Riss asked.

She smiled with her cheeks still puffed up with food.

Riss was grateful for Tice's happiness. He wished that he could feel the same way day-to-day. There were so many things to be worried about. He didn't know how he would feed his sister in a few days. He didn't know if they could make it out of the jungle in a few hours or survive the journey.

He looked in the jungle. There were so many trees that he couldn't see clearly in front of him past ten feet. He did know that there were animals there. There was something close wrestling through the leaves and breaking branches as it came closer to the two of them.

Riss's heart began to race. What if it were a jaguar, or a crocodile, or a giant snake? Could he outrun those things? Could he save Tice from being eaten alive?

Tice was oblivious to the noise. She was still working on swallowing her bread. There was no way that she'd last.

"Maybe we should find another way," he said trying to be calm.

"Do you know another way?" she asked.

"No, but I don't think this is a good idea."

Riss was always sure about everything. When he made up his mind that was that! "Why?" Tice became afraid and finally heard the sounds coming out of the jungle.

Riss stood to his feet and motioned for her. "Come close to me."

Tice didn't hesitate and ran behind her brother. She closed her eyes and held onto his leg. She just knew it was a monster plant coming to eat the both of them in one munch!

But it wasn't a plant. Two men emerged. One was tall and very thin; the other was tall and wide. Both men stared at Riss before speaking a word. They appeared very serious. Then the big man smiled showing that he was missing a few teeth. The thin man spoke. "Hello."

Riss was afraid, but did his best not to show it. He reached behind him and made sure to hide Tice as best he could. They were men coming up from the south, but they might have known northerners. "Hi."

Tice poked her head from behind Riss to see the men. The only other adult she had seen was their caretaker before she abandoned them. Those men were much bigger than Riss and even Mal. They looked like they were dragged through the mud, stuffed with pillows, and covered with fuzz from a caterpillar's back.

The big man pointed to Tice and asked, "Is that girl sick?"

Riss pushed her back behind him. "She's my sister, and she was born this way. There's nothing wrong with her."

The two men began to walk closer to them. The thinner man walked close enough to get a better look at Tice from behind Riss's back.

20

"I saw a person with her color skin from Eastern Pearl, but I've never seen eyes like hers."

Riss didn't know what they were talking about. He hadn't ever seen anyone who looked like Tice before, nor had he heard of the Eastern Pearl. If there were people like her, then that's where they needed to go. "Where's Eastern Pearl?" he asked.

"East," the big man said.

Riss wanted to reply smartly. Of course, Eastern Pearl was somewhere east. How far east was a good question. Would they need a boat? Was it even possible to get there? Either they were men who wouldn't help them or they were men who didn't know the answers.

The thin man saw the sack sitting behind Riss. "What's in the bag?"

Tice answered without thinking. "It's food."

"It's nothing you should be concerned about!" Riss said.

"Did you steal that food?" the thin man asked.

Yes, was the answer. He didn't want to admit that to those men. They were probably scavengers who went looking for and stole food themselves. They didn't deserve an answer and Riss didn't care if they scolded him for it. What he did care about was what Tice would think.

He spat out an answer that was quick. "It's our food. I'm sure there's some in the jungle for you guys."

The thin man smiled. "All the food to eat is too much trouble to get. You're welcome to try."

"No, thank you." Riss gently nudged the sack of food away from them and toward Tice.

"I think you should give it to us."

"Why?" Tice grabbed a hold of the bag and held it tight to her chest. It was food that Mal gave to her and Riss. No one else had the right to take it from them!

"It's payment for coming through our jungle."

"We're not in it yet," Riss said smartly.

"But you are going in there."

Riss stretched out his hands to protect his sister. He pushed her up against the boulder, to keep her safe on all sides. They were stronger than him, but he wasn't going to let them hurt her. He wasn't going to let them steal from them without a fight. "We're just passing by until we can find a town or something."

"We're taking that bag," the thin man warned.

"No!"

Tice screamed as the two men bombarded them. The big man grabbed a hold of Riss's shirt and threw him on his back. The thin man latched onto the sackcloth, but she wasn't going to let it go. She closed her eyes and forced down two tears. She screamed and fought for it with all her might. She didn't let go until she felt a swift hand to her face.

She fell down on the ground and held her face. It hurt, but she was too stunned to cry. People had said mean words to her, but no one had ever hurt her.

Riss rolled off of his back and jumped on the big man's back. He folded his arms around his neck and did his best to pull him off his feet.

"Get off of me!"

"Give us back our food!" commanded Riss. "That's all we have in the whole world! It's ours!"

Tice knew her brother was brave, but something about him made her brave too. She knew she was too small to stop them. He must have known that too, but she knew it was wrong to sit on the ground and cry.

She got on her feet and charged the big man. "Let go of my brother!" She couldn't jump as high as Riss did and land on his back. She wasn't higher than the man's leg, so that's what she grabbed.

Tice was barely moving him at all. The big man laughed wildly, even with Riss trying to choke him. The thin man laughed as well.

Then something began to happen to Tice. She had been laughed at her whole life. They would call her Pale Face or Evil Eyes or something like that. Riss and Mal were always there to protect her, but it never made all the laughing go away. Well, she was sick of the laughing! No one was going to laugh at her anymore.

She thought about what she should do. She punched his leg, but that didn't do anything but crack her knuckles. "Ow!" she screamed.

The men laughed harder.

That's when she did the only thing she could think of. She bit him as hard as she could.

"Ow!" He hollered and kicked his leg forward.

She went flying onto the grass and felt broken. It reminded her of when an older girl threw her doll and broke its head off. She cried for her dead doll, just as she began to lightly whimper from the pain.

The big man looked down at his leg to see Tice's little teeth marks imprinted in his skin with pricks of blood beginning to seep through. He roared and threw Riss off of his back. He landed a clear foot over his sister.

The big man was furious, but the thin man motioned him to follow him into the jungle. Tice watched through her tears as they disappeared behind the trees.

It took Riss a moment to see if he were alright. He took in a good breath and then let it out. He was in pain, but he didn't think anything was broken. "Are you alright, Tice?"

She wiped her eyes, but she wasn't done crying. She wasn't hurt as badly as she first thought. She just didn't understand why people who didn't even know each other would want to hurt one another.

Her back was facing Riss so he couldn't see how hurt she was. He knew that she probably wouldn't blame him, but he thought it was his fault. What could she have done? He was the older one. Now they didn't have food for that night or the next day. They had already been without for too long. He couldn't let that happen!

He got up on his feet and ran into the jungle as fast as he could.

Chapter Two

"Riss?" Tice couldn't believe that she was just left by her brother! She looked around. If she waited, nothing was going to get her from behind, but something could always come from out of the jungle. She couldn't stay alone!

She gulped down all her fears and ran as fast as she could after her brother. She was surrounded by green. It even covered the sky when she looked up. Green was a lovely color, just like her brother's eyes. She didn't see what could be so wrong about the jungle if it were covered in such beauty.

"Riss!" She spotted him up ahead, but she would never catch him. Her legs already felt like they were going to wobble off of her body. She never had to run across anything but flat land. Now she was running over rocks and tree roots that looked like they were purposely rising up to trip her. She was mindful of the big ones, but her luck wouldn't let her escape all of the smaller ones.

She fell and landed flat on her belly, and all of the air was knocked out of her. But even worse, she was covered in mud. Only the back of her hands and legs were dry.

Tice sat up on her butt and turned around to see the thin roots that had sprouted out from a very fat tree trunk. She pouted and kicked at it. To her surprise, a leaf jumped off of it. She screamed and jumped back.

How was it possible that a leaf could jump? It might have been dangerous, but she needed to know.

She climbed on all fours and followed it two hops over. It didn't look very dangerous. It was actually very cute. It was a fat leaf with black eyes, a mouth, legs, and arms. It reminded her of something that Mal brought home once. It hopped and made strange noises when its throat got big. She reached out to touch it, but then it quickly hopped away.

"Tice!" Riss yelled.

She got up on her feet and ran toward her brother. When she saw him, she gasped. "What did they do to you?"

His nose was bloody, and his face was red and turning purple around his left eye and on his cheeks. His eyes were also red like he had been crying, but that couldn't have been why. Tice had never seen him cry before.

Riss hadn't cried yet, but he was holding back his tears. He didn't manage to get anything back from the thieves. He felt more worthless than he had ever felt in his whole life. "We have to hurry before it starts."

"Hurry before what starts?"

The sky answered in a thunderous roar. Tice screamed and grabbed a hold of her brother's waist. He was a little annoyed by the mud, but he was also dirty from being punched and knocked into the ground. He rubbed the back of his head and sighed.

He held Tice in his arms as he tried to outrun the rain. The tree tops seemed to cover up the sky until the rain started pouring from overhead.

Tice wrapped her arms around her brother's neck and peered over his back to look at the scenery. She had never seen so many colors. Reds, blues, pinks, and yellows were everywhere. There was grass as high as she was and some of the flowers bloomed like a pretty dress while others spiked out like sharp knives. Some were bigger than her whole body while others were only starting to bud. "Please stop! I don't mind the rain! I want to see the flowers."

Riss wanted to set her down, but he had never seen rain come on so fast and out of nowhere. The heaviness wasn't in the air. The sky had become cloudy, but they weren't storm clouds. It was still hot up until a few minutes ago. Something wasn't right. Darkness should have never come on that fast. Soon Tice wouldn't be able to see any of the fantastic colors.

"Please stop!" she begged. "I want to see!"

Another burst of thunder exploded in the sky. Then the trees shook as creatures began to flee from all around. Birds of red, blue, and yellow began to emerge from the trees and flew away in front of them. There were other creatures that she hadn't noticed before like a black-faced fellow as big as her with long hairy arms and legs. He climbed away and hid.

It was silly to her. Didn't they live there? Weren't they used to a little rain? "I'm scared." She held on tighter to Riss.

Riss wasn't sure how much further he could go with her in his arms. The more they ran the more open the jungle was. They were no longer covered by tree tops. They were soaked through the bone, and the mud was pulling on his feet with every step he took.

They came up on a small creek that would soon become a rushing stream from the rain. A few feet from it was a cave cutting into the backside of a small mountain. He crossed the water and nearly slipped, but he made it over safely.

"Where are we going?" Tice asked.

"Up here!" The opening to the cave was a little bit above his head. They couldn't be sure what was inside, but it was better than drowning or getting sick and dying.

Then the sky screamed. It wasn't a sound made from pain. It almost sounded like a high note at the end of a song. Light unlike anything they had ever seen was streaming across the sky. It was bright, stunning, and lit up the sky to make it day again. The ground began to shake as the sound became louder until it they could feel the streaming light near.

Tice could not keep her eyes off of the sky. She couldn't find words to describe how it made her feel on the inside to see something like that. She had a strange thought. How many people from all over the world were looking at the streaming lights? How many small children were looking up at the sky and wondering what it was or what it meant? She had seen a shooting star before, but the lights were different. They were the beginning of something bigger than her. She didn't know how she knew that, but she did. "What do you think it is?" Tice asked.

"I don't know," Riss said, "but we've got to get to a safe place." He pushed Tice up on his shoulders so she could climb inside. She wasn't very athletic, so it still took a big push from him to get her in.

There was nothing but darkness in front of her and behind her there was a sky striped with colors. She obviously wanted to stay out in the jungle until the light had stopped, but Riss would hear nothing of it. She got a final glimpse right before he climbed up and forced his way in.

Riss grabbed both sides of Tice's face so she would look in his eyes. There was still enough light for her to see him. "I'm gonna go first. If there's anything dangerous, I want you to crawl out as fast as you can. Do you understand?"

Tice nodded.

He scooted past her and started crawling forward. As the cave got deeper, it became less narrow. There wasn't a speck of light except for the light coming in from behind, but neither of them was really afraid. Riss couldn't afford to be, and Tice was still trying to figure out what the light meant. She almost wished that something bad was waiting for them so they could go back outside.

The cave began to widen until she could stand and hunch her back. She let out a short scream when her brother lifted her up and sat her down gently to avoid tripping from the brief drop. They could both stand up straight, but she didn't let go of his hand. Tice was finally feeling afraid of the dark.

The ground began to shake, and she held him tighter.

"I'm here," he told her, "we'll be safe here until the storm is over." The earth shook again, and dirt fell from the roof of the cave and on top of their heads. Tice tried not to think about it and take her brother at his word. Riss, on the other hand, was afraid of the cave collapsing.

He thought about grabbing her and getting out before that happened. There were only a couple of estimated feet around them. They wouldn't have enough air if they were trapped inside. But whatever was up in the sky wasn't going to stay. It was loud and shaking the earth because it was close. They needed some type of cover. Either way, he knew something bad was about to happen.

Then, the entire cave shook. The rumbling knocked them both off of their feet. The light shining from outside made everything bright white for a flash, and then it just became darker and darker.

Riss wrapped his arms around Tice, and she buried her head into his chest. She screamed and cried. The ground was shaking so much that neither of them realized they were shaking from fright. They squeezed each other until they couldn't breathe as the cave lit up from light brighter than the sun had ever made the sky. They were forced to close their eyes, and when they opened them back up, it was dark again.

Riss slowly reached out with one hand while holding onto Tice with the other. A pile of rocks were blocking the way they came in. "We're trapped." He started to cough from inhaling the dust that surrounded them. It was so dark that he couldn't even see Tice's red eyes right in front of him.

"Can we get out?" she asked while still keeping her head in his chest.

"I don't know." He slowly let go of her, but she continued to latch onto his chest. "Tice, I need you to back up as far as you can while I dig through these rocks. I can't see, and I don't want to accidentally hit you. Alright?"

She wanted to protest. She didn't feel safe without Riss. Still, she let go of her brother and scooted away with her hands and feet. The further she moved, the more panicked she was. The cave seemed much smaller when she first came in. It felt like her heart had completely stopped by the time her back pressed against the wall. She bit her lip and held in her tears. "I'm s-safe."

"Good." Riss stood and leaned on top of the pile. It was unbelievable that the two of them weren't crushed during the cave-in. Riss tossed as many rocks to the side as fast as he could. Tice was already panting heavily. She might have gone mad long before the air went away. "Just hold on. I promise I'm going to get us out of here." No one else could take care of her. It was his responsibility. No mother. No father. It was just Riss and Tice together, and it wasn't time for them to die.

Riss grabbed a hold of a heavy boulder, but it was too big for him to toss as easily as the other rocks. He grunted as he strained his muscles to lift it. When he finally moved it out of place, a light flickered.

"What's that?" Tice asked.

If she hadn't said anything, he wouldn't have been sure that he saw it himself. "I don't know." Riss once again grabbed the boulder. He closed his eyes and lifted with his knees. His arms felt like they were going to pop off, but he lifted it up.

There was a light that was shining under the rock. It was blinking from bright to dim and hummed. Tice got up to follow the sound and the blinking light. She was curious to know what could possibly give off its own light in the darkness. It wasn't warm enough to be a fire.

Riss did his best to toss the boulder, but it didn't make it far past his foot. He huffed out a large breath of air and curled his arms to dull the stress on his muscles. He didn't know how he could get the two of them out of there. It was good that they had a mystery to keep them occupied.

"What do you think it is?" Tice reached out to touch the shining ball of light, but Riss pushed her back.

"Stay behind me," he warned. She did as she was told and stepped back as he began to dig through smaller rocks. The more he moved, the more shimmers of light broke through. After he moved another heavy rock, a pile poured through. They both stepped back to keep from touching them when they rolled on the floor. They were both oddly entranced by the small orbs.

Then one gained speed on Riss and bounced up against his foot. Riss's shoes were thin so he would have felt if it were hot. It was hard but not heavy. It almost looked like glass with something trapped inside. It wasn't a liquid, a solid, or even a gas. It swirled and called out to Riss with a beautiful voice.

"Be careful," Tice said softly.

He couldn't help himself from reaching down to grab it. "I've never seen anything like this before." It warmed his entire body. His body wasn't in pain anymore from the heavy lifting or the fight from the men.

Tice's eyes bucked as she saw her brother's swollen eye and cuts disappear. It happened so fast, she questioned if they were ever there at all.

Riss watched the light inside of the orb moving and rushing in a circle. He couldn't take his eyes off of it. It was the loveliest thing he had ever seen. And then, it swirled faster until the orb became a blazing red.

31

"Watch out!"

Riss's dropped the orb as his hands caught on fire. "My hands!" He backed away to keep his sister safe.

"Put it out!" Tice screamed. "Put it out!"

He shook his hands furiously, but the fire wouldn't go away. He blew on his hands, but it wouldn't extinguish. His mind was racing with many questions of if he would survive. He watched his sister crying and his mind was overcome with what ifs. What if he would lose his life and she would have to be alone? "I can't! I can't! I..." Then the flames rose from off his hands to an inch above his palms. His hands weren't even burned. The flame wasn't even hot. But the most important thing was that when he thought to make it small, it dimmed down to the size of a coin in his hand. "I can control it," he said slowly. He gulped and thought to make the fire bigger. Then it roared and rose in his hand into a ball bigger than his entire head. "I'm making the fire."

"How are you doing that?" she asked in wonder.

"I don't know." He looked down at his feet. The orb that was once bright red was now frosted white and dim. "I think it's the stones. They must have done this to me. There's no other explanation." He smiled genuinely excited. Riss always thought himself to be strong and brave. Even when Mal would best him in fighting, he always knew that he was great and could defeat anyone one day. Wielding fire made that possible. What was more powerful than an open flame?

Tice walked up to her brother slowly. He was still making the fire grow small and large. She wondered how he could stand it. It was far too hot for her to get close to him. She figured that the fire was his gift. Maybe there was another one for her. After all, there were so many. She would settle for simply looking normal. "I want to touch one."

"No!" He yelled so loud, it made her jump. Riss closed his hands and made the fire go out. "You can't."

32

She felt like she had been beaten down by his refusal. She hung her head low and looked down at her tattered and dirt stained sandals. "But it made you special. I want to be special too."

Riss frowned and patted her on the top of her head. "You're already special," he said. "You don't need those stones."

She didn't believe him and shook her head. Strange didn't mean special—not in a good way. They were forced to run because she was different from everyone else.

Riss tried to reason with her. "Besides, we don't know what will happen if you touch it. I just caught on fire. What if something worse happens to you?" Riss didn't mean to cause her any harm. It was just that Tice was already so fragile. A warm day was too much for her pale skin to bear. She could barely run without falling, and she was as weak as a field mouse.

She looked at him with serious eyes. "Do you really think something bad will happen?"

"I don't want to take any chances." He bent down and grabbed her shoulders. Her eyes were strange, but they were beautiful to him. No matter if she were lost among a sea of faces, he could always find his sister. "You're too precious to me. Do you understand?"

She nodded. "Yes. I do."

He smiled. "Good." Riss nicked her in the chin playfully. "Now you stay here and don't touch anything while I'm gone."

Tice's eyes found the entrance. It was still covered with rocks that were big, small, and glowing. "Where are you going?" she asked confused.

"I'm gonna find those guys who took our food and get it back."

Tice forgot about the question of how he could escape. She forgot about the fact that he was willing to leave her alone in a scary cave with

33

powerful orbs that set people on fire. There was only one fact that she couldn't ever forget. "But they hurt you!"

They did hurt him. They stole from them and then they beat him up. He didn't like feeling humiliated. He wanted to show Tice that he could still take care of her, and he wanted those men to know that too. "Yeah, and now I can take care of myself."

"Please don't leave me alone!" she begged.

"I'll be back soon. Nothing bad is going to happen to you. I promise." Riss stepped to his left and stretched out his hand. He didn't want to take a chance of destroying any of the orbs—if that were possible.

Tice watched the palm of her brother's hand turn bright red just like her skin would get if she stayed out in the sun too long. He didn't look like he was in any discomfort. He had his eyes closed and looked calm. Then, Tice jumped back as the flames shot from his hand. She wanted to watch, but backed away without thinking. She couldn't believe that he could stand there with the fire being so hot, even if it were coming from his hand.

She shielded her eyes from the bright light of the flames. She opened them when they stopped aching. Riss had made a hole in the wall, leading right outside to the bright day. "Wow."

Riss was also amazed but smirked. "Don't doubt me, Tice. I'm going to take care of you."

"I know."

Riss climbed through the hole that was still smoking and oozing with melted rock. It didn't faze him at all, but Tice could still feel the heat. She had to stand at the very back of the wall to feel comfortable. If he had become that powerful, then maybe he would be okay.

But she did wonder if he could really control it.

"Hurry," she said quietly as the remaining orbs began to blink and glow.

Chapter Three

There were five men all together. The smallest man in the group was the man who robbed them. Fortunately, the biggest person was a man who Riss had already fought. Their camp was set up in a cave. The entrance was narrow, had a source of fresh water, and a canopy overhead. They had piles of food, clothing, and coins stacked up. They must have stolen from everyone they came in contact with. They didn't need what little food Riss and Tice had to survive.

Riss was going to really enjoy picking them apart. He didn't care what he had to do to take care of his sister as long as she was safe.

There were a lot of people who didn't believe he'd be able to take care of her. When he was little, his mother was afraid when she was born. Red eyes? The doctors had never seen anything like it. Then her skin was as white as a cloudy sky. Riss's father was angry didn't believe that she was his.

The doctors explained that Tice had a sickness, and they all tried to love her. Riss was jealous of all the attention she got as a baby. She couldn't do anything by herself, yet he was too little to help. His mother claimed that she was the most fragile child she had ever seen.

Then right after Tice had her first birthday, a strange man visited his family. He said that Tice was special and some other things that frightened his parents. After that day, they never acted the same. It wasn't long after that they wanted to get rid of her. When they explained what they were doing, Riss was furious.

They said that they were going to give her to people who took care of special people. Riss heard terrible rumors, but his parents refused to believe them.

The night before his parents were supposed to give Tice away, Riss refused to leave her. He told his parents that if they got rid of her, he was leaving too. He thought that would change their minds, but they claimed that Riss couldn't stop their decision.

That's when Riss wrapped her up in a blanket and ran away with her in the middle of the night. He never told Tice what really happened. He told her that they got sick and passed away. He was always afraid that his parents would come and ruin his lies, but they never did.

He looked at his hands, squeezed his fingers together tight, and made a wish. He wished that he wasn't dreaming and that what he could do was real. He opened his hands and watched the fire grow and dance in his hand. He really could control fire!

He closed his hands and snuck a little closer. Riss thought he was pretty smooth. They would never know he was coming until it was too late. He inched in on his toes, being as careful as possible.

Then, he kicked a rock.

One of the men looked up and saw him. Riss moved out of the way quickly to hide behind the rock wall. Maybe the bandits hadn't seen him. Riss closed his eyes and took in a big breath. "I can do this." He let his fear rush over him and then he pushed it out. He was ready.

Just as he opened his eyes, he felt two big hands grab him. He let out a small yell in pure shock.

The man held him against the wall as the others began to come out. He didn't say anything. He growled in Riss's face and breathed a terrible smell on him.

Riss turned his head. "All that fresh water and you don't even bathe?"

"You think you can just come in our jungle and say anything you want?"

Riss crossed his arms and smirked. "The rules of the wild seem to be that the strongest takes charge. Since I'm the strongest, I think you all should bring me whatever food you have and then leave my jungle."

They began to laugh. Riss would have been angered usually, but they didn't know any better. He waited for his opportunity to arise. "Or what?" they asked.

"Or this." Riss placed his hands on the wrists of the man holding him. It only took a split second to make him drop Riss. Riss ran a few feet away, turned around, and raised his fists ready to fight.

The man hollered and looked at his newly formed burns. "What did you do?"

Riss smirked. "Like I said, I'm in charge here." He opened his hands up and created two fire balls.

All of the men stepped back on instinct. None of them wanted Riss to defeat them, but they were mystified. The thin man who robbed Riss stepped forward first. He was stubborn and thought it could have been a trick. "Any circus freak can come up with a little fire. You and your weak sister don't scare us."

Riss closed his hands. "You're not?" He was offended. "I'm going to make you scared," he warned. Riss reached out his hands and blasted fire at his attackers. He didn't really think about it. His rage fueled his power more than what he thought it would.

All of the men began to run. Riss never truly had the upper hand before. It felt good to be the strongest. He continued to chase them all with a trail of fire until they were gone.

"You better run!" he yelled. He was satisfied with his handiwork.

Riss kept a smile on his face until the smell of smoke began to come through his nose. The trees were beginning to burn with brilliant colors of red and yellow. It was much too radiant for him to control.

He closed his hands and tried to calm it down, but the flames he threw weren't bending to his will. He stood in shock with his mouth opened wide. The luscious jungle was engulfed in power. He had to do something, or it wouldn't be safe for him and his sister.

He reached out his hands, closed his eyes, and spoke to the flames. "You have to go down. You have to go down!" He wouldn't open up his eyes until he was sure. If he saw the flames, then he would lose hope in himself.

"Go down! Go down! Go down." He finally opened his eyes to see. The fire was gone, but so much of the earth was scorched. He never wanted something so terrible to happen.

Tice was safe from those men thanks to Riss, but he was a curious person and decided to explore the abandoned hideout. There were kerosene lamps, stacks of food, and gold coins. Everything was probably stolen, except for some of the fruit. Riss gathered up what he could in the sack and in his pockets, but he planned on making many trips back. The spoils of the wicked now belonged to the just!

But then, her terrible scream echoed across the jungle.

Chapter Four

Far away in the heart of darkness, a small flash of light glittered across the sky. It started as one brilliant flash and then broke out into a shower. While some stretched across the land to places beyond what many can comprehend, a light found its way into the deepest hole.

And through a tower of steel, a pair of green eyes peeked through a hole tiny enough for a baby mouse to crawl through. The owner of the eyes—a young boy—had to stand on the tips of his toes to reach, but he hadn't seen the sky in years. He was beginning to forget what it was like. The streaming lights were a wonderful reminder of how the sky looked when it opened its arms up to the light.

But most importantly, the light had fallen, and it was close.

"You have to find it."

The young boy landed flat on his feet and turned around to meet the small voice. She was the strangest girl he had ever seen with white hair, pale skin that was even lighter than his own, and red eyes. "Who are you?" the boy asked.

"You have to find the light, Davin."

"How do you know my name?" he asked. That wasn't the only question he wanted to ask. He didn't understand how she got inside the room. He had locked it. She didn't even make a sound until she spoke.

"You have to find the light."

Davin woke up in a cold sweat. As he rose off the hard floor, he hit three people that were crowded next to him.

Davin looked around. It was too dark to see anything, but he was certain that there was no odd girl in the room. It was still filled with small boys, all younger than him. He lay back down and closed his eyes. It was difficult to become comfortable in a hot and crowded room, but he had grown accustomed to living uncomfortably.

After a brief nap, a man knocked on the door and claimed that it was morning. Davin had to take his word for it. There wasn't a speck of daylight to offer any testimony. One of the boys opened the door to their room to let the light from the hall seep in.

Davin was hoping for a change, but it seemed like the beginning to any other day. He marched the boys down the halls in a single file line, passing the rest of the cells up the stairs and to the cafeteria. He let them all pass by once they got to the food line so they could eat first.

Even the cafeteria was dim. It was filled with lamps, but it never compared to the brightness the day could bring. There was simply too much dark steel and stone to make it seem like it was ever day. Some of the youngest boys thought that the sky had died. Davin wished he was that naive. Some days, the thought of living in a giant coffin made him nearly mad.

But Davin never showed his feelings. He kept a smile on his face and a spring in the step of his skinny legs. If he couldn't be strong for the younger boys, then no one else would be.

Breakfast smelled terribly delicious. It was delicious because it was all they were accustomed to and their scarce meals were always a blessing. It was terrible because it always smelled terrible. Davin remembered better meals, but he never complained about the food. It wasn't worth the price of not eating.

40

Davin was served a piece of hard bread and a bowl of red soup. He smiled wearily to the server, who was around his age, taller, and thicker. He was dirty and always wore a frown on his face. Davin didn't understand why. He might have been a prisoner like the rest of them, but at least he got to eat the leftovers.

Davin took his place at a table filled with the youngest boys from his room and one little girl. She had her hands placed on his seat at the bench until he arrived to take his place. "Thank you, Mina."

She smiled. Mina reminded him of the girl he had seen last night. She was just as small, maybe six-years-old. They had the same baby face and light hair. But Mina's hair was blonde, and the stranger's hair was white. Actually, everything about the stranger was white—her hair, her skin, her clothes. The only colored thing about were her red eyes.

"You seem distracted, Davin," said the boy sitting across from him.

"What's the matter?" asked another.

"Nothing," Davin smile. "I had a dream last night."

The entire table went up in a roar of astonishment. "Tell us!" they chanted. The onlookers from other tables glared at Davin. That's why Davin sat with the young children. They always appreciated and believed in his gift.

"If you really want to know…"

"We do, Davin. Tell us! Please!"

Davin smiled harder. "It was about yesterday when I snuck out of our room to see the hole in the wall on the fourth level. It was very small, but I saw outside. It was raining and dark. I thought maybe it was night."

"Do you still think that?" another boy asked.

"No. I think that it was just a very bad storm. Remember that the ground began to shake?"

They all nodded.

"I wanted to see the sun, but I think I saw something more beautiful than that, or at least more beautiful than my memory of it. There was light running across the sky. It was more powerful than fire. It was brighter than it too. I've never seen anything like it."

"But you've told us this," another boy said. "Are you sure it's not a memory and that it was a dream?"

"I'm sure," Davin said. "I can't remember a little girl that I've never seen in my life." He placed his hand on top of Mina's head, and she smiled. "She was no bigger than Mina. She was strange but beautiful. She told me that I had to find the light."

"The light from the sky?" Mina asked.

"No. It's not in the sky anymore. I think it's here somewhere. I think that's why the ground shook so much."

"Will it make it look like day?"

"Where do we find it?"

"How do you know it's real?"

"I don't know any of those answers," Davin said. "What I do know is that we have to get it somehow. Everything will change for the better if we do. There's a reason why I had this dream. It was instruction from something I think we can believe in. We've got to."

"That's the stupidest thing I've ever heard!" said an older man that had begun to walk by the table during Davin's story. The kids believed that he was over one thousand years old. They told stories about each hair on his white beard being another year on his life. That, of course, wasn't true. He was much too fiery to be that old.

He had given Davin a lot of trouble, but Davin never disrespected anyone older than him. "Why do you think it is unwise?"

"Because it's ridiculous! All you had was another silly dream. You're not special. None of us are. We're cursed."

"Davin's not cursed!" Mina yelled. "Davin's brave and he's smart and—"

"He's going to get all of us in a lot of trouble," the old man yelled. "Why do you think they put us in here? They don't like us because we have dreams. It's bizarre, and there's no place for it in the real world. We'll be in here until our bones are dust if we don't stop having dreams."

"It doesn't matter if people don't like who we are. It doesn't change anything about us," Davin said.

The old man frowned up his face tight. "They should let me go! I don't have dreams anymore. I haven't for a very long time. I'm normal now."

Davin sighed. "That must be very sad for you, Mr. Petey."

"Don't you dare pity me, Boy! I'm going to be free before I die, and it won't be because of your dreams."

"I didn't mean for everyone to think that I was the only way we could be free," Davin said. "I don't even know if that's possible. I do want you to be free one day, no matter the cost. I wish you happiness."

He glared. "There is no happiness here, Boy."

Mr. Petey walked away, but eyes from the rest of the inmates were still on Davin. Whether they thought Mr. Petey was right or wrong, it was true that they were in there for their dreams. Davin was the most vocal about his dreams and encouraged the younger children to speak freely about them. He was a very loved and despised boy.

He tried to ignore the gawkers and began eating his food. The bread was too hard to bite, so he dipped it in his soup to soak it. It was probably best to get it all over with quickly. The smaller kids liked it more. They probably didn't remember what real food tasted like. Davin was also beginning to forget.

The sun, the sky, the smell of wet grass on his feet, and the feel of fresh dirt between his toes were all things he was forgetting, but in his heart, he was refused to let go.

A few minutes after the food line had finished being served, a man dressed in a black uniform came inside the cafeteria to blow a whistle. It was barely enough time to feed over a hundred people, but the children had learned to scarf down food. They had to leave so the next rush of people could be fed.

Mina took Davin by the hand when they both stood up. He looked down at her beaming smile and offered her one in return. They went out the cafeteria, down the stairs, and then down another staircase to the end of the hall. The younger kids like Mina were allowed to go to a large empty room to play. Davin was far too old to do that since he was fourteen.

He let go of Mina's hand at the edge of the stairs and waited for her to leave, but she stared at him with a smile on her face. The older kids were watching and shaking their heads from up the hall. They misunderstood and believed that Davin was going to try to get out of his responsibilities. He had never done such a thing, but they always looked for something negative to say about him.

"Mina," he asked, "why don't you go?"

She tugged on his pants and signaled him to bend down with her tiny index finger. He did as instructed after the last child ran by. "I had a dream last night too," she said softly.

Davin was glad to hear that. Not many people were choosing to share their dreams, even though just about everyone there was having them. "What was it about?"

"It was about my mother." Mina's eyes sparkled at the memory of it. "I never really got the chance to meet her. The older girls say that when I was on the way in, she was on the way out. They tell me that I can't

44

remember what she looked like because I was too little, but I do remember her when I dream. She had pretty yellow hair like me and you."

Davin did know Mina's mother. She was named after her, and she did have long yellow hair. She began to get sick when she was pregnant, and medicine was never allowed to be given out to any of the residents. She was very kind to all and made sweets in the kitchen and snuck them to the children. Mina's mother had given one last gift to the world before she died: Mina.

Mina was so much like her right down to her sweet smile. "I can know her even if she's gone. That's how I know that our dreams are good."

Davin wrapped his arms around her. "Thank you for telling me that."

"You're welcome." She kissed him on his cheek before running down the stairs to the rest of the children. There wasn't much for them to do, but kids had a way about them. They could usually take nothing and make it into the most significant game in the world. Some of them were kicking cans like a ball; some were scraping rocks against the ground like chalk. Some girls had taken torn fabric and spare buttons to make dolls.

Davin would have found something fun to do with the children, but today was his first new assignment.

"Come on," said a guard from down the hall. Davin made sure not to make eye contact. The guards always made it seem like they were ready for a funeral. Davin wasn't afraid, but was wise enough not to try and make it his own.

He caught up with a line of older boys. One of them was almost his friend named Alm. He used to have bright red hair and freckles. His hair was so dirty, it looked brown. He was a year older, but a little shorter. "It's taken you long enough," he said.

"I'm sorry," Davin said. "Mina wanted to tell me something."

"Mina always wants to tell you something. You're too old to hang out with those little kids. They're not going to let you corrupt their easily bendable minds."

Alm was always depressing. Davin thought it was funny for some odd reason. "Then why will they let me hang out with you?"

"Because our minds are already made up," he spoke bitterly. "It's hopeless."

"Nothing is hopeless."

Alm began to mock him. "Why, because you have dreams?"

"Because I believe." It didn't matter that everyone else thought he was crazy. What mattered was that he knew he was right. "One day, I'll be free. One day, I'll be able to feel what it's like to have the sun on my skin."

Alm's eyes widened, and his mouth dropped.

"What is it?" Davin asked almost in a panic.

Alm couldn't believe it! "Are you telling me that you don't know what they're making us do?"

"What are they making us do?" Davin was clueless.

"They want us to make this facility bigger by digging up more land." Alm hinted at his point, but didn't want to give Davin the satisfaction of admitting that his dreams were possible. He waited a little longer before finishing his statement. "We have to work outside."

"Outside?" Davin was so excited that his voice cracked. "I haven't been outside since they brought me here. I don't know how long that's been, but it seems like another life ago."

"You've been here for seven years, Davin."

"How do you remember that?"

"Because," Alm said restlessly, "you've been a pain in all our sides since you arrived."

"Quiet!" yelled the guard at the end of the line. The facility wasn't surrounded with that many guards compared to the number of dreamers, but there was more than enough fear to keep them in check. They were armed with whips, clubs, and swords. Davin had never really seen them discipline anyone, but he had heard some stories and seen some scars.

He didn't say much about the direction they were going. He wasn't familiar with all of the twists and turns of the facility. Though he had enough time to search around, the guards never let anyone roam around free. The only time the doors weren't guarded was the day before. No one was around, so he made his move. He wanted to look for a way to get outside, but then he saw a room with a hole in the wall. He looked through it and that's when he saw the light. He probably should have taken his chances with freedom, but he didn't regret watching the strange storm. Besides, he was going to get his chance to finally see the sun.

When they came to the door at the end of a narrow and empty hallway, his heart busted open. He was amazed at the real sunshine pouring in from the outside. He anxiously pushed on Alm to make him walk faster.

Then, he was bathed in the sun. He shielded his eyes from the pouring rays. It had been so long. Candlesticks and lamps could never compare to it. His skin already felt like it was healing. He reached his hands toward the sky and breathed in the warm air. For the first time in a long time, he felt alive.

"Walk!" The guard behind Davin jabbed him in the back with his club. Davin let out a small holler but caught himself. Davin didn't really have meat to protect himself. "Walk!" he jabbed him again.

Davin opened his eyes and followed his team up a staircase that sat at the side of the building. It still felt like he was in his own grave. He really didn't start to feel better until he reached the final top step. He was once again above ground.

"Seven years?" he asked himself.

"That's right," Alm answered. "Seven years."

Davin looked around. Where was the green grass? Where were the trees to offer shade on a blazing hot day such as that one? Why did it look like death?

He turned to look at the building. He stayed underground for half of his life? And even with all those people trapped underground, there were still three levels above the ground and guards watching from the roof. It wasn't nearly as big as he remembered from the outside, but it was still intimidating. Black stones and steel—no wonder why the land was afraid to grow!

"Hurry up!" The guard jabbed Davin in his back again harder than the last two times.

Davin gritted his teeth and walked faster until he was side-by-side with Alm. "They're pretty strict out here." He spoke quietly so the guard wouldn't hear.

"Yes, they are."

"Do you think they're hot?"

Alm rolled his eyes, "We're all hot, Davin."

True. It was a hot day. Davin and all of the other men were dressed in thin brown pants and a thin brown shirt with long sleeves. The material was pathetic and tore easily, but it must have been considerably cooler than the buttoned up black uniform that all of the guards wore.

The land was a desert. He remembered blue flowers and a field of wheat. Even a lake used to be near. He thought it was oddly beautiful when he was young. *It's a camp. You'll only be there for a short while. You can come home when you're better.* That's what they told him. He was foolish enough to believe.

Off into the distance, there was a white tent stationed. It seemed strange to Davin. Why would they work so far away? It must have been something dangerous or something they didn't want people like Davin to see.

Something inside Davin's chest opened up. He couldn't describe the feeling. He just knew deep inside himself, there was an answer in that tent. "What's over there?" he asked Alm.

"I don't know. They didn't bring us out to work yesterday, and it wasn't there the day before."

Then, it lit up. Davin could see the shadows of at least thirty men who surrounded the entire tent, shoulder to shoulder. There was no way to be sure, but it might have been the light that fell from the sky.

"Shut up!" The guard hit Davin in the back hard enough to knock him down on his knees. That time, he couldn't help but let out a loud yell. He took a second to get his air back, but his body was in shock.

Alm stood and watched. He was about to reach out to help Davin up, but the guard glared at him as a warning. Alm didn't care much for Davin, but he didn't want to see him get hurt.

Davin didn't want or expect any help. He got up on his own two feet. He couldn't give the guard the satisfaction or take the chance of having the guard hit him again. He kept his eyes forward and followed the line.

The building looked the same on all sides, so it was hard to tell what part was the front and which was the back. Davin assumed that he was led to the back because that's where a group of men were already in the ground digging. Everyone had to climb fragile wooden ladders to get to the bottom of the hole. Davin looked over the edge and observed. It gradually got deeper as it stretched across the yard. He didn't want to get on a ladder if it was going to collapse.

It didn't matter much though. The guard behind him once again became angry with his slow pace and struck him. It wasn't as hard as the last hit, but it was hard enough to make Davin lose his balance and fall in.

49

Everyone looked at him in shock. Davin obviously needed help, but they didn't know what the consequences would be. There were guards down in the hole armed with whips. None of them wanted to face that punishment.

Davin's chest, stomach, and face hurt the most. He never had a broken bone before, but he guessed that his entire body had shattered. What had he done to deserve such a beating? The guard couldn't have simply hated him alone. It must have happened every day to all of them. How could they stand such a thing?

He lifted his head up first to rest on his chin. When he opened his eyes, an unforgettable pair of red eyes was staring into his. "Go find the light."

How did she get there? Could other people see her? No one else was mentioning her out loud. Everyone always called him crazy. Perhaps he had finally snapped.

"It's nearby," she said. "You have to find the light!"

He found the strength somewhere in his body to stand. He held his stomach while the guards laughed at him. Davin didn't mind that much. He still had a little white girl staring at him with red eyes.

No one else seemed to be looking at her. They could have been hiding it, but no one looked confused at all. Was it possible that he was imagining the whole thing? He knew he wasn't dreaming.

The little girl pointed back in the direction of the tent. It was just as he expected…Or imagined.

She smiled. "Believe in yourself, Davin." If nothing else in the world was real, Davin knew that her smile was. "Only you can do this."

Davin knew that there was always something different about him, but he never realized that he was meant for something that important. "Alright."

Alm placed his hand on Davin's shoulder. Davin turned his head away for a brief second, and when he turned back to that little girl, she was gone. "I'm fine."

"Are you sure?"

"Yes." For her to disappear like that, she couldn't have been real, but Davin was certain that he wasn't insane. "I'm sure."

Alm picked up a shovel and handed it to Davin. "We should get to work." Alm was worried about Davin. He was acting weirder than usual.

Davin took the shovel and began to dig. The earth was dead, hard, and very difficult to break up. Why would the guards make them work like that? There must have been a more effective way.

Some were diggers; some of the men took the dirt out of the hole and took it out by the bucket full. Alm had to climb up the ladder back and forth with the dirt to empty it. He was already tired after a half hour. Davin didn't know how he could push himself to keep working. He also couldn't believe how much they had done as a whole. It was on its way to stretching across the entire back wall. They probably wanted it to reach all the way down to the fourth level.

Throughout the day, every man he knew that was his age and over were out working. But it wasn't enough to really handle a job like doubling the size of the facility.

Davin noticed Mr. Petey working. He couldn't move as fast as any of the others. Why make him work? He was obviously sick. He stopped every few seconds to cough.

It was hard work for anybody. The sun was blazing down on Davin. He was beginning to understand why he had been the palest young man in the facility. His skin was already beginning to tan. His body was exhausted, so he took a moment to rest.

"What are you doing?"

Davin turned around to the voice calling out. He thought for sure that he would be physically punished again, but Davin wasn't the one in trouble. The guard stood a full head over everyone. He especially looked like a giant while hovering over Mr. Petey. "Get up!"

Mr. Petey always did as he was told. He would have gotten up if he could. He was hunched over and coughing on the ground. He had spilled the buckets of dirt that he was supposed to be carrying. Mr. Petey wished he was young again, but those days were long behind him.

The guard raised his hand to strike with his whip. "I warned you!"

Davin ran over as fast as he could. He couldn't make it before the first lash or the second. Mr. Petey screamed but all of the air was gone after that. He raised his arm to stop the guard, but he had no compassion.

"Leave him alone!" Davin ran in front of Mr. Petey. "He can't take anymore!" He couldn't think until after he was struck in the back. Davin closed his eyes and yelled.

"Get out of the way!" The guard ceased the beating, but he was ready to strike again.

Davin's didn't want to feel that pain again, but it must have felt even worse for Mr. Petey. He outstretched his arms and tried to be brave. "You're working all of us too hard!"

The guard cracked the whip on the ground close enough to make Davin jump. "We need this facility to be twice as big so we can bring more of your kind here."

Davin was shaking, but he wasn't going to move. He opened his eyes and looked at Mr. Petey. He was also shaking. His eyes were open wide and filled with fear. His lips were chapped; his body was covered with dirt, even the inside of his fingernails. He was scraped and cut up. Mr. Petey was mean-spirited, but he didn't deserve that. He had already collapsed from exhaustion. "You don't have the right to treat people like this!"

"People like you aren't supposed to exist at all."

Davin heard that before. He was a mistake. He was cursed. Well, he never believed any that. He knew that he was blessed, no matter what anyone told him. Because of dreams, Mina could find love. Because of dreams, the boys knew how to still have fun. Because of dreams, Davin could be free.

"Well, we are, and you can't treat us like this," he yelled. "Not forever!"

"Oh really?" he asked. The guard cracked the whip again, but Davin stayed still and didn't flinch. He was afraid to be struck again, but he was more afraid of what would happen to Mr. Petey. Davin could take it. He had to!

Just as the guard raised his whip, a light burst from above. The wind blew, and a cloud of dust poured while screams loomed over them. Davin held onto Mr. Petey. He wanted to protect him the best he could.

When Davin could no longer feel the dust on his face, he opened his eyes. All of the guards watching them in the hole were unconscious. Not only that, but the dust hadn't passed over. It was hovering above their heads.

"Are you alright, Mr. Petey?" Davin asked.

He couldn't answer. He hadn't opened his eyes since before the dust storm brushed over. He was breathing heavily and holding his chest.

Another adult walked over to the two of them. He was twice Davin's age but also had twice the fear. "He has a bad heart."

"We already knew that," Alm said smartly.

"I think he means he's sick," another man said.

Davin gently set him down on his back. Mr. Petey had always been cruel. Davin never understood why, but he didn't want to see him die. He was still one of them.

Davin looked around. Another kid around his age had gotten the courage to poke one of the guards with a shovel. They were indeed unconscious. The light had somehow done all of that.

The choice they had to make was so obvious, yet it came off of Davin's lips as a whisper. "Why don't we run?"

Then another man spoke with anger. "Why would we do that?"

"Because no one is watching us," Davin said. "We have a chance to get free. There is nothing here to stop us other than our own fear."

Then Mr. Petey desperately grabbed Davin's shirt collar. "If we run, they'll find us." He was struggling to breathe. "I was sick of running when I was a young man. I can't bear it now that I'm old."

They couldn't all run. The men couldn't leave the women and children inside. The old men like Mr. Petey certainly couldn't run. There would be other guards ready to find them. There wasn't enough light in the world to change that.

There was only one thing Davin knew they could do. "Then maybe we should stand up and fight."

Alm responded mockingly. "We're all weak compared to them, especially you. How would you expect to defeat them?"

Everything Alm said was true. Davin was weak. He had his bravery, but it might have easily been stupidity. Fighting naturally wasn't the way to go, but there was something strange happening to Davin. He was becoming more confident. He was becoming stronger. "I don't know if I can. We just have to try—we men."

Davin knew by their faces that he hadn't convinced them. Someone must have tried to convince another group of men at least once in the past seven years. Were those men too afraid to try? He wouldn't let himself fail another seven-year-old boy.

He tried again. "There are children buried underground that are living just to die if we don't do something now. No one fought for me. I want to fight for them now."

They all looked at each other. Some were shaking their heads. Some were simply shaking from fright. It was only natural. Then another boy around Davin's age asked, "Is it worth our deaths?"

Davin wanted to gulp at the thought, but he instead answered as bravely as he could. "If it's worth the victory, then it's worth our deaths."

A revelation seemed to come over their faces. Davin rose to his feet and continued to urge them on. "I believe that, but I also believe that we don't have to die." Davin could feel strength deep inside of him. There was something that started deep in his belly and flowed throughout his body. "Something is happening to me. I keep seeing a little girl. She tells me to find a light—the same light that I saw yesterday. It fell from the sky and now it's here to give us hope."

"You're as crazy as ever, Davin." Alm meant it, but it wasn't a usual mock. He was excited!

"There is no hope for men like us," another man said.

Davin didn't know what to say to convince them otherwise. If he had to fight alone, he would. Finding the light was his duty.

"You're wrong." Mr. Petey's weak words surprised them all. "Davin, come here."

Davin bent down beside him and grabbed a hold of Mr. Petey's hand. Mr. Petey remembered what it was like to have smooth hands without a wrinkle. He remembered what it was like not having a care in the world. Oh, he wished he could be young again!

But Davin wouldn't be a young man anymore. He would either grow to be a man like him or free man with his head held high in pride. In a way, Davin was wiser than all of them.

"I've been living my whole life as a coward," he admitted sadly.

55

A sparkle came to Mr. Petey's eyes as he reminisced. "I used to see marvelous things that could only live in the depths of a child's mind. I loved my dreams, and I clung onto them. No matter what, I knew that there would be better days.

"But when they came for me, I was afraid. I tried to be strong like you. I told the others to never give up dreaming. I told them not to lose what made them special just because it caused us pain. I was an inspiration, so I had to become the example.

"They punished me in ways I can't say. I can't remember unless I recall them from my darkest nightmares. I stopped speaking of my dreams to make them stop. It wasn't enough. I wanted to leave and go home. I had a family that I wanted to see.

"I told them that I didn't have dreams anymore. I lied over and over to myself every day that I lived. Then one day, it became true. I haven't had a dream in years, and I miss it very much.

"That's why I envy you, Davin. You are who I used to be. You are brave and have a kind heart. I don't know what you can do to save us. I'm not sure if I should believe in you, but we need to believe in something.

"That's what this is all about. They don't want us to believe. If people have dreams, they'll begin to have hope. And when we learn to have hope, we'll begin to have faith."

"Faith?" It was a word Davin wasn't sure he had ever heard, but it was powerful. He somehow knew that it meant to believe in something bigger than yourself. Faith to Davin meant that everything that he believed in was true even with no evidence in front of his eyes. His freedom was real.

"That's why they keep us here. They want to destroy us." Mr. Petey had another coughing fit. Davin believed that Mr. Petey could get better, but Mr. Petey was a man ready to go.

"I want everyone to follow Davin to the ends of the world if you have to." Davin was surprised. Even with all Mr. Petey had said, his vote of confidence was overwhelming. "I know that you're going to change the world. I only wished I would have believed in you before."

Then Mr. Petey smiled with what little strength he had left. "I saw…" he whispered.

Davin barely heard him, so he leaned in closer to hear. "Saw what?"

"I saw…The little girl."

Davin's eyes widened. He knew that the girl was real, but a confirmation was amazing! And from Mr. Petey no less!

His eyes grew heavy and fell. His grip on Davin's hand faded, and he let go. "Mr. Petey?" Davin shook him, but he didn't open his eyes.

Everyone took a moment of silence for Mr. Petey. If Davin was ever to lose his dreams…It would be a terrible life. He couldn't imagine what it must have felt like for Mr. Petey to lose his gift. Davin wouldn't let that happen to another person as long as he lived.

He stood on his feet. Every man with the ability to dream surrounded him. They were all older than him. Davin was the strangest, the most hopeful, and the most foolish. It was a difficult task, but he had to rally those men. "I know you guys don't feel comfortable trusting a person that I've seen in my head. I think it's weird too."

He paused. It was difficult to speak with tears in the back of his eyes and his throat grief stricken. "I don't know what she is or what she means. All I know is that I trust her. I believe that things will change if we find the light."

"But there are more guards than what you think," another man said. "There are archers stationed on top of the building to make sure that we don't run."

Davin didn't know that. It added speed to his pounding heart. He had fear. There was no question about it. He gulped it all down because he had to. "I'm going to fight if I have to. I'll die if I have to, but I'm not going to let them rule me with fear anymore."

He waited for their hesitant reply. Alm and some others began to slowly nod. Everyone looked at the guards spread about. There were about forty armed in the pit with them and some of them were beginning to move.

The light in the distance began to flicker brighter than the sun. Davin was beginning to feel a rush in his stomach. He couldn't wait any longer. "Run!"

Every single person did as he instructed. They headed off to the ladders. There weren't enough to get them all out before the guards woke up. Some of the men who could crawl up began to. Alm did it with ease. Davin tried, but he began to slip halfway down. He let out a short yell until Alm outstretched his hand and grabbed Davin. They smiled at each other in a brief amount of respect and then resumed the escape.

The dust cloud ended once they got out of the pit. A bell was sounding off from the top of the building, and all of the guards were screaming to get them. Some of the men were stopped before they could get out. Davin heard them scream, but he knew he couldn't afford to turn around.

Those who could, continued to run, but they scattered. Davin only had about ten men—including Alm—behind him on the search of the light. The tent was down, but Davin couldn't see what was giving off the light. The guards who were surrounding it were already up and waiting for them.

A voice shouted from behind. "Look out!"

Davin turned around for a second and looked up. The archers were preparing to shoot. He turned around and ran faster than he knew his legs could move. He never knew that he could run faster than Alm. He had never felt such strength to do it. Something amazing was happening to him!

He heard the sound of the arrows whizzing through the air like a silent deadly scream. He saw men being hit and falling. He wanted to help them, but he couldn't. It wasn't out of selfishness. He knew if he could get to the light, their hopes wouldn't be in vain.

He blocked it all out. He took out the noise, his allies, his foes, and the fear. All he left himself was the power surging throughout his body. He pushed himself to run even faster. There was a guard waiting with his feet planted into the ground. He was three times the size of Davin, but he didn't see him. He saw past everything and saw the light. He plowed through the man as if he were a child and kept running. Another guard came flying at him, but he jumped out of the way. He didn't need to think about it. He just somehow knew how to dodge or defeat every man in front of him. He was going to make it!

Then, he was hit.

Davin fell to the ground flat on his face. His heart was pumping so fast that he felt it in his skull. He gritted his teeth and tried to block out the pain, but he knew that he had been shot more than once in his back. He was bleeding and perhaps even dying.

"Davin!" Alm ran for him, but another guard tackled him before he could make it. He began to shout hysterically, but Davin couldn't hear him anymore.

He had done a great thing that day. He gave Mr. Petey back his hope. He gave all those men back their dignity. He fought for all of the people like him: the dreamers. He fought for himself. Hopefully, that was enough to start a fire in someone else's heart.

But it wasn't enough.

What did it matter if he tried? His memory would be honored *if* the story were ever told. His mission was far too great to fail! He had to do something. He had to get up.

The light was so close; he could feel it. As it blinked, his whole body pulsed. There was a new life flowing through him. It had to be enough. He had to be enough!

The guards marveled as Davin stood. There was no humanly way that a man could get up after that, let alone a boy his size. They were stunned enough to let him get close enough to see it. The light was coming from an orb resting at the bottom of a small crater.

Davin reached the edge of the crater just as a man tackled him. He was pinned on the ground, but he wouldn't let that stop him. He was too close. He was too important to fail. That light wasn't just for him. It was for Mina, Alm, and Mr. Petey! It was for every dreamer.

His legs were pinned, but he moved himself closer with his arms. No one could believe Davin's strength! They were afraid of him, but they were even more afraid of what would happen if he were to touch the strange light. Another man jumped on the other leg, but it felt like nothing to Davin. Then another one came to hold down his back, and another came to grab his arm, and then another.

If Davin had to move by his chin alone, he would do it. He did do it! "Just an inch," he told himself. "Just an inch!" It was so close. He could see himself in its reflection. He fought and wiggled until he could get an arm free. He only had a second before they would grab him again. He stretched out his hand. It was so close to his fingertips. All he had to do was reach!

Chapter Five

Tice kept her head pressed against her knees and under her folded arms. She was in a cold, dark room. The only light was from the stars shining through a steel barred window higher than what she could reach.

There was a fight going on from the outside, but she wasn't afraid. When all the sound disappeared, her door creaked open.

She slowly looked up to see a young man coming in. He had beautiful green eyes, blond hair, and white skin. His skin wasn't pale like hers, but she had never seen another person who had ever come close.

"Some things are worth dying for." Then he walked up to her and reached out his hand. "But your work isn't done yet."

Tice had never seen a boy who looked so strong and handsome before. He had a kindness in his eyes that she knew she could trust. She reached out her hand and grabbed his.

"Are you awake yet, Tice?"

She opened her eyes but wasn't sure. She stared for a while before she remembered that she couldn't see. "I'm awake..." she said weakly. She continued to lie on the cold floor of the cave. She wished so much that she could see her brother. She knew he was looking at her with sadness. Tears began to fall from her eyes and onto the ground. She whimpered silently.

Riss reached over and brushed the loose strands of hair off of her face. He hated himself for what he allowed to happen to her.

Tice sat up and reached out for her brother. She found his legs first and then patted her way up to his chest. Then she hugged him as tightly as she could. "Did you get any sleep?" She did her best not to sound upset.

"No," he said. "I'm not tired."

"Yes you are. I can hear it in your voice."

He held her tighter and kissed her on the head. "I'm so sorry." He broke down and began to cry over her.

"It's not your fault."

"We should have never left the orphanage. I'm not strong enough to protect you all by myself." He never should have left her alone with the strange orbs from the sky. But he was blessed with the ability to control and make fire. Why would it give to him and take away her sight?

He found her crying and screaming. She had to cry herself to sleep, and she slept most of the next day. He did his best not to sleep at all. He was afraid to move with Tice from the cave, but he very well couldn't trust the orbs after what they had done.

Tice didn't know what it would be like for her not to see anything else for the rest of her life. She was terrified at first. She never really liked looking at herself, but it was better than not being able to see at all. She wouldn't be able to see Riss and his green eyes anymore. She could never find that pink flower and put it in her hair.

The only time she could still see was when she closed her eyes and tried to remember or when she would have a dream.

She had never seen that boy before. He was saving her from something. The dream felt important. She never had one that wasn't silly before. It was odd. "Maybe it won't be that bad, Brother."

62

Riss didn't believe her. How could she live her life without walking with her sight?

"There are worse things in the world."

"Mother, I want to go and play," said a young girl of thirteen. She was pretty, kind, and many other sweet compliments that her mother gave her every day while she looked out at the beach and felt the ocean breeze on her face.

"You're special, Diene," was her mother's excuse for that day. She would always pat her on the back of the head gently and offer a smile. "Maybe someday. It might be soon—might not—but someday."

Diene understood. She was special. She was different.

It wasn't fair.

All of the other kids laughed and ran barefoot against the shores while she watched them every day from her porch. She wanted to laugh with them. She wanted to dance with them. She wanted to run.

"Come on," her mother said. "Let's get you off to the doctors."

Diene held on tight to the handles on her chair while her mother pulled it back and wheeled her away. Diene kept her eyes on the group of children still running about with strong legs. They took it all for granted.

Diene was grateful for what she had. Every day her mother and father would take her into town. Her mother would help her get dressed in a pretty, long dress and a pair of white sandals that never got dirty or worn out. Her mother would brush every strand of hair on her head carefully, and then braid it all up. Diene always insisted on doing it herself, but her mother always wanted to help.

Her father would be the one to carry her around and put her into her wheelchair. She felt safe when he pushed her around town. Every time she held her head up, he would be looming above her with a loving smile.

It wasn't all that bad being crippled—not when she had people who loved her and made her feel whole again.

Her parents did their best to make sure Diene got outside every day. Some days she didn't want to, but her parents always gave her incentive. Her father would buy Diene something every trip. They didn't have a lot of money after paying for all of her medicine, but they would buy her something sweet to eat or a new ribbon for her hair.

That day, Diene and her family passed by a store and she saw a beautiful green dress sitting in the window on a wooden manikin. It had been sitting in that window for weeks, but she had never tried it on or even asked her father to stop pushing her chair so she could get a better look at it. She didn't want to burden them.

But she was beginning to get desperate. "Mother," she said meekly, "you know there is a dance coming up soon."

Her mother looked down at her surprised, but Diene didn't look up to see her mother's shocked face. "Do you want to go?" she asked carefully.

Diene didn't want to go to the last dance her school had, but things were different then. She was maturing, and so were many handsome boys. "Yes." She was trying not to blush.

Her parents looked at each other wearily. Neither of them thought it was a good idea, but neither of them had a good idea how they could stop her without hurting her feelings. "I was thinking that we could stay home and have a nice meal," said her father.

"Oh…" she said sadly. She did enjoy their company, but she ate alone with them every night. She didn't have a single friend outside of school.

Her mother leaned over to be closer to her daughter. "I can make your favorite meal."

She really couldn't disappoint her parents after all they had done for her. "Alright."

Diene tried not to show how discouraged she was, but how could she not be? She wanted—more than anything in the world—to be a normal girl.

She tried not to think about the dance. After her father bought her a sweet snack to eat, they took her home and fixed her dinner. Her mother gave her medicine and brushed her hair at least a hundred times before letting her sleep. Then her father took her to her room, tucked her in her warm bed, and kissed her forehead. "Sleep well for me," he said.

"And be there when I wake," was her reply every night.

Diene closed her eyes and made the same wish she made two nights ago when she saw a shower of stars streaming across the sky. Hopefully one of them would make her wish come true. She wished that somehow, someday that she would stand up on her own two feet. She wished it until she fell asleep.

"Wake up."

Diene opened her eyes to see a young girl with white skin and white hair sitting on the foot of her bed with her back to her. Diene would have screamed if she wasn't too afraid to make a noise.

She pulled her covers up over her head to hide. She thought, "Maybe she'll go away if I don't look at her."

Then the bed began to sink in around her, and the sheets began to rustle as something began getting closer.

She whimpered and struggled not to cry. "If I look, she'll take my life!" She bit her lips together so she wouldn't scream.

But then, heavy breathing was right in her ear. Diene didn't know much about apparitions, but if they were not alive, they shouldn't be able to breathe.

She finally got up the courage to slowly peel the covers away and stared into her red eyes.

She couldn't help it and prepared to scream. She opened her mouth, but the ghost's little, warm hands fell on top of her lips. "Don't!" the ghost warned.

Diene's eyes had been filled with frightful tears. Her parents were close. If she fought the ghost off and screamed, her parents would hear and come to her aid, but all she could do was let the tears slip down her face.

"Don't cry," the ghost said, "I'm not trying to hurt you."

She let go of Diene's mouth. Diene could still feel the warm touch of the ghost's fingers. It was as if she were a real person. "Who are you?"

The ghost smiled. "I'm your friend."

Diene didn't really have friends, except for her mother and her father. "What do you want?"

"I want to help you." The little ghost smiled and walked over to her door. "You have to follow me."

"Follow you?" Diene asked. "I can't move."

"You have to follow me if you want to walk."

"To walk?" Diene felt her heart begin to race. For as long as she could remember, she had never taken one step. She tried many times to make her legs move, but not even her toe would wiggle in the slightest bit. It was a worthless cause. "It's impossible."

"Nothing is impossible." The ghost girl didn't wait for Diene and walked out of her room.

"Wait!" Diene looked to the left of her bed where her wheelchair was. She had never tried to get up on her own. She felt pitiful, but if there were even the tiniest bit of a chance that things could change, then she had no choice but to act.

She threw her covers off of her and scooted her body over to the edge until she was close enough to pull the wheelchair to her. It was heavier than what she thought, and she wasn't as strong as she should have been, but she wouldn't give up until she got her body in the chair.

She wanted to wake her parents so they could help her, but they would never believe. She barely believed it herself. They would tell her to go back to sleep and not to believe, because disappointment hurt so much that it was better not to try. But Diene was sick of sitting still!

Diene was tired from getting into the chair, but she wheeled herself out of her room. The ghost was in the next room watching. "Can you help me?"

"You have to do this yourself." The ghost continued to walk until she headed to the front door and outside.

Diene was beginning to sweat. It was the hardest thing she ever had to do, but she was going to keep moving. She followed the little girl and pushed through the door until she was outside on her own for the very first time of her life.

The little ghost walked down the ramp and headed off to the shore. Diene was beginning to wonder where the little ghost was going to stop. She was afraid when she went down the ramp very fast, but she missed the speed once she hit the sand. Her arms were sore, and when she got to the little girl on the shore, it all seemed to be for nothing.

"How am I supposed to walk?" Diene asked the ghost.

She pointed out toward the water. "It's in there."

Diene looked at the ghost confused. "What is?"

"The light."

Diene remembered a light that fell from the sky. She didn't know it was so close. "Are you going to get it for me?"

"I can't. You have to go get it yourself."

Diene looked out into the water. She didn't know how deep it was and even if she could use her legs, she couldn't swim. But the issue was that she couldn't even stand up or feel what it was like to have the sand squish in between her toes. There was no way she could do it.

She began to cry. "But I'm afraid."

"If you get it," the girl said, "you'll be able to walk."

Diene knew somehow that what the little girl said was true. There was just no way to get to it. "But I could die."

"I wouldn't ask you to do this if you weren't capable." The little girl smiled. "Have faith."

Diene had begun to cry harder. "I don't know what that is."

The little girl reached over and touched Diene's hand. "You will."

Diene opened her eyes and saw into the little girl's eyes. She was kind, and she knew that she meant the best. Diene didn't know if she would be okay, but she did know that she had to try. "Okay."

She was still crying, and her fingers were shaking, but she gripped onto her wheels and began to push herself toward the ocean. As the water touched her legs, she couldn't feel it, and that frightened her all the more. It was harder to push herself into the water, but she continued to do it.

"Have faith!" the little girl shouted.

Diene took a deep breath for courage and swallowed it to push down her fears. When the water was high enough to reach her waist, she began to feel the cold water. She sobbed harder, but she continued to go deeper. Somehow everything had to work out. Somehow, something had to change.

When the water was up to her chin, her lips were quivering. She was amazed that she could still roll the wheelchair, but she did. Before going under, she took a deep breath and watched as the water came into her eyes.

She shut them tight once it hit. She kept her mouth closed, though she wanted to scream. She had no choice but to believe that the light was nearby.

Then, she felt warmth on her face and opened her eyes. There was a green ball swirling with light floating up in front of her. She could barely believe it, but it was time to start believing in something.

When she reached out to touch it, she felt its warmth all over her body, even on her legs. It was an incredible feeling. But as it grew brighter and brighter, she became afraid and screamed.

She closed her eyes as hard as she could and thought about getting away as fast as possible. When she opened her eyes again, she was once in her room dry and standing on her own two feet.

She had no words to say or thoughts in her mind. She touched her legs, and she could feel every single one of her fingers on her skin. Diene began to cry and scream hysterically.

Her parents woke up in a panic and ran to their daughter's room. When they saw her, they screamed, cried, hugged, and kissed their daughter.

Diene had never really known what it meant to be truly happy until that moment. "I can walk! I can walk!"

Then her mother grabbed her face frightened. "You mustn't ever walk in public. It's very important!"

Diene didn't know what to say. She looked into her father's eyes, and he agreed. "But why?" she asked.

Her mother held her close into her chest. "Because this is called a miracle and they're not supposed to exist."

Diene's parents made her swear to never walk, run, dance, or to let the people know the truth. She did as she was told, but she did not explain how she could walk. She questioned whether or not the little girl was real or if she really did wheel herself out into the ocean. She didn't really receive an answer that she could understand.

Her wheelchair tracks were in the sand, but there were no tiny footprints. She watched from her window as her parents retrieved her wheelchair from the water. She wasn't sure what happened, but she had learned something.

She knew how to believe. "Thank you."

Chapter Six

"Brother, please no!" Tice had never disobeyed her brother before, but she felt like she had no choice. No matter how hard he pulled on her, and no matter how much he yelled, she wasn't going to take one step. She made her body go limp and fell on the cold, hard ground. It hurt her bottom, but she wasn't going to give in.

Riss glared at his little sister as a warning, but he soon remembered that a stern gaze would never work on her again. He began to feel guilty and loosen his grip. "Please, Tice. We have to." He knew that he should have been tougher with Tice, but he couldn't bring himself to do it. She couldn't see because of him.

Tice leaned back until her entire body was across the ground. "No!" she yelled. "I'm not leaving!"

Little did Tice know, but she just gave her brother exactly what he needed. He was the older brother. He made the decisions, whether he was right or wrong. There was no way that he was going to let her lay on the ground and con him into staying. "Get up, Tice."

"No!"

He spoke more forcefully. "I said get up!"

"No!" she yelled louder.

Riss had enough. He forced her on top of his shoulder. She began to kick and scream, which made it difficult for him. He couldn't carry their supplies and her while she acted like such a spoiled child.

He set her down and grabbed her shoulders. He knew that she couldn't see him, but he looked her right in the eye and asked, "Why don't you want to go back to the orphanage?"

Tice was about to scream. She felt so strongly not to go back. The only reason why she didn't shout in her brother's face was because she didn't understand why herself. "I don't know," she admitted quietly.

Riss was angry, but it was hard to stay that way while his sister looked miserable. "Is it because of your eyes?" he asked.

She didn't think that was the reason, but she wanted to go back before. She never wanted to leave in the first place. It was the only thing that had changed. She wasn't going to say yes or no unless she knew, so Tice simply shrugged her shoulders.

Riss figured as much. "You want to see your friends again, don't you?"

She nodded.

"Well, then don't worry about your eyes. Everyone will still love you." He smiled. "I bet Mal cries every night you're away."

She laughed. "No, he doesn't."

"I bet he does." He played with her hair, just as he knew Mal would. Tice scrunched up her face, and he chuckled at her. She was beginning to be more like her old self. He admired her strength. He knew that he would never be the same again.

He took a sack and filled it halfway with bread and some fruit that she would be able to carry while he carried a full sack that was heavy. His friends back at the orphanage would be happy to see them return with food. They might have even agreed not to speak of Tice's dreams.

"Are you ready to go?"

No. The answer was no. Tice still felt strongly that they shouldn't go back. "Sure."

He gently touched her back and began to nudge her toward the exit of the cave. Tice was hesitant to step forward. She was afraid of the dark, and now everything was permanent darkness. At least her brother was there for her. He wouldn't let anything bad happen to her.

"Here you go. Be careful." He helped her climb into the exit, and he was right behind her while she crawled. To him, she was already helpless. Not being able to see was going to make it worse.

"Hold on." The hole in the wall was a couple of feet off of the ground, so he helped her up and squeezed by her so he could help her out.

Tice usually enjoyed being a child, but she was beginning to feel like a burden, and that was very bothersome to her.

Riss took their bags and set them on the ground. Then he reached out his arms for her. "Come on."

Tice puffed up her cheeks, but did as she was told. She was too afraid to jump, so she reached out her arms until he grabbed onto her and lifted her up off the ground.

Riss thought that it wasn't so bad taking extra care of her. Tice never complained about anything. As long as she stayed sweet, he could reciprocate. "All set to go?" he asked.

Tice wasn't sure how she should answer. She couldn't see where they were going. She didn't know where they were or what would be in their way. "I suppose," she said.

As they walked together, he made sure to mention if there was a twig or something in the way. He would pull her arm and led her away from anything that she might trip over. She wanted to walk on her own, but it would have been less terrifying if Riss carried her on his back or let her sit on his shoulders. She didn't like him tugging on her arm, but she didn't want to tell him that he was hurting her. She didn't like that she didn't know what she was stepping on. Riss was doing his best to lead her away from harm, but her thin shoes were worn and too small for her feet.

They both continued on pretending. He pretended like he knew what he was doing while she pretended to be okay with it.

After a while, Tice began to wobble about, and her legs began to itch. She tried to ignore it, but it wasn't long before she began to moan and lose her will to walk.

"Tice?" Riss caught her with his arm and pulled her up, but she moaned louder. He didn't want to rest in the jungle, but he couldn't refuse her. With her condition, taking the smallest steps took the greatest of time.

He sat his bag down and carried her over to a nearby rock. There was no way the two of them were going to survive on their own with her being weak, sick, and blind. He knew that going back was the right choice for them. "We can rest here," he said, "but not long."

Tice breathed out heavily. "Why?"

"Because there are dangerous things out here."

"But what about your fire? Can't you protect us?"

Riss appreciated her confidence in him, but he knew that he didn't deserve it. "I'll try, but it's better to be safe." It was odd talking to her while looking in her eyes, knowing that she wouldn't see his face and respond to his reactions. He missed how everything used to be. "I don't think we should have ever left."

"Why would you say something like that?"

Before he could answer, the two of them heard rustling from the trees and broken twigs. "What is that?" she asked.

"Be quiet." Riss picked Tice up and carried her behind a thick tree. He had to set her down to retrieve their sack cloths, or else a traveler would know that the two of them were near.

He was successful in running off the bandits who stole from them, but he wasn't sure if he could face them again. He had burned a lot of trees, and he was embarrassed to tell Tice that he lost control.

He held her close to his chest while she whimpered afraid. He was frightened himself, but he was going to do what he had to in order to keep her safe. The noises in the jungle began to get louder. Riss held out his free hand and began to concentrate. He could feel the life of the fire in his hand beginning to grow. As soon as he opened up his hand, there was a tiny flame.

Tice lifted her head, feeling the heat from her brother's hand. She wished she could see the colors, but at least she knew it was there and that he was willing to protect her.

He whispered, "Don't be afraid."

She gulped and nodded.

The traveler was near. They both could hear him breathing. It was time. Riss slowly tilted his head around the tree and moved his eyes to the traveler. "Mal?" His flame disappeared in shock.

"Mal?" Tice was so excited! She tried to run around the tree, hoping to see him. She tried to follow his voice, but was facing the wrong direction.

Mal laughed. "I'm right here, Little One."

Riss grabbed Tice's hand before she could wander any further.

Mal was still smiling at the sight of seeing them. It was comical how helpless the two of them looked. Tice's once white dress was brown with dried mud and fresh dirt. Riss's clothes were torn. Their hair was messy, their faces were dirty, and they were tired. "What have you two been doing?"

Tice tried to come forward, but Riss held her close.

"What's the matter?" Mal was still smiling, but he was beginning to realize that there wasn't anything to smile about. He noticed that Tice's

75

red eyes were now a pale blue with pupils barely visible. Her red eyes were a little unnerving when you first saw Tice, but you got used to them. With her eyes being so light, it washed out the rest of her body as if she were not from their world at all.

"She can't see," Riss admitted quietly.

Mal let out a short, hysterical chuckle. "What?" He didn't mean to laugh, but it was something he always did. When he wasn't strong enough, he would lie with a confident smile. When he was sad, he would fib with a dashing smirk. It was the same when he went through a loss. He never meant to. It was just his way of protecting himself.

"It's true," Tice said.

The laughs never lasted that long. He couldn't lie quite that well. "What happened?" Mal was a little angry at Riss. Of course he knew that Riss didn't let it happen on purpose, but Tice was like his little sister too.

Riss hardly knew how to explain it all. "There was a light that fell from the sky."

Mal interrupted impatiently. "I saw it."

Mal was really making things difficult for Riss to explain. Riss already felt guilty enough. "What happened was—"

"The light messed up my eyes." Tice spoke quickly, and Riss looked down at his little sister with a lot of questions. She felt him staring, and she knew why. "You know how sensitive my eyes are."

"You should have been looking after her!" Mal yelled.

"Don't you think I know that?" The anger was good for Riss. It took his mind off of the guilt. "It was an accident!"

Mal came up to Riss fast and domineering. The two boys stared at each other fearlessly, waiting for the other to back down. Surprisingly, it was Mal who backed away from Riss and bent down to touch Tice's face. "Are you okay?"

Mal's touch startled her at first. She had to remind herself that he was her friend. "Yes. I'm fine."

Riss was a little amazed and still felt the rush of anger from Mal's accusations. It upset him that Tice and Mal could suddenly pretend like it was old times again. "What are you doing here?"

Mal ignored Riss's words to stare into Tice's eyes. The closer he looked, the more they looked like glass. "I don't understand how this could have happened, even with her condition."

"I don't have a condition!" she yelled. "I'm fine!"

He was taken aback by her short outburst. Tice was never defensive about anything. He played along and smiled at her. "I know you are, Little One."

"Come on," Riss said, "tell me why you're here."

Tice tugged on her brother's pants. "I'm hungry."

The three of them agreed to rest and talk. Riss gathered up some wood for a fire and went through the sacks they had for a meal while Mal sat with Tice. Riss wanted to tell Mal about what had happened to him, but he was going to wait until Mal had told his story first. He looked behind him to make sure Mal was busy holding Tice before setting the wood on fire with his will.

The three of them enjoyed bread, cheese, apples and finished off the milk. There was even some honey. Mal was concerned how they got the extra food, but he was glad to be eating it himself.

"So what happened?" Riss asked again.

"I came to find you both."

"To bring us back home?" Tice whined.

"No," Mal said sadly. "There is no more home."

Riss was shocked. "What do you mean by that?"

Mal swallowed his last piece of bread and took his time to wipe his hands free of crumbs. It was hard for him tell Riss the truth. "I mean that there isn't any more home. The rest of the kids decided to leave and venture out into the world like you did. They tried going north."

"Why would they leave like that?" Riss asked.

"I'm not exactly sure, but none of us wanted to live there forever." Mal shrugged and smiled, trying to lighten the mood. "I think they just finally realized that they could go out on their own and find a better life for themselves."

It was hard for Riss and Tice to believe that their home was gone in a manner of days. Everything they knew had changed, and there was nowhere for them to return to.

"What about you?" Riss asked. "You were supposed to take care of them."

"There were some other kids around my age who felt up to the challenge." Mal did feel like they were his responsibility, but not a lot of people would look out for someone who looked like Tice. "I needed to find you guys and make sure you were okay, but I wish I could have gotten here sooner to prevent Tice's blindness."

Riss felt very grateful to have his best friend with them, but he was insulted. "There was nothing that could have been done."

"How do you know that?"

"Because I do!" he yelled. "I can take care of Tice."

Mal was surprised with Riss's anger, but just like he did in serious times, Mal laughed. "I know you're her older brother, but I'm older and stronger than you. It just would have been nice if—"

"You're not stronger than me," Riss insisted quickly.

Tice knew her brother well enough to know he was brash. "No, Riss!" she pulled on his arm and begged. "Don't do this."

Riss pulled his arm away from Tice and folded them with his head held high.

Mal didn't understand Riss's cockiness. "You haven't beaten me once!"

"Things are different now." Riss was excited that his time to be the strongest had finally come. "I would show you, but my advantage is very unfair."

"And what's that advantage?"

He smirked as he held out his hand toward Mal. "This." When he opened up his hand, a flame appeared.

Mal jumped back at the sudden small burst of fire. He didn't expect or understand it. But the longer it burned in Riss's hand, he realized that the power belonged to Riss. "How did this happen?" he asked amazed.

Mal came closer to the flame, and Riss became more arrogant. "Oh, I don't think someone like you could get something like this."

Mal was offended. "If you can, I can!"

"Riss," Tice pouted, "stop being such a jerk!"

Riss closed his hand to put out the flame and smiled more. "Do you remember the light that fell from the sky?"

Mal did see it with all of the other kids at the orphanage. They all thought it was strange, and none of them knew what it was. "Yes. What about it?"

"Some of it fell down to where we were, and it gave me these powers."

Mal couldn't believe that such a beautiful light could even exist, and he would have never thought it would have been so powerful. "Take me to it."

"No!" Tice begged the both of them. "You can't go there. The light is what took away my sight. It might do something worse to you!"

Mal looked at little Tice. She already had so many problems. He didn't know how she would survive, but he was stronger than her. "I'm willing to take that chance."

At first, Riss didn't know what to do. He liked that he finally had the upper hand, but Mal was his friend. "I'll show you where it is."

Tice began to pull on Riss's arm. "No! Please, Riss! Don't do this."

Riss was surprised by her outburst. "Calm down, Tice. I'm sure nothing bad will happen. Mal is the toughest guy that I know."

She still had her hand on her brother's arm, but she stopped pulling and pouted. "So you think I'm blind because I'm weak?"

"No. That's not what I meant." Riss sighed. "Will you please calm down and trust me?"

She couldn't see her brother's face, but she knew him so well that she didn't have to. She knew that his eyes had doubts and that his lips spoke lies. "I've always trusted in you. I wish you would start trusting in me." She let go of him and sunk her head down.

The boys felt bad, but neither of them was going to discontinue their plans. It was Mal who scooped Tice up into his arms and kissed her cheeks. "Come on. We're all friends, and we look out for each other. If I learn to wield fire like Riss, we can protect you better."

Tice laid her head against his chest, but she wasn't happy. There was a prickly feeling on her skin and rumbling in her stomach. She wasn't scared. There was just something wrong with taking Mal to the light.

She didn't understand why. He still smelled like trees and the wind. His voice was the same. His arms still felt just as strong as when she used to feel safe in them. There was no change in him, yet something was wrong.

When they got to the cave, Riss and Tice both felt the same warmth from the light when it gave him powers and took away her sight.

It glowed radiantly, and one of them was so bright until a light burst from the inside out and changed them. Now the light was still and dim.

Mal sat Tice down on the cold cave floor and approached the light with an awing curiosity. They burned so much brighter in the sky. He was expecting something different. "How does it work?"

"I'm not sure," Riss told him. "One of them began to glow red, and when I touched it, I created a fire."

Mal carefully looked at all of the small orbs. There had to be at least one that was glowing a bit brighter than the others. When he didn't see one, he began to touch them all.

Tice heard them fall and clack against the ground. "All I did was look at it," Tice said.

That made Mal even more frustrated. He touched every orb that he could, but the more he touched them, the more they began to dim.

Riss was in shock. "I guess you can't do it."

Mal became angry. He always licked Riss clean when they fought with each other. Riss couldn't be stronger or more capable than him. It was impossible.

"I don't…" Tice's small voice quivered. "I don't think you're supposed to have it."

Mal was so angry that he ran out of the cave and away from his friends.

"Mal, wait!" Riss called after him, but he didn't want to leave Tice alone. Besides, there was nothing that could be done when Mal was upset except for giving him some space.

Mal kept walking through the forest without really watching where he was going. He had never been so embarrassed in his life. He kept moving until he felt something in the wind and stopped. He looked around, but he couldn't see anything around him except for trees and a darkness among the light of day that seemed to whirl through them.

"Hello?" He felt a chill go down his spine. "Is anyone there?" He looked around, but he didn't see anyone.

"Hello."

Mal turned around startled from hearing the voice suddenly behind him. There was a woman there. She was tall, thin, and her skin was the same shade as Tice. Her eyes were different though. He had never seen any person with yellow eyes.

"Who are you?" he asked.

She smiled friendly, but there was something malevolently wicked about her. "Do not be startled. I am only here to help you."

"I'm not scared," he said quickly. "I'm strong enough to take care of myself."

"But not strong enough to wield the power of the light?" she asked with a smirk.

He narrowed his eyes at her suspiciously. "How do you know about the light?"

The woman was strange indeed. As she talked, she circled around Mal, but she it was as if she never took a single step. She glided along the ground with not even her long flowing dress making a sound while dragging across the jungle's floor. "Everyone called of the light saw its beauty, but there are those who are chosen by it and those who are too weak."

"I'm not weak," Mal insisted.

She appeared quickly behind him and touched his shoulder gently. "Then why is it that your friends wielded its power with such ease, and you have nothing?"

Tice had always been incapable of taking care of herself and Riss wouldn't have been able to do anything without his Mal's help. It didn't make sense to him. "I don't know."

The strange woman smiled and glided around to face Mal once again. "Cheer up, Child. I can help you."

He didn't trust her, but nothing could be worse than being unable to take care of his friends. "Help me how?"

"Give me your hand." She slowly stretched out her hand and uncurled her fingers from a fist until all fingers were extended toward Mal. In her palm, a darkness began to radiate.

Mal was scared, but he was too proud to show it. He looked at the darkness and was intrigued by its beauty and wanted to know more of it and its power. "What is this?"

The woman reached out her hand further toward Mal until the darkness began to show in his eyes. The stranger didn't have to utter another word to persuade him. He reached out his hands and touched it.

"The next time you touch the orbs, you will have the power to wield it, and you will carry a flame of your own."

The darkness disappeared, but Mal could feel it on his hands and under every inch of his skin. It burned, but he found pleasure in the pain. "Who are you?" he asked the woman.

She stood up conceitedly and smiled until her yellow eyes became dim. "My name is Sakai, and I am from where the light once came."

"And where is that?" he asked.

She shook her finger at him. "So many questions for such a small child! Do you want my help to become powerful or do you not?"

He smirked, mirroring her expression. "I do."

"Good." Before Mal's eyes, she began to disappear as if she were never there at all. "All you have to do is touch the light and the power will be yours."

Mal didn't know what to believe, but he knew the power in his hands was real, and once he touched the light, the darkness and the power inside of him would grow.

Riss was beginning to become worried about his friend. He waited for Mal to return inside the cave with Tice lying in his lap. She was becoming bad company. She hadn't spoken a word to him after Mal left and refused to do so.

He sighed angrily after a while. "Why are you so angry?"

She puffed up her cheeks to conceal her anger, but that wasn't enough. She had to yell. "You were being a showoff when you showed Mal your fire! You didn't care that his feelings would be hurt."

"I thought he'd be able to get the light too!"

She raised her head up. "But it's not for everybody!"

"How do you know?"

She hesitated. "I don't know." Tice sunk her head back on her brother's lap.

"Well, then you don't know." Riss was beginning to become irritated with everyone questioning his capabilities of being in charge. "Remember that I'm the big brother, and you're the little sister. I know more than you do."

Tice didn't say anything else. She closed her eyes. He treated her like she was small because she was, but he also treated her like she didn't know anything because she couldn't see anything. Tice wished that she could see something!

When she opened her eyes, she felt something punch her in the stomach and jumped up. "Riss!"

"What's the matter?"

"Mal," she said. "Don't let him come in here."

"Why?"

"Please!" she screamed. "Don't let him touch the light!"

Riss didn't understand, but he listened to Tice and ran out of the cave. He was surprised to find that Mal was fast approaching the entrance. "What's going on?" he asked nervously.

"I want to try again," Mal said.

Riss didn't understand why Tice was so upset earlier, but he could see that something was wrong with Mal. His eyes were much darker than before. "I don't think that's a good idea."

Mal glared at his friend angrily. "You're supposed to be my friend, but you don't want to share the power."

"No. That's not it."

"You've always been weak. You were so happy that you were stronger than me that you lied about how you got the power!"

"That's not true!" Riss did want to make Mal jealous, but he certainly didn't mean to anger his friend that much. "Listen to yourself. Something is wrong!"

"The only thing that's wrong is that you're in my way!" Mal ran as fast as he could and charged into Riss's chest. Riss wasn't strong enough to push Mal back, and they both fell to the ground.

Riss hit the back of his head on a rock and began to feel dizzy. He couldn't get up or grab Mal. "Don't do this!"

Tice reached out her hands and walked until she found the orbs. Then she threw her body on top of them. She had been afraid to touch them ever since she lost her sight, but she knew that she had to protect them with all of her might.

Mal came into the cave and grew angrier when he saw Tice protecting the orbs. Had he not been good to her? Why was she trying to keep him away from the power? "Get out of the way, Tice."

She closed her eyes and held them tighter. "Please don't do this!"

There were orbs all across the cave. Tice's tiny body was too small to hide them, but he didn't want to pick up any on the floor. He wanted to punish her for trying to keep the power for herself.

Tice felt him grab the back of her dress, and she screamed. "Please!"

He didn't listen and threw her back on the hard ground. "You can't keep this from me."

Tice felt all of the warmth leave the room immediately, and a cold wind swept all around them. The darkness appeared from Mal's hands, and it spread to the orbs.

Mal was confused. He didn't feel any stronger. There was no fire in his hands. The orbs began to shake until they floated and flew out through the cave exit.

Riss saw them fly past him, and he got up to watch them fly away. "What have you done?"

Mal came out of the cave to see them off. He began to run after them, but they were moving much too fast. It was hopeless. "I don't understand."

"You did it, my boy." The two boys turned around to follow the voice of a stranger. It was Sakai with a great and twisted smile on her face.

"Where's the power you promised me?" Mal asked her.

"Oh, you will have the power and so will many others. The light fell from the sky to find those who might save this world. Now with your greed, anyone may have this power. But it will not be light. It will be my darkness."

"Take it back!" Riss yelled.

"I can't. Your friend is the one who opened the door and spread the darkness to your world. I could have never done it on my own."

Mal was horrified. "I'm sorry." His hands began to simmer slowly.

"Your hands!" Riss stepped away afraid.

Mal held his hands up to his face so he could see. He could feel the heat. It didn't burn Riss when he used his fire. Why was it hurting him? "Help me!"

Riss didn't know what to do to help his friend. Mal's fingers caught on fire, and it began to spread across his hands to his arms. It was too hot for Riss to take, so he stepped away. "Make it stop!" he begged Sakai.

"I'm making him better," she said. "He wanted to be strong. Soon he will be a warrior."

Mal was screaming as his skin began to turn black. They were the strangest flames they had ever seen. They were black with no warmth but burned just like fire. "Help me!"

"Riss!" Tice screamed for her brother from inside of the cave.

Riss ran inside to retrieve his sister. She was crawling on all fours trying to find a way out. "What do we do?"

She wrapped her arms around his neck. "We have to run."

When he got back outside, Mal had stopped screaming. He had been completely set on black fire, and his eyes were glowing bright red.

"Mal?" Riss asked.

He was calm, but began to laugh. It was the most unsettling laugh Riss had ever heard. Tice held onto her brother tighter. Riss tried to concentrate and control the flames, but when he did, the trees in the jungle began to burn with black fire.

"Run!" Tice screamed.

Riss did as he was told, and the fire began to spread. In the distance, Sakai's constant laughter could be heard as the jungle continued to burn into the ground. Tice remembered the beauty of all of the colors that was once in the jungle, and she wept at the sound of everything crackling and popping into the night.

87

Chapter Seven

Eastern Pearl was once a place known for great beauty and sophistication. There were flowers surrounding every home and the farmlands were plentiful in crops. Every home had food on the table for dinner, and children had cake afterward if they were well-behaved. The people were not afraid to roam the streets at night, and the day was always a time to work and play. King Raymon kept his people prosperous.

There was one tree in the castle's garden that was his daughter's favorite. They would sit together under its shade and laugh with each other while his wife watched from the balcony with her hand on her growing belly.

The last day they spent together under that tree, King Raymon kissed his daughter's cheeks and placed a locket around her neck. "This is for you, my Princess."

She smiled bright and held the golden heart in her hands. "What is this for?"

"So you can always have my heart." He held up a matching necklace. "Is it alright if I have yours as well?"

"I want to have the honor, Daddy!" He gave her his locket so she could put it around his neck. "Now we can always be together."

"Always, my precious. Always."

That was years ago. Samara wondered if that tree were still standing. The only thing she knew that remained from that day was the locket that she still wore every day. "Always, Daddy."

"Princess Samara?" a man asked from behind her bedroom door, "is it alright if I come in?"

She sat up in her bed. She was fully dressed for the day, but she had nothing better to do all day than lay and worry about her father. "Come in."

He was one of the many guards who had watched her. She didn't know his name. There were far too many servants to remember, and she always thought that she wouldn't be there long in Cavastinova. "Here you are, Princess." He was holding a letter in his hands.

That was enough to put an anxious smile on her face. "Give it to me quickly!" She reached out her hand for it and jumped off the bed. She snatched it from the guard and marveled at the letter's seal. "That is all."

He bowed before her and exited the room.

Samara held the letter in her chest. It was her father's seal. He hadn't sent a letter in three months. It was either good or bad news. She took a swallow of courage and opened it up.

My Dearest Samara and Raymon,

There have been many days when I wanted to hold you both in my arms. I apologize that the circumstances have kept us apart. No more. It is with great joy that I write this letter to you. The war is over. Lord Rovin has been captured, and his armies have surrendered. It is now safe for the both of you to return home.

I have business that I must attend to. Otherwise, I would sail all the worlds to hug you both again. Instead, you two shall

have to greet me. King Valdor has been informed and will ready a
boat for your safe travel.

Until then,
Your Loving Father

Samara had tears in her eyes when she finished the letter. She couldn't keep it to herself and ran out of her room to find her brother. He was always in the same place. She ran past his room and down the palace halls to another. She hated going inside, but she would not let it take away her good mood.

"Brother?" she opened the door, and he was inside lying on a bed with his mother.

"Samara?" He lifted his head up.

"Come here," she ordered.

"Why don't you come in here?" he asked.

She glared at her brother slightly. He knew good and well why she wouldn't go in there. "Do as you're told!" she said sternly.

He sighed and kissed his mother's forehead before jumping off of the bed and coming out to the hall. "What is it?"

She held up the letter. "Father said we can come home to Eastern Pearl!"

He smiled, but it was more for his sister's benefit. He didn't remember what life was like there. Cavastinova was the only home he had ever really known.

"We'll leave immediately!" She began to spin in the middle of the hall; she was so thrilled! "We can see father again!"

Raymon kept his head down. He didn't know how to bring up what he wanted without upsetting his sister, but he had to. "But what about Mother?"

90

Samara stopped and looked at her little brother. He was innocent, and she loved him dearly. He looked just like a smaller version of her father with a rounder face. She hardly got angry at him for that reason, but she did become irritated. "She's never going to wake up. Father is alive and loves us. That has to be enough."

Raymon lowered his head to stare down at his feet. He didn't want to leave his mother. He would sleep in her bed some nights and wonder what she was doing while she laid there asleep. Was all the world still or was she somewhere beautiful? He didn't know, but he wanted to be there for her.

"Don't do that, Raymon." She grabbed her little brother's hand and smiled. "You're the future king of our people. You have to be strong like father."

Raymon lifted his head enough to see, but he hid his eyes so she wouldn't see that he was about to cry. "I'll try."

The two of them walked down the halls of gold and marble stone to the throne room where King Valdor was waiting for the two of them. He was a slim man with a bald head, goatee, and a thin face, but he was tall and strong. Everyone always showed King Valdor great respect.

Samara and Raymon both bowed in his presence. "King Valdor," Samara said.

"Rise."

They both stood up straight, and she began to speak. "My father sent me a letter this morning. I expect that he sent you one as well."

"Yes. Eastern Pearl is finally safe from Lord Rovin and his evil forces. I will have a ship ready to take the both of you home tomorrow."

Raymon spoke up quickly. "What about my mother?"

Samara looked at her brother wide-eyed. "Raymon!"

King Valdor smiled wearily at the boy. "She will remain in my care for now. I fear she might be too sick to travel."

Raymon tried to bite his tongue, but he couldn't keep himself from speaking. "Then I want to stay with my mother!"

"That's enough!" Samara said. "We're going home to be with our father."

"I understand him," said King Valdor.

Samara looked at him surprised. "You do?"

"Of course. Your mother is a very kind and beautiful woman. Though she has not been awake for many years, she is a gift." He got off of his throne to walk down to touch young Raymon's shoulders. "I promise that I will take good care of your mother."

Raymon wrapped his arms around King Valdor, but Samara was not grateful for his words. She did not like King Valdor. She knew her place, and she knew that she owed him a great deal, but she would be glad to be gone. "Thank you, King Valdor." She grabbed her dress and curtsied. "We will never forget your kindness."

"No," he let go of Raymon and walked back to his throne, "I suppose you won't."

The night was busy for the palace. Assigned guards were preparing to leave with Raymon and Samara. A ship was loaded with supplies for the journey that would take a few weeks. Samara watched the men bustle about because she was far too eager to sleep!

Raymon also could not sleep. He lay with his mother again and waited for her eyes to open. "I've never really known you, Mother. I want to know you."

The morning came all too fast for him but had taken a century for Samara. As soon as the sun rose, she helped her brother get dressed. They didn't carry anything on board the ship themselves, though King Valdor had many suits and dresses for Samara and Raymon packed away on the ship. The only thing in the entire world that Samara cared to bring with her was her brother and her locket.

As they boarded the ship together, Samara had to hold her brother's hand and smile. "Cheer up! Think of this as a brand new adventure."

He frowned. "I like my old ones." Raymon wasn't much like Samara. She liked to explore, to dance, and to sing. Raymon barely spoke and would rather spend his time thinking. He didn't like to hear things about the war or his mother's sickness. He liked to think of better things like when she would finally wake up.

Samara didn't understand her brother, but she thought he was reluctant to see their father because he begged him not to leave. He hadn't seen him in two years. That's a long time for a boy not to see their father. "You're going to grow up and take Father's place one day, and then you'll understand," she told him.

King Valdor was watching the children from the dock. They both waved to him once they got on deck. "Be safe!" he yelled. "These are troubled times."

Samara felt bad for her little brother, and didn't want to see him upset. "Do you want to play a game?" she asked.

"Not really."

She sighed irritably. "You know, you can't just sit and mope around until we arrive back home."

"Yes I can." He walked away from her to go search for his cabin.

She shook her head and watched the ocean waves and the sky as they set sail off to her beloved home. The ship couldn't move fast enough for her, even though the home she had known for many years disappeared sooner than what she expected. Time seemed so vast to her, like the water that surrounded her.

She spent the next few days watching the water, hoping to see her land. It probably looked different than what she could remember. Six years ago was a long time and she was only a child.

93

She did get bored and sought her brother's company, but he would only lay on his bed and stare up at the ceiling. By the third day, Samara had enough. When she marched into his cabin, she stood at the foot of his bed firmly and said, "Get up!"

He lazily sat up on his bed but did not get out of it. "Yes?"

"I know you're sad about mother, but you can't be depressed forever. Remember, you're the—"

"Future king," he answered. "Yes, I know. But if I'm supposed to be the king, then why do you treat me like such a baby?"

She stuck her head up higher. "Because I'm an adult, and you're a child."

"But you're twelve."

"That means I'm at least five years smarter than you." She smiled.

He didn't. "I wish I was like you and father, but I'm not."

She frowned and climbed in his bed next to him. She didn't mean to be an overbearing sister, but it was her job to take care of him, just like it was his job to grow up and to one day be the ruler of the greatest kingdom in the world. "You have a lot of time to grow up," she said. "I'm different than I used to be. We change."

"How?" he asked.

"The world makes us change." She kissed him on his cheek and hugged him tight. If the world were a better place, she would be more playful with him all the time. But it wasn't.

A bell began to sound off, and the two of them looked at each other excited. They dared to believe it was their homeland and ran up to the deck.

"What's going on?" Samara asked the first crewmen she saw.

"A ship is approaching."

"A ship?" Raymon asked. They both ran to a group of crewmen at the bow looking out at a large ship. "Who are they?"

Samara wove her way through the crew to get a closer look. The ship had big, black sails. No normal, friendly ship would ever have such a thing. The captain was among the gawkers looking frightened. That was never a good sign. "Are we going to be okay?" she asked him quietly.

"Of course." He forced a smile on his face. "You and your brother had better get down to your cabin. We'll take care of everything."

Samara knew what a man full of fear looked like, and the captain certainly fit the description. Samara did as she was told for the sake of her little brother and took his hand. "There's nothing to see here, Raymon."

"But what kind of ship is that?" he asked.

"It's nothing." He was fighting her touch, but she pulled him until his feet stopped stumbling behind and obeyed her guidance. They both went back into his cabin and climbed back into his bed.

Samara didn't say anything, but Raymon could tell that something was wrong with his sister. She actually looked worried. "What kind of ship was that?" he asked.

"It's nothing!" Samara lay down and closed her eyes. "I think I want to take a nap. We should both sleep, Little Brother." She could hear her own nervousness in her voice, but she didn't want Raymon to know that she was afraid.

Raymon did notice, and that frightened him all the more. He lay down next to his sister and wrapped his arm around her stomach. He wanted to be back at the palace with his mother, but Samara looked a lot like her. They both had raven black hair and blue eyes. There was something about his mother and his sister that made him feel safe.

She hugged onto Raymon and kissed his forehead. "We're going to be okay." They had to be! She hadn't seen her father in years. She wasn't going to let anyone stand in her way.

They both closed their eyes, but neither of them could sleep. Their hearts were beating too loudly. When they heard a noise, they would

95

flinch and hold each other tighter. It wasn't long before a bell began to sound and the two of them began to hear men yelling. The noise began to get louder, no matter how much they wanted it to go away.

They both sat up and pressed their back into the wall. Raymon was too afraid to open his eyes, but Samara was looking straight ahead at the door. She knew that sooner or later someone would come through, but she didn't know whether they would be friend or foe.

The most frightening thing was how the noise suddenly ended. Where was the sound of cannons firing or the clashing of swords from honorable men who would fight to their last breath? Where was the struggle?

They could both hear creaking coming from behind the door. Samara let go of her brother to run to block the door, but a man began to open it before she could reach. She screamed and pressed all her weight against it, but the door flew open and knocked her to the ground.

"What do we have here?" he asked. The man was large with dark blond hair and brown eyes. One of his eyes was completely white with a scar slash above and beneath his eyelids. "I believe Captain Saxson would like to see you."

Samara crawled away frightened, but he grabbed onto her foot and dragged her closer to him. "Run!" she told her brother.

Raymon was too frightened to do anything but shake on his bed like a leaf. "Samara…"

"You're coming too, Boy."

Samara began kicking, screaming, and scratching the man with all the strength she had. The pirate had on many furs and was unable to feel much damage, but he did find her annoying and flung her on his shoulders. "Calm down, Girl!"

She wouldn't stop fighting. She beat on his back, pulled his hair, and hollered in his ears on purpose. She did anything to try and slow him down so her brother might take the chance to run away.

But Raymon didn't get away. Despite Samara's best efforts, the pirate grabbed him like a doll and carried them both up to the deck of the ship where the entire crew of twelve men were huddled together and surrounded by at least twenty men with swords pointed. He sat Samara down in front of a man with a big, black hat with a dark, red feather. "Be nice for Captain Saxson," he warned.

Raymon and Samara both took his wise council for at least a little while and ceased resistance. The Captain's presence was quite overwhelming. "And who might you two children be?" Captain Saxson was a big man with long, tangled blond hair and a long thick beard. He had scars and tattoos all around his body. "Hmm? Are you the children of the captain?"

Samara was terrified, but she had been raised with dignity and a sense of great pride. She stood and raised her head gallantly. "I am Samara, Princess of Eastern Pearl, and he is Prince Raymon, the future king."

Raymon had not yet stood to his feet, but he did so after his sister introduced him so grandly.

Captain Saxson's eyes narrowed just a tiny bit. "Eastern Pearl, you say?"

Samara noticed the look in Captain Saxson's eyes. She didn't know what it meant, but she assumed that he knew of her father's bravery and skill. It was enough to give her a little bit more courage. "Yes, and I demand that you let us go, and your lives will be spared."

The pirates erupted into a great laughter so much that it felt like Samara was being pushed around by the sound of their voices. Captain

Saxson was the loudest. He replied in his grungy voice. "I'm not very concerned about my life."

Samara wasn't going to let a no good, filthy pirate talk down to her! "We're not worth anything to you dead. If you kill us, then my father will hunt you down to the ends of the earth, and you will regret this day." She smirked confidently. "Leave us alive and you will receive mercy and perhaps a ransom if the king is feeling generous."

Then there was a deafening silence. Her crew and the pirate crew didn't know what the price would be for speaking to Captain Saxson in such a manner. Captain first glared at Samara with his mouth dropped a little bit. Then after a long pause, he laughed. "You are quite the spunky little girl!"

The crew breathed a sigh of relief while the pirates laughed again. Captain Saxson was very pleased with Samara indeed. He slapped her in the shoulder and asked, "Ever consider becoming a pirate?"

Captain Saxson reached out to stroke Samara's face, but she jerked her head away before he could touch her. "I think I'd rather die."

He cocked his eyebrow at her. "You think?"

"Well," she gulped, "we still are negotiating."

"Ha ha! I like this girl." He rubbed his dirty hands in Raymon's hair next. "What about you, Little Man? Do you have anything witty to say or does your big sister think for you?"

Things were just as they always were. There was a bad situation, and Samara took it and made it her own. He never understood how she did it. He tried many times, but he often made things worse.

Still, he didn't want to be known as the boy who…Who was Samara's little brother! Raymon stuck out his little chest and said, "You're very ugly."

"What?" Captain Saxson blurted out angrily.

Samara's eyes bucked, and she pushed her brother back behind her. "Leave him be. He's only a child."

Captain Saxson was angry, but he calmed down. "That he is. But we mustn't forget whose child he is." He began to pace around Raymon and Samara dramatically. "Your father, King Raymon, believes that he can control these seas as well as his kingdom. However, these seas are mine, and he will not ever forget that."

"What do you mean by that?"

He stopped when he was once again in front of her and smirked. "Since I like you, Girl, I will be merciful. Instead of killing the entire crew, we will keep them in the brig and let them go when we please."

His crew went up in a joyous roar. Samara was rattled, but someone had to take charge. "I demand that you set us all free!" She let go of her brother to step closer to Captain Saxson.

He was amused with her. He actually thought of taking her with him, but an example had to be made. "I will only let you and your brother go free." He signaled his men, and they began to transport their new prisoners to the ship. "Enjoy that freedom for as long as you can."

Raymon took his sister by the hand as they watched their caretakers leave. "You can't leave us alone here!" Raymon didn't want to become a pirate, but they had a better chance with Captain Saxson than being abandoned.

Captain Saxson turned around. "Be proud, Boy! You are a prince. You should die with some respect."

Samara was near tears, but she refused to cry. She absolutely refused to let those scoundrels see that she was terrified and needed their help. "You don't think we can handle the ship?" she yelled. "Well, you're wrong!" She continued to shout to them as they began to sail away. "I'm going to keep me and my brother safe. We're going to go home. I'm going to see my father!"

She held in her tears by all means necessary. She sniffed, she blinked a few times, but then she kept her eyes closed. "It's going to be okay," she told her brother. "It's going to be okay."

She felt a tear on her cheek regardless and touched it surprised. But then she realized once she opened her eyes back up, the water belonged to the ocean.

"Samara..." Raymon began to tug on his sister's arm to try and lead her back down below.

Samara didn't understand why the waters had become so uneasy. There wasn't a black cloud in the sky. She walked over to the edge of the ship to watch the water swirling and bubbling up as if it were coming to life.

Before the ship was carried away, she looked out to the waters to see Captain Saxson's ship. They hadn't gone that far, yet their ship was fine. The Captain was watching from the bow of the ship with his arms stretched out toward them and a smirk on his face.

Samara was frozen in panic. "He's doing this..."

Raymon ran and grabbed his sister's hand. "We have to go."

The ship began to toss and turn and the both of them slipped and fell. Raymon was knocked unconscious on impact, but Samara was still awake to see a giant wave of water rise out of the ocean like a hand to choke the lives out of them.

She opened her mouth to scream, but the water hit her so quickly that the force took all the sound away from her. She blinked for a second and then her brother was gone. They were both trapped in the cruel inevitability of ocean's depths.

There was no way she could survive. She managed to cry. Her tears wouldn't matter when lost in the immensity of the ocean. Everything around her was dark, and it was so cold that it felt like nothing.

Until she saw a light.

Chapter Eight

"One week ago..." Riss was in the orphanage wrestling Mal. Tice was cheering him on as loud as she could. She wasn't the only onlooker, but the only one that really mattered. As long as the three of them were together, that was all the family they ever needed.

"Only one week ago," Riss thought to himself. Things had progressed into quite a different phase. He watched his best friend burn alive and turn into a monster, she lost her sight, and his home was abandoned. Even if he wanted to go back home, he was too afraid to face Mal and the strange woman who turned them against each other.

What was he to do? He had to get Tice somewhere safe. She couldn't see any dangers in life and he had proved to be unworthy to be her protector.

While lost in thought, he missed a small rock in the path he was traveling on and tripped. He fell flat on his stomach and hurt himself, but he was in better shape than Tice who had been sleeping on his back. Riss fell on her hands, and she hit her head on the back of Riss's. She hollered and began to whimper from the pain. She didn't mean to be a baby about it, but Riss had been hardheaded his whole entire life.

"Oh, Tice! I'm sorry!" He lifted his body off of his sister and held her. He tried to rock her back and forth to keep her from crying as if his parents would see and slap him in the back of the head for not properly taking care of the baby.

Tice was barely aware of what was going on. She had been sleeping, and the next thing she knew, she was hurt and was being cradled in her brother's arms. "I'm fine," she said through her tears.

Riss set her down on the ground, but he still felt worthless. "To be honest, I'm not sure what we're supposed to do now."

Tice frowned. But if her brother didn't know what to do, then maybe he would finally begin to listen to her. "Where are we?"

"I'm not sure." They had barely made it out of the jungle alive. There was still lush vegetation around, but Riss could smell the scent of the ocean in the air. "Near the ocean."

Tice wondered what that strange smell in the air was. She had never been to the ocean, and she really didn't care much for the smell. "What if we go back up north?"

"Not an option," he said sternly.

Tice sighed. Her plan wasn't as simple as she thought it would be. "Well, I think we have to find a boy."

"A boy?" he shrieked. "What boy?"

She laughed at the way her brother's voice leapt into a higher pitch. "A boy from my dream. He had yellow hair and white skin."

Riss didn't like that at all! "You're too young to be dreaming about boys." Tice was only six-years-old. She wouldn't be ready for boys until he was at least dead. "Besides, that bandit said that he saw someone with white skin from Eastern Pearl. Remember?"

"Yeah..." Eastern Pearl would mean that they would have to go east—not north. But she did feel strongly that they were supposed to go north. It was like there was something alive inside her stomach.

"Is something wrong?" he asked.

She thought about it carefully. It was important to go north, but going to Eastern Pearl seemed okay. "We should take a boat there."

"How do you know it's across the ocean?" he asked.

She thought about it long and hard. "I'm not sure."

He glared at her oddly. "But you do know?"

She shrugged her shoulders. "I suppose."

Riss didn't know what to do with her. He hadn't been making any right choices, but she was beginning to make less sense every time she opened her mouth.

Tice also felt the same way with her brother. He made perfect sense with his decisions, but they didn't feel right. She wasn't sure how to make him realize that, but she didn't have any other choice but to try. "Riss, we both know that the light gave you powers, and even though something bad happened to Mal, he got powers too."

"Yeah. What's your point?" It was bad enough that he couldn't get the image of Mal burning out of his mind. He didn't want to hear about it out loud from his innocent little sister.

Tice knew that she was upsetting her brother, but she still spoke up quietly. "Maybe I got powers too, you know?"

Riss looked at Tice carefully. She had her head lowered, and her eyebrows were heavy like she was going to cry if he disagreed with her. She was always weak and small. "How is not being able to see a power?" he asked carefully.

Maybe at first, she believed like Riss did, but she was beginning to believe in herself. "My dreams are realer than they've ever been. I know things that don't make any sense, but they're right. I knew that something bad was going to happen if Mal touched the light, even before that strange woman appeared."

That was true, and Riss could feel a sting to her words. "So what are you trying to say?"

103

Tice tried to press her lips together to stop herself from speaking her mind, but she couldn't help it. "I'm saying that maybe you should listen to me for a change!"

He was shocked. Riss wanted to command her not to speak to her older brother like that, but there was really nothing he could say to stop her from being right. He was lost, and she was somehow managing to find her way while stumbling through the darkness.

It was time to trust her. "What's going to happen?"

"Happen to what?" she asked confused.

"The world…" He spoke quietly. "…After what happened with Mal?"

"I'm not sure." She wished she could tell him that she had pleasant dreams of a world where everything would be good again, but she couldn't see anything other than darkness. "I do know that something bad is going to happen to a nice girl and her brother because of what we let happen."

That wasn't what he wanted to hear, but he was going to trust that she would have some more insight as they went on their journey. "Where are we going to find a boat?"

Tice smiled and jumped to her feet. "If we hurry, we'll make it!"

Riss stood up and took Tice by the hand. They had no more food, their clothes were ruined, and he could feel that a hot sun would soon rise fully into the sky and begin to beam down harshly on them. But for the first time in the past couple of days, he felt like he had some kind of direction and a purpose. He didn't have the answers, but Tice must have somehow known what to do. "Okay."

"Always, my princess. Always."

Samara opened her eyes and saw into a pair of familiar blue eyes. "Father?" Was it truly possible? Those eyes and blond hair belonged to her father, but his shadow was much too small.

"Samara, wake up!" Raymon continued to shake his sister until she became fully conscious.

When she realized that it was her little brother, Raymon, she rested her head on its side and watched the sand as she thought. She remembered being on the boat. She remembered Captain Saxson controlling the water with strange powers. She thought she and he brother were going to drown in the water. Then there was a light, and that was the last thing she saw.

"How did we get here?" Raymon asked her.

Samara honestly wanted to lie on the beach and cry to herself until she felt better and understood everything that was happening to her. Instead, she pulled herself together as much as she could and sat up for the sake of her little brother. "I think the more important question at the moment is: where are we?"

Raymon inhaled the air deeply. It was so clean and pure. "Whatever this place is, it sure is nice."

Then it suddenly dawned on Samara what that place was. She stood on her feet and turned around. In the distance, she could see a castle. It looked different from the wounds of war through the years, but she could recognize the stones.

Her eyes immediately began to well up with tears, and she ran. It was her home. She told herself that her father was waiting under their tree. The white flowers were probably blooming.

"Sister!" Raymon ran after her, but he wasn't fast enough to keep up. "Where are you going?"

"Father!" she thought. "You've been waiting for me all this time!" The kingdom began to become familiar as she ran through its streets. She saw them differently through the eyes of a child. She remembered the

105

shops where she would get sweets. She remembered the swings where she would play with children were. She didn't even realize that the kingdom was completely empty.

The palace walls had been destroyed and crumbled. She didn't care and climbed on top of the ruble to enter through the garden.

In the spring, there were so many white flowers that covered the ground and floated through the air that it looked like it was snowing. Samara loved it because it was the beauty of winter with the warmth and liveliness that spring was supposed to have.

But things were different that spring. "Father?"

There were no trees. The soil was lifeless and covered with swords sticking up through the ground. The land had been disturbed so much that she knew good and well that the swords were tombstones of fallen soldiers.

She was trembling as she walked through the graveyard. She had no thoughts, yet warm tears began to run down her face. There was a coldness that overcame her. She didn't understand why yet. She simply continued to walk.

Even though there were no thoughts to guide her, her heart guided every step she took. That memory of her father holding her under that tree and giving her that locket was real. She found her father's locket again in that same spot hanging from a golden sword.

"Papa…" She dropped to her knees and cried. She held her chest and screamed from the aching that she felt. She could feel that it was him. She just knew when she saw that necklace; there was no mistaking it.

Her father was gone.

Raymon finally caught up with his sister. He was too young and naive to understand what he was walking through until he saw his sister hunched over and crying.

"Samara…" He wanted to say something to make her feel better, but he had never seen her that way. He also felt terrible that he didn't feel the same. He was sad, but he couldn't remember much about his father beyond his legacy and the incredible weight that it placed on his young shoulders.

Raymon did the only thing he knew to do and he hugged her as tight as he could. As he tried to comfort her, he began to cry.

Samara was at a loss for the first time in her life. She was supposed to come home, be a princess, and reunite with her loving father. There wasn't supposed to be anymore suffering. There was supposed to be peace. "What could have happened?" she asked aloud.

What she received was a crack of thunder close enough to make her and her brother jump and hold each other in fear. They looked up and saw a spark flash in the terrible eyes of their enemy.

Lord Rovin was free.

"Raymon's children have arrived?" Lord Rovin was a young and handsome ruler with dark hair and eyes. He towered over Samara and Raymon, which only made him seem all the more invincible. He always wore armor and spoke smoothly with sophistication. His charm made people want to follow him, but there was always something twisted in his smile.

"Well, this is most unexpected." His fingers at his side were sparking with blue lightning from each tip of his fingers.

Raymon was the only one who paid any mind to it. Samara was in a shocked daze from seeing her father's greatest enemy standing over his grave. "You did this?" she asked.

"There's no other being in the world with such power." He laughed and raised his hands close to his face to watch each lightning bolt travel in its strange occurrence from finger to finger. "Just when your father thought he had won, I used my powers to complete my mission here."

No. It couldn't be that simple. He was talking about taking lives! "A mission?" she asked quietly before raising her voice into a deep rage. "That's all this is to you?"

Lord Rovin did not possess any trace of remorse on his face. "You look so much like your mother."

She stared at him with such a fire. She hated Lord Rovin and wished that he would disappear forever!

He could see her desire for the worst for him in her eyes. "But your eyes have the same look of your father."

He stretched forth his hand, and the lighting began to flash. She felt her heart racing. There was nowhere for her to run, but she didn't care about her life. She wanted to keep her brother safe—the heir to her father's proud throne.

She lifted up her hands and closed her eyes. She began to feel a tremendous pressure on her head, and she didn't know why. She felt like she was being pushed, yet she knew that she wasn't touching anyone except for her brother who was holding onto her from behind.

She opened her eyes, and it was the most frightening thing she had ever seen in her life. The light was so bright that it was practically blinding. The lightning was flashing blue from Lord Rovin's hands. She knew that it was powerful, and strong enough to destroy her and her brother like it did her father, but it was surrounding and bouncing off of them.

Samara was somehow fighting off Lord Rovin! She could feel it. The more she wanted to protect her brother, the easier it was to push his lightning away. But it was difficult, and his lightning was becoming stronger.

She closed her eyes and gritted her teeth. It was beginning to hurt her head more as she fought him. She couldn't hold on for much longer!

Raymon was trembling as he held onto his sister from behind. His father probably died bravely in battle, but he wasn't his father. He wanted to live at least until he wasn't a coward anymore. "Please leave us alone!" he yelled.

As soon as he spoke it, the lightning stopped. Both of the children questioned if it was over and if they had lost their lives, but their fear was still too real.

Samara opened her eyes first. Lord Rovin was still standing over them, but he was looking at them with a strange expression. He was angry, but he was…Baffled? He did want to hurt them, but he laid his hands down at his side and smiled before beginning to walk away.

Raymon opened his eyes and peeked from behind his sister. He couldn't believe that Lord Rovin decided to give up. It was too good to be true.

Samara wasn't at all grateful though. As she saw Lord Rovin's back facing hers, she became very angry. That man somehow escaped her father's custody and killed him. Just like Captain Saxson, he had strange powers and tried to kill her. Well, she discovered that she somehow had a power of her own. She could feel it deep inside her.

She was never going to let someone else hurt her ever again. She was never going to cry. She was never going to be afraid, and she would never ever be weak again!

She stood up on her feet and began to run. The only thing that stopped her from chasing down that evil man was her brother who had grabbed a hold of her wrist. "Let me go!" she told him.

"He's too strong," he begged her. "He killed father. He'll kill us!"

She didn't believe him, but she didn't want to leave her little brother with him crying on his knees.

She would have to teach him how to become a strong warrior. "I swear to you, Little Brother, Prince Raymon, heir to King Raymon—the rightful and only true ruler of Eastern Pearl!" She screamed loud enough for Lord Rovin—the coward—to hear.

Then she softly spoke a promise that she vowed on the fabric of her very life. "You will be king. You will restore glory to this kingdom, and I will make Lord Rovin bow before your feet."

But that wasn't the only thing she wanted to do. She couldn't stand the sight of Lord Rovin. She couldn't take the thought of him. She wanted him expelled from the world in all manner of form. No body, no memories, no honor. "I will avenge my father!" she screamed to him. "I will avenge him!"

$$\diamond$$

Riss had begun carrying Tice in his arms once again. The sun had completely risen, and she was beginning to actually change into a color. It was hard to walk fast while carrying her in such a way, but he was trying to shield her as best he could. He knew that her skin was probably already stinging, but she didn't complain out loud.

But just like he knew, they were right near the ocean. And just as she said, there was a boat loading up at a dock. It was unbelievable to Riss and becoming scary. Tice was just a small girl. How could she possibly know such impossible things?

"Hurry up!" she told him.

He had to set her down so they could both run together. Riss could barely wait until he was on that boat. By coming so close to the water, he was beginning to feel secure. Mal wasn't going to chase them across the ocean.

Tice was excited to finally get on with the journey. She felt like she was becoming a different person than who she was days ago. She was much stronger.

The ship was huge, and the crew was finishing loading up supplies when Tice and Riss ran up to a man barking orders at the rest of the men. "Hurry! If we're late for any of our deliveries, I'll cut your wages in half!"

Tice slowed up her feet and instinctively hid behind her brother. He had such a grunting and loud booming voice that it intimidated her.

Riss was intimidated himself, but he had conned more than one adult in his lifetime. "Are you the captain?" he asked.

"Who wants to know?" He turned around, but was confused when there was no one eye level to match the voice he heard. When he looked down and saw two children standing there, he was obviously annoyed.

Riss lowered his head to appear like a fragile child. "I suppose I do, Sir."

He was a tall, fat man with a big belly and a grey beard. He always looked like he was glaring. "I'm busy. Get lost."

"But we need to get on your boat."

"My boat?" he laughed harshly. "What in the world for?"

"Because..." Riss began to fake tears and sniff. Usually he and the older kids would steal food to bring it back to the orphanage, but sometimes, pity worked just as well. He could cry on the spot if he needed, and he always had a good baby face. "My sister is sick, and she's dying, Sir."

The Captain bent down and leaned in closer to get a better look at Tice. Where her skin wasn't white, it was bright red from being burned. She was sweating and looked extremely uncomfortable, and her eyes were glazed over and a very strange blue. Plus, she was afraid and fragile. She couldn't see him, but she felt his body over hers' and she stepped further behind Riss.

111

"She's blind and her skin burns easily. They're the side effects to her terminal illness." Riss began to let the tears flow out slowly like a true professional. "We wanted to travel to Eastern Pearl because they're the only people with the cure for her illness, but I fear she won't survive the journey on foot." He covered his face with his arm for drama. It was his best performance yet.

"There is no other way to get to Eastern Pearl than by boat," The Captain said. "I'm curious to know of how you know of its medicines and not of its geography."

That was a minor setback in Riss's opinion. He latched onto The Captain's coattails and sobbed harder. "Then we are doomed without you, Sir. Doomed!"

He pulled Riss off of him immediately. "Eastern Pearl is not my first stop, nor is it my last. It's better that you pay for a ride on a traveling boat, and not an exporting ship."

"It has to be this ship!" Tice yelled out without even thinking.

The two of them looked at her oddly, but The Captain brushed it off quickly. "I should be going."

He began to walk away, but Riss swallowed his pride and reached out to grab his coattails again. "I lied. She's not sick and dying, but I am telling the truth about her eyes and her skin. We need to get to Eastern Pearl, and we can't afford to travel around anymore."

The Captain was still annoyed with Riss and pulled his coat away from him again. He didn't seem to have any pity in his heart for the two of them. "Eastern Pearl has been riddled with war and has only recently become liberated. I do not see how they would be in a position to help aid your strange sister."

"Never mind why we want to go. We have to go there!"

He sighed. He couldn't believe that he was actually beginning to break. "Where are your parents? They must be worried."

"They're both dead," Tice said quietly.

Captain Mayes suspected trouble out of them. He didn't know what it was about them that gave that impression, but he knew. "Every man on my ship has to pull their own weight. You two can't possibly keep up."

"I'll pull mine and hers." Riss reached out his hand and opened his palm to reveal a small flame. "Please."

The Captain had seen many strange things in his travels, but he marveled at the flame floating in Riss's hand. He couldn't find any sort of trick to it. He wasn't in any sort of discomfort. The boy truly mastered the flame. "How is this possible?"

Tice spoke up before Riss could. "It happened a few days ago."

Riss took Tice's interjection as a warning to be careful with his words. "My sister has an ability too. Sometimes, she just knows certain things."

The Captain looked at the both of them and glared. He found it very hard to believe that she could be anything other than an ordinary girl. "Like what?"

Riss answered with a smart tone. "Like you would be here at this exact time."

The Captain wasn't sure about Tice. He got the feeling that Riss wasn't being completely honest with him, but he liked that he had backbone. The glare on his face began to form in a curious smirk. "Follow me."

Tice and Riss jumped and cheered silently when The Captain turned his back. When the Captain turned around, they forced themselves to calm down and followed him onto the boat a bit more maturely.

Riss held Tice's hand tightly and led her up the ramp of the ship to begin their new adventure.

Samara stood in front of her father's golden sword and gazed at it. Her heart had broken so much that she knew he was in that grave, but somewhere in her mind she wished that he was on a journey on his way to see her once again.

Raymon was standing by his sister's side afraid to say anything to her. He had never seen her so distraught. "Are you going to say anything?"

She didn't respond.

Raymon had never been to a funeral before, but he convinced himself that the best way to start growing up was to move forward. "Thank you for fighting and protecting our home."

Samara felt tears in the back of her eyes, but she fought them off. She swore to herself that she wouldn't cry. "I promise that we'll do our part and get our home back." When she saw her father's matching necklace on his sword, she began to be flushed with an overwhelming amount of memories. "But if it's alright with you, I think I have to take this back." She couldn't let him have her heart anymore because he was gone. She couldn't let anyone have it again, so Samara took his locket and placed it around her neck.

Raymon wondered to himself why Samara didn't give him her necklace. He knew what it meant to her. Maybe it was because he was a weak crybaby. "I'm going to try and be strong like you were, Father. I want to make you proud." But truly, he wanted to make his sister proud.

Samara was just so angry! "How could this have happened? The war was over. How did Lord Rovin get the power to destroy our father?" She clenched her fists and closed her eyes tight. The anger was the only thing keeping her from being sad.

"I think I can answer that," said a voice from behind.

The two of them turned around and saw a pale woman with yellow eyes. "Who are you?" Samara asked.

She smiled until her eyes closed shut. "My name is Sakai."

"Sakai?" Raymon asked confused.

"Yes." She bowed in what seemed to be respect for the two of them. "I am a traveler and an oracle of sorts."

Samara reached out and gently nudged her brother behind her back. "And what do you know about Lord Rovin and our father?" she asked demandingly.

Sakai stood up straight and opened her eyes. "I know that Lord Rovin was not the only guilty party. The power that he possesses was never meant for him. It was only meant to be possessed by sweet children such as yourself."

"So I do have an ability?" Samara asked surprised.

"Yes." Sakai began walk closer to them as if she were gliding. "You have one of the strongest abilities there is." She walked behind Samara and placed her thin, long fingers on her shoulder and whispered into her ear. "You will soon discover the extent of your great power."

Samara was in awe of it. She wasn't somehow imagining blocking Lord Rovin's lightning. She protected herself and her little brother.

But there was something that Sakai said that made Samara angry. "If Lord Rovin weren't meant to have it, then how did he get it?"

Sakai giggled out of sheer excitement and turned to walk in front of Samara once again. "An evil boy corrupted the power of the pure and beautiful light. He turned it into something dark for those who have evil in their hearts to destroy this world. Because of his evil, the darkness corrupted other light from around the world and changed Lord Rovin, Captain Saxson, and many other men into monsters.

"It is up to you to stop this boy and his corruption. By doing this, you will also be avenging your father."

115

She thought about it carefully. It was a lot of responsibility, but she was well willing to do it. She always had the world on her dainty shoulders. "How? I don't know where he is."

Sakai smirked. "He will come to you."

"But how will I know who he is?" Samara asked.

"He is a young wielder of fire." Sakai smiled once again before beginning to fade away in front of their very eyes. "Believe me, he won't be hard to mistake."

Raymon was frightened when he saw the woman disappear. She couldn't have been human. But it frightened him more that Samara had a look in her eye that was unlike anything he had ever seen in her before. He tugged on her tattered dress. "What are you going to do, Samara?"

Samara could feel her powers in her so strong then. Sakai told her that she was one of the strongest. She couldn't let more evil spread, and she couldn't let her father's killer go unpunished. "I'm going to do what I swore I would do," she said. "I will avenge our father."

✧

Riss had taken Tice down to a crowded room where many other men had their bunks placed. The two of them would have to share the bed, and he wasn't happy about Tice being exposed to so many older men, but he didn't have much of a choice. "I hope we're doing the right thing, Tice."

Tice didn't like the smell of the place and the men were very loud and rowdy, but she wasn't going to let that, her stinging skin, or anything else bother her. "Don't worry. Eastern Pearl is the right place."

Chapter Nine

Alm was watching the barren earth from a hilltop high above where he had just come from. It was strange finally being free. He had felt the wind on his face before, but not like that. There was a sweetness in that dusty air that he could not explain.

But nothing was more unexplainable than his former inmate, Davin. He was standing at the highest point of the cliff top looking down heroically like something the children would dream about. He used to be one of the smallest boys, but he grew muscles instantly as if he had been a properly fed boy with extensive exercise. Neither was the case. His newfound strength was astounding.

Alm never really cared for him much. Davin always talked too much about his hopes and dreams and got them all in trouble. Things were definitely different though. Davin had become a leader who everyone instantly respected. How does a boy become such an inspiration?

Alm was intimidated when he walked up to Davin. "What are you doing?" It was clear what Davin was doing. His question was really, "What are we going to do next?"

Davin was still trying to understand how simple everything became. When he touched the light, there was some kind of explosion. He felt it from the inside of his body, and then it came out and knocked all of the men who had guarded the light away. Everything was surrounded in dust, and he knew he had been injured, but he didn't feel afraid.

When he could see once again, his eyes had changed. There was a swirling yellow light in his head that showed him a path of what he should do. He knew where to run, when to duck, who he should hit, and how hard he should do it.

He began to run and follow the lights. He had never been that fast, nor had he hit anyone in his life before. None of the guards could keep up with him, and Davin knew how to counter every move they made against him.

His first move was to save Alm from a guard who began to drag him back in toward the entrance, but not before disciplining Alm with his club. Alm had been struck in the back and didn't have the strength to struggle anymore. He closed his eyes and waited for his bondage or the release of death.

Davin grabbed the guard's hand before he could strike Alm again. The guard looked at Davin surprised and was unable to defend himself before Davin head-butted him into the ground and out of consciousness.

Alm was shocked. "Davin?" Where had the skinny, annoyingly happy, and positive kid gone? "What happened to you?"

"I'm not sure." Davin wondered what he must have looked like for Alm to be looking at him so strangely. "We've got get everyone inside."

"Why?"

Davin raised his hands and clasped his fingers into a fist. When he looked up, he saw that he had caught an arrow inches away from Alm's face. Alm was too blown away to yell in fear like he wanted to. Davin's power was amazing.

But it didn't faze Davin at all. It was as if that ability had been within him his entire life. "We're all sitting ducks out here with the archers. You guys work on trying to get everyone else free from inside. We greatly outnumber them."

Truthfully, Alm didn't want to be separated from Davin. What could he possibly do to compare with Davin? "And what are you going to do?"

Davin smirked. "I'll be in with you in a second." It was all clear to him. He knew already that he was going to win as soon as he started fighting. The more he fought, the more confident he became in that fact.

Davin ran for the walls and began to climb them with the speed of a spider. An archer spotted him during the climb and tried to shoot, but Davin moved his head and dodged it with ease. The archer tried again, but Davin moved to the left and then to the right if he needed to.

He got to the top and jumped up over the wall. The archer aimed again, but Davin jumped clear over him and punched him out. After that, all of the archers noticed that Davin was up there with them, but he had begun attacking them before they could really defend themselves. He knew which enemy to hit first by how fast they turned or how quickly they drew an arrow from their quiver. He couldn't fight them all before he was shot at, but he knew when to roll, move, or bend back. It was as if they were the child. They were all down before he managed to break a sweat.

He entered through the door leading downstairs. There were guards coming up through the stairwell, but Davin attacked them quickly. One of them took out a sword and reached out to strike him, but Davin took his hand and twisted it until he couldn't hold onto it any longer. Though Davin knew he was bigger, he was still smaller than the guards and able to slip through them with ease. When more began to come, he grabbed one by the arm and tossed him into the others.

He continued to run and defeat whoever was in his way. He wasn't sure exactly where to go. He had never been that high up before in the facility. He had only been on the first ground level. He began to figure it out as he went along, especially as other guards began to come and try to face him.

When he went down two more levels, he began to run into more of his own kind. They weren't very good warriors, but there was enough of them and they were desperate for freedom. Alm and the other men had managed to get down to the lower levels and began to hold off the guards as the women escaped. They were afraid to move at first. The brave and little Mina was the first to begin to run toward the doors. After the women got the hunger in their eyes, it wasn't really much of a fight.

The guards tried to beat them down and hold them back, but there was no stopping them as they headed toward their freedom, and since the archers were gone, there wasn't anything they could do once they got out of the doors.

Davin was the very last to leave. Mina tried to stay and wait for him, but Alm took her in his arms and ran with the rest of his people. Davin was soon to follow.

It was all so surreal. Davin could hardly believe that he had gotten them free. It was as if he had never been there at all, like it was all some kind of terrible dream. But he knew when he looked at his friends that it wasn't a nightmare. What they had been through was terrible, and he couldn't let that happen to any of them ever again.

"Mr. Petey would be happy," Alm told Davin.

He smiled. "Yeah. I guess he would be." He wished Mr. Petey would have been able to experience freedom. Maybe he would have even begun to dream again.

"Davin!" Mina ran to his side.

"Mina!" Davin lifted her up and hugged her tight. It was good that she would be able to grow up and become an ordinary woman. "Now we can dream and be proud to do it."

She hugged his neck and kissed him on the cheek. "I've always been proud because you made me proud to be who I am."

He lifted her up in the air and let her stretch out her arms as if they were wings. Lifting up Mina wasn't a hard task, but Davin used to be so weak that he couldn't hold her up for long. Now she was so light!

"You certainly are different," Alm said.

"It was the light that the little girl told me to find," Davin said. "It made me strong enough to get to it, and when I touched it, a power exploded inside me. I felt completely different—sort of like being reborn."

"You should come celebrate with us," Mina said.

Davin sat her back down and tapped her on the nose. "Oh. Really?"

"We are celebrating being free, but we wouldn't be free without you."

He patted her on the head. "I'll be there shortly."

He kept a smile on his face and a light heart until she had ran back down the hill toward the other survivors. Alm recognized that serious expression; he just didn't recognize it on Davin's face. "What's the problem?"

"None of you really think that this is over, do you?"

Alm was stupefied. "Sure. We escaped. We've got a couple of days lead on the guards. We can outrun them if we want to." Alm assumed that everything was as good as it could get.

Davin shook his head at Alm. Maybe a few days ago, he would have been like everyone else—just happy to be free—but he could see so far beyond that now. "We're hungry, we're tired, and their hearts aren't really ready for a fight. Some of them don't even believe that we should be free. Some of them still think that we're dreaming."

Davin watched all of his people. They were singing, dancing, and laughing with each other. They never got the chance to do any of that before. It made him smile, but there was still so much they were naive to. "Let them soak in this freedom for a few days. After they begin to realize how precious it is, they won't be able to go back to how things were."

Davin looked a bit more seriously. "They will be threatened again, but they'll be ready to fight for their freedom."

Alm didn't like hearing that they had to fight or that they weren't safe anymore, but he trusted in Davin's word and tried to be brave. "So we sit around for a couple of days and wait for them to attack us?"

He shook his head. "I said they'd be ready to fight. I didn't say that they would win."

"How do we become ready?" Alm asked.

"With time and training," Davin said. "Maybe I could show you guys some of the things that the light has shown me. But until then, I'm going to fight first."

"Wait! Why?" Alm asked in a bit of a panic. Davin had become amazing, but to fight alone was ridiculous.

Davin smiled. "I have to protect you, Mina, and everyone else."

Tice lay on her brother's lap while he held her in his arms. She didn't like riding on the ship. It made her feel nauseous. The only thing that made her feel better was her brother rubbing her back. "Do you think all of this happened for a reason?"

"What do you mean?" he asked.

"I mean when we left, the light came. When you left the cave, the light started to glow, and then I couldn't see. But now I have dreams about people who get powers. I think people all over the world are changing for the better."

"And that's why Sakai came and used Mal." Riss thought she was being silly at first, but it was starting to make sense.

"She wants to stop who we can become." Tice rose off of her brother's lap. She felt compelled to do something, but there was nothing she could do while on that ship.

Riss was angry just thinking about it. He understood that Sakai was merely using him and Mal to get what she wanted. It was his responsibility to stop whatever she did and to get Mal back to his old self again. "Don't worry. I'll set things right."

Tice tried to lie back down on her brother's lap and find comfort in his words, but she couldn't get the peace of mind that she wanted with so many loud men in their cabin. There were many of them in the middle of the room playing a game with cards and dice. They yelled with every roll. Tice and Riss also had to share a bottom bunk while a very large man slept on the one above. It made Tice afraid that he was going to fall through and squish them to death.

The men began to get even louder when a very pretty woman came down into the cabin. They whistled and spoke a lot about her beauty, but not in a very polite way. Riss thought she was a very beautiful woman as well. He actually began to blush as she began to make her way over to him.

"Hello." She had a very sweet voice and kind eyes. She had long black hair and skin like Riss.

"Who are you?" Tice asked.

"I'm Captain Mayes niece, Evva. Come and follow me."

Riss wasn't going to argue with her. He grabbed Tice's hand and followed Evva out of the crew cabin and down the hall of the ship up to a higher level. She led them to another cabin, one much nicer and open than the crowded room with the crew. "My uncle told me about you both. It must be very hard to live in a world like this all alone."

Riss tried to sound mature. "We have each other."

"That's true. If it weren't for my uncle, I don't know what I'd do. That's why I like to help people." Evva really only saw Riss as a small child. His attempt at charm went right over her head. "You both can stay in here with me."

"Really?" That was too good to be true! Her cabin was large, spacious, and comfortable. There were books, a very comfortable looking bed, a table, chairs, and chests full of clothes. It was actually like an acceptable living space. He hadn't slept in a real bed since the day he left his home.

"Not everyone in the world is cruel," Evva said. "Try to remember that."

A full smile came to Riss's face. "Sure." He was entranced by her beauty. He hadn't really been around a young woman before. All of his acquaintances were dirty, scrappy girls with a lot of edge to their personality. It was nice to meet a sweet woman for a change.

"Now you two haven't bathed in a while have you?" She asked nicely, but it was clear that she was the adult, and they were small, irresponsible children.

Riss's pride began to evaporate. "Not really…" He was ashamed to admit it. He was used to roughing it, but they must have looked ridiculous.

"I'll take…" Evva took a hold of Tice's hand. "What's your name?"

"Tice."

"I'll take Tice and then you can use my washroom."

Riss was hesitant about letting his little sister out of his sight, but he didn't protest it. Evva seemed like a very nice person.

There was already a warm bath waiting for Tice when she got inside. She didn't really know what she should do. She had been able to take care of herself for a while, but it was like she was moving in reverse. She couldn't see the bath, and she wouldn't be able to see whether or not she was clean. It made her feel like less of a person.

Evva was very patient and helpful. She helped Tice take off her dirty gown and got her in the water. Tice kept her eyes closed the entire time, because she didn't want to get soap in her eyes when Evva began washing her hair.

"Is it scary being out on your own?" Evva asked while massaging Tice's head. At least that soothed her.

"My brother has always taken care of me."

"Is the water too hot?"

"No, Miss." Tice had never had a bath quite like that before. Usually, it was just a scrub down with a worn out washcloth and some water. The older kids were lucky if they could bring soap to the orphanage, and it usually didn't last that long.

Evva enjoyed taking care of Tice. She never had a little sister before, but she always wanted one. "I've never seen a person who looks like you," she told Tice.

"I thought people from Eastern Pearl looked like me."

"No. I don't know anyone with skin as white as yours, and then it's like you're supposed to be a different color. You look like the rest of us, but you're not."

"Well, I don't see any colors anymore." Tice sunk her head in the water until she was completely submerged. She didn't mean to be a child, but she thought that there were people like her somewhere in the world. She had no idea how completely alone she was.

"I'm sorry if I upset you."

Tice came back up to breathe in some air. There was no point in hiding. Evva was being very nice to her. "No. It's alright."

She patted Tice on her head affectionately. "I'm going to get you something new to wear. Do you mind staying here alone for a little while?"

She shook her head.

"I'll be right back."

Tice hadn't been alone since her brother left her in the cave. She didn't mind when Evva asked, but she began to become fearful. She told herself that Evva was nearby. She would have to learn to be by herself in the dark. She had no choice.

Tice jumped when she heard the door close, and she hid under the water again. It was stupid. There was nothing out there that was going to hurt her. She took a moment and hugged herself and let the water pull and tug her gently along. She wondered what it would be like if she opened her eyes. She knew that she was blind, but she was curious. Sometimes she liked to pretend she could see.

When she opened her eyes, she closed them back up quickly. The water touching her eyes startled her, but she tried again right away. She could feel it all around her, but there was nothing but darkness. She at least thought that maybe her eyes could see wavy darkness, but it was the same old same old.

But then something strange happened. She swore she saw something. She squint her eyes, and it began to become clearer. There was something green in the water. There was something far away—farther than the length of what the water should have been—swimming toward her. It was something large, very dangerous, and it was coming right for her!

"Ahhh!" She screamed and began to crawl backward to get away from it. When she hit something hard, she stood up on her feet and reached to climb out of the bathtub. She was in such a panic that she kept slipping and could get out, but she continued to scream until she felt arms wrap a soft towel around her.

"What's the matter?" Evva asked in a fright.

Tice couldn't see that she was safe, and she didn't feel safe. She still felt a chilling sensation all over her body that continued to loom even after she realized that she was in Evva's arms. "I saw a monster."

"A monster?" Riss had come inside the washroom with Evva once he heard Tice scream. He had never seen her cry and shake with fear like that, not even when she had lost her sight.

Evva held her close and kissed her forehead trying to calm her down. "It must have all been in your mind, Tice."

A day or two ago, Riss would have sided with Evva, but he knew better than to count his little sister out like that.

He waited until after Evva got Tice dressed in a new white dress. It was very big on her and held up by belts. Evva had to leave her alone on a bed while she went to go get her and Riss dinner.

Riss quickly washed up and changed into a pair of slacks and a shirt that were too big for him as well, but he was grateful for what he received.

Evva brought the two of them a meal of bread, fish, fruit, and goat cheese. Riss wolfed all of his food down quickly, but Tice was still startled and took her time taking everything in.

Evva observed the two of them with a curious smile. She loved children, but they were a strange bunch. "You know you'll have to work tomorrow, Riss."

"I know." He didn't care about that. He was just waiting to be left alone with his sister again so they could talk. "Will you take my plate? I'm finished."

"Sure." She took his and Tice's plates away to the kitchen.

127

As soon as she left the room, Riss asked his sister, "What kind of monster was it?"

Tice couldn't get the image out of her mind ever since it appeared. She was haunted by those giant, yellow eyes. "It was a snake."

"A snake?" Riss wrapped his arms around his sister once he noticed that her eyes were welling up with tears again. He kissed her and rocked her in his arms. "Come on. I'll take care of you."

She knew that, but she couldn't shake the feeling.

"Is it after us?" he asked.

No matter what she did, no matter how tight she closed her eyes, or how much she thought of something else, those yellow eyes were still watching her. "I think so."

Davin had been looking out into the distance for intruders for the entire day. All of his people were beginning to wonder and worry, but no one bothered him. As wonderful as Davin was, his power was even frightening to some of them.

But not Mina. Mina ran up to Davin alone and tugged on his hand until he looked down at her sweet face. "What is it, Mina?"

She smiled. "I made a song for you, Davin."

"Really?" Davin was humbled, but he did not want to leave his post.

"Yes. Please come and listen!" She pulled on his arm until his feet began to follow. His people had gathered wood and started a fire. They were still hungry, but at least they weren't cold. There were five boys and another little girl waiting near the fire for Mina. "You will love this!" she teased.

"I'm sure that I will." Davin took a seat next to Alm while the children began to sing:

Davin is brave
Davin is strong
He knows what is right and wrong
When he touched the light
All was right
Now we sing praises in the night

"That's a very nice song," Davin said.

Mina was the loudest for having such a quiet voice. It was clear that she cared for Davin the most out of everyone there. "Now we feel safe because you're always going to protect us."

Her words began to convict Davin. They all did think that they were safe and free. How could he let them go on any further with such false hopes? "I need everyone to listen."

He stood up, and the noise completely dissipated. Though not everyone was comfortable with Davin, they were all wise enough to listen to him. "About our safety...I think it's important that I go back and face some of the guards."

There was an eruption of disapproval. He expected it, but not in the extreme intensity that he received. "But that's insane!" one man said. "You can't stand up to an entire army!"

He let them yell for a little while, and then talked over them as best he could. "I'm sure they wouldn't send an entire army. There's probably just going to be a few to scout for us, then they'd send reinforcements when they see what we can do, and then they'll properly prepare to take us all back."

"It's too dangerous!" It was like none of them had listened to a word he had said.

"The truth is that someone is already after us!" he yelled, and it silenced them all. They were all petrified. He lowered his voice once he had their attention once again. "They might have slowed down their search because they're afraid of us or the light, but there are men on the way. I have to slow them down."

They all looked at each other. Many of them were too afraid to speak what was really in their heart. One man dared to ask Davin, "What are you going to do when you find them?"

"What do you mean?" he asked confused.

Mina grabbed Davin's hand again and shook it. When he looked into her eyes, he saw how concerned she was. "Promise that you're not going to hurt anyone."

"I wasn't really planning on it." He hadn't thought about it. He only knew to fight. He didn't think about how far he'd have to take it, and he wouldn't know how far he'd have to go until he was in the midst of the battle.

"Then you're not ready to save anyone," said an older man, very sternly.

Alm rose on his feet and clenched his fists. "What is that supposed to mean? If it weren't for Davin, we'd still be in cells!"

The man didn't raise his voice, but his tone was very serious. "It means that we're dealing with evil people." He was pleading with Davin in his eyes. "You have to put a stop to all this right now."

When he thought about how those men treated Mr. Petey, he knew good and well that those men were evil. There was no reason to keep so many innocent people like Mina down in a cage like an animal. There was a strong chance that even if he fought them off, they would still come back. They would never give up because of what was driving them. It wasn't greed. It was more than hate. It was evil. "Do you realize what you're asking me to do?"

For the first time since he gained the powers from the light, Davin felt his age again. He didn't want to take anyone's life, but it was possible that he might have to.

The man came and put his hands on Davin's shoulders. They weren't familiar with each other, but he sympathized with Davin. "I can't imagine what it must be like to have all that weight on your shoulders. You're too young for this type of responsibility, but nonetheless, it's yours."

Davin slowly looked up into the man's grey eyes. He imagined that his own eyes were full with just as much uncertainty as that man's. "There's always a better way," Davin said.

His grip on Davin's shoulders tightened. "Not for people like them."

"But there is for people like us." Davin knew that the man's eyes were burning with a desire to be safe. Freedom was a beautiful gift. Davin knew that he had to fight, but to kill...? "I promise I'll do what I have to do in order to survive, but only what I have to."

The man let go of Davin's shoulders and backed away. He was frustrated, but there wasn't anything that he could really do to change Davin's mind. He was innocent.

Chapter Ten

It had been days since they mysteriously arrived on the shores of Eastern Pearl, and all young Raymon had done since his arrival was watch his sister. She didn't say much to him. He knew she was devastated, but she never cried. All she did was stare at her stretched out hands.

"Aren't you hungry?" he asked.

"No."

"But you haven't eaten since the day before. We should find you something very nice to eat."

"I said I'm not hungry." Samara didn't raise her voice, but Raymon knew good and well how irritated she had become.

He sighed and left her alone to finally explore on his own. He didn't like staying in the garden. It crept him out. The empty city streets were also very strange to Raymon, but at least there weren't any graves around.

He found a ball left alone in the streets. Raymon took what small piece of joy he had left and kicked the ball all the way back to the palace. Samara didn't even notice that Raymon had gone anywhere. It made him feel small and even unimportant. Maybe if he convinced her to play with him, she could be happy again.

He carried the ball on top of the rubble and kicked it until he returned to his sister. She was still sitting in the same spot she had been sitting in for the past few days with her hands outstretched. Her eyebrows were narrowed and pressed against her focused eyes. "Samara."

"Not now," she snipped.

He sighed and sat the ball down at his feet. "But Samara—"

"Not now!" She rolled her eyes at him and continued to concentrate. She could feel the same power that saved her erupting from her hands. She couldn't control it though. It would come in small bursts. She couldn't see it, but she knew it was there.

Raymon didn't know any of that. He really thought his sister might have been losing her mind from the grief. He decided that the only right thing to do was to force her to play with him. That way, she would remember what it was like to be a child.

He nudged the ball with his foot gently at his sister so it would nick her knee.

Pop!

Raymon screamed and fell on his butt as soon as he heard the sound of the ball exploding. He had tears in his eyes. It was the only thing that had cheered him up, and she somehow destroyed it.

Samara slowly turned and looked at her brother with a smile that frightened Raymon. "I'm getting the hang of this."

"But you..." He looked at the bits of ball spread across the ground. "You destroyed my ball."

She glared at her brother and shook her head with disbelief. "You think this is some kind of game? Lord Rovin seeks our lives. If we don't do something, he's going to have them."

Raymon closed his mouth tight. He didn't handle pressure on him very well. He thought it was his fault when someone was angry with him. He did do his best to explain. "But I just wanted to play a game with you. I thought it would make you happy."

Any other time, Raymon's big baby eyes would have softened her up into a submission, but she was much too angry inside. "Defeating Lord Rovin is the only thing that will make me happy ever again." She turned away from him and tried to continue working.

"When you fight Lord Rovin," he asked fragilely, "what are you going to do?"

"I'm going to hurt him!" she yelled.

Her words were like a slap in the face to Raymon. He didn't want to ask, but he needed to know. "How bad?"

"Real bad." She tried to ignore her brother and continued to feel her powers in her hands. It was some kind of shield, but she would learn to make it a weapon.

Raymon placed his chin on his knees and hugged his legs as he watched his dedicated sister. He was afraid of Lord Rovin, but more so of what his sister might become.

$$\Leftarrow$$

Davin hid silently behind a giant rock. He could hear the guards from his long time prison fast approaching. Though he was sure he would be able to defeat them, he was concerned about his ability. He was trying not to see all what he should do in fear of what must be done.

He closed his eyes so he wouldn't see, but he could still hear. Without thinking about it, he listened to the beat of the ground. The constant vibrations of the earth and the pounding of horses' feet treading across the land were his guides. He would have never thought about anything like that before the light changed him. There was nothing he could do to stop his abilities.

Davin opened up his eyes and took a deep breath. It was time.

Davin climbed the rock and jumped off the top without even thinking about it. There were ten of them that came on horses. Clearly, they were just scouting the area. Davin kicked the first one off the horse. By the way he held his head up, Davin knew he was in charge. He punched him in the face and knocked him out.

The other men were shocked. Some of their horses were startled. Davin took that opportunity to begin grabbing the men and throwing them off of their horses. He knocked off four men before the others backed away. It was a mistake on their part. Davin had just enough time to fight the four men and knock them out. That was five down—five to go.

Davin smirked at those remaining with confidence. He knew his exploits were making them afraid. He knew that appearing cocky would make them frustrated and startled enough to start making huge mistakes.

One of the men took a net and began to ride toward him. When the guard threw it on Davin, he pulled on the net so fast that the guard flew off of the horse and into Davin's elbow. He was out as soon as soon as he hit the ground.

Davin got the net off of him and threw it on the next man that charged. Davin pulled him off of the horse easily. He had a sword in his hand, so Davin kicked him in the face as soon as he got on the ground.

There were only two left.

One of them began riding away. Davin let him go for the meantime to focus on the one that still wanted to challenge him. Davin's last opponent drew an arrow from his quiver and aimed it at Davin. He didn't move. The guard was startled by his boldness, but still fired the arrow at Davin. Davin barely moved but caught the arrow when it was only an inch away from his heart.

Davin snapped it with ease, and the guard was left in complete dread. Davin walked quickly and tipped the guard off his horse by his foot. As the guard laid on the ground whimpering in fear, Davin placed his foot on the man's face and pressed it into the ground.

"Please, don't kill me!"

Davin could hardly believe that his oppressors were nothing more than cowards. How could his people been their prisoners for so long? "I'm not going to kill you," Davin said.

The man was still whimpering. "You're going to let me go?"

Davin thought about the words that his elders gave him. He knew that the only way to guarantee that his people would be safe would be to kill those men. He didn't want to. There had to be another way. "Promise me that you won't come after me and my people anymore."

The man wouldn't say anything, so Davin pressed his foot harder against his skull. "Promise me!"

"Okay!" he yelled. "I promise!"

Davin knew by his voice that he was lying. He was saying whatever he could to escape. "I know if I let you go, you're going to come back with more men, and you're going to hurt my friends."

The guard hesitated. Surely he thought Davin would kill him if he admitted the truth, but he was too afraid to lie. He was simply following orders! "We have to."

"Why?"

He was so ashamed to die by the hands of a treacherous child. "Because you're an abomination."

"An abomination?" Davin asked. "What you do to people like us is the abomination!" Davin removed the guard's bow and took an arrow from his quiver angrily. The guard closed his eyes tight and began to cower even more. Davin wasn't going to end his life. He took aim toward the other conscious guard and fired the arrow in the man's shoulder. He instantly fell to the ground.

Davin got on his knees so he could grab the man by his hair. "Listen to me," he threatened, "this is your last opportunity to stay away from us. We will be safe." Davin threw his head against the ground. "Now attend to your injured friend if you want him to live."

The guard slowly stood on his feet. He was skeptical whether Davin was speaking truth about his mercy. He was still shaking from Davin's amazing might. He had been taught that the dreamers were dangerous, but he never could have imagined that boy.

As he began to walk over to his horse, Davin stopped him. "You can walk."

He was hurt but would not argue with the boy. The guard was mostly embarrassed about his miserable defeat and would take the boy's misguided mercy and return it with vengeance one hundredfold.

"Get out of here," Davin warned.

He began to run away toward his fallen comrade. The only two conscious were gone, and eight of them would be knocked out for a while. Davin had some time to get his people farther away. Taking nine out of ten horses would slow them down significantly.

All in all, it was a good battle, but a disheartening one. Davin had no choice but to make some hard decisions about what he should do.

✧

After days of watching his sister do nothing, Raymon was finally at his breaking point, and he was concerned that Samara had somehow surpassed her own. "Samara…" He asked her quietly.

"I'm busy," she said quickly.

He was a timid person, and Samara had never been. He didn't usually bother arguing with her, but he would never survive in a world

137

where she had gone mad. "I think you should take it easy. We've been through a lot."

Samara chuckled. "Do you think I've gone insane, Little Brother?" she asked.

He shrugged his shoulders embarrassed.

She smiled and shook her head at him. "I'm not crazy, Raymon." She reached out her hands toward him. "Feel this."

Raymon looked, but he didn't see anything. He squint his eyes, but he still didn't see what he was supposed to feel.

"Just try to put your hands between my hands."

He questioned her with his eyes, but reached. He didn't know what happened, but his knuckles cracked as his hand bounced back. He gasped. "What was that?"

She smiled happily. "It's my ability."

Raymon smiled as he spread his fingers against her invisible ball of power. It was strange, but he couldn't doubt her. He did question what she would do with that power, but he did know that his sister would protect him no matter what. "We're going to be okay."

Samara didn't really think the two of them would be safe. Lord Rovin would come after them again. The only thing she was sure about was that she was going to be ready when he tried to hurt them again.

✧

When Davin returned to his people, he had a lot on his mind. He had to get them moving again. He had some horses, but not enough to make a real difference. It was his responsibility to keep them safe somehow against all odds. But no matter how spectacular he had become, it was still too much for Davin's young shoulders.

Davin was met with many fearful questions and enthusiastic pats on the back. They all asked him about his battle. A great deal wanted to know of Davin's wrath against the scouts. Only a few wanted to know about his mercy.

He stood before them all with a burdened heart to address them all. "I know you all have questions about what I did. I promised that I would only do what I needed to do, and I kept my word. I fought them all off." He could see the satisfaction on most of their faces, but the older men were still asking questions with their eyes.

"I didn't kill anyone," Davin said. Many men looked at him disappointed, but Davin didn't care. "I'm glad that I didn't."

Truth be told, it was the easiest thing to do, but sometimes the hard way was more profitable. There would be repercussions for the things done and not done, but none of his choices could be undone. He had to move forward, and he would have never come to the revelation that he needed if not for the difficult path ahead. "I didn't ask for this responsibility, but it's mine. I should help those who cannot help themselves, but I shouldn't have to do it alone."

Everyone waited breathless for Davin to explain.

He took a deep breath. "I've decided that everyone here is going to learn how to defend themselves." There was a rush of noise that followed from men and women of all ages. None of them knew how to fight. They only knew how to be in bondage.

Davin knew that, but it was time for a change. "They will send men after us. If something happens to me, you all have to go on." He held his head up high and spoke boldly. "If you want your freedom, you have to fight for it yourselves."

They all looked amongst themselves. No one spoke for a while. Their silence said it all, but it didn't matter to Davin. He was going to make them fight. There were only two options: fight or die.

Chapter Eleven

"I have to do this!" a young girl told herself with sweat dripping down her face and tears in the back of her eyes. Her body was sore, her arms felt heavy, and her mind was nearing the breaking point. "I have to do this!"

"But you can't. Can you?"

She slowly looked up and stared at her oppressor from his feet up to his snarling face. He was three times her age with decades of experience trumping hers. Did he have to look at her with such disgust? Wasn't it reasonable that she was weaker than him? "I am trying, Sensei."

She reached out for help, but he slapped her hand away viciously. "That is not enough, Kumiko."

As he walked away from her, she pressed her head down on the wooden floor. She was frustrated, but she wouldn't dare cry. If her father were to find out what a failure she was, she would lose all of her honor.

She collected herself within a minute's time and stood. The soles felt like they were on fire. Even her toes tingled from being beaten once again. She had much shame as she walked through her home and saw the many faces of her father's workers staring at her in defeat. They wouldn't dare ever speak a word of mockery toward Kumiko. It would cost them their lives if she ever requested her father to destroy them.

One of the maids drew Kumiko a warm bath while another prepared a kimono for her to wear. Another washed her hair while another massaged her hands. They did it all without asking her what she wanted, and even though she was only fifteen, none of them would dare look her in the eye. It would be a sign of disrespect toward her and her father. The servants only did what they were meant to do: to serve.

No one could deny that she was a beautiful girl. Many boys did like to gaze at her. She was a graceful flower as she walked through the halls of her mansion with her raven hair and kimono flowing behind her as if she controlled the winds themselves.

Many of her father's men were already waiting for her to come into his war room. When they entered, they bowed their heads in respect, just as she bowed before her father's feet. "I am honored to be in your presence, Father."

"Rise, Kumiko."

She did as she was told and took her place next to her father. He was a strong and fearless man with a sword always at his side. He was known as a cruel and ruthless man. But just as many feared him, his daughter loved him all the more.

"How was your training?" he asked her.

She was ashamed of her defeat. She was sore, but she would never dream of revealing her weakness to him. "It is going well, Father."

"I heard you struggled today."

He was simply stating what he had heard. He didn't mean to shun her or be harsh, but she felt his words crush her. "I'll defeat my Sensei, Father. It will only be a matter of time."

"It pleases me to hear you say that, Kumiko. There is no such thing as a defeat. There is only a prolonged victory." Every time he spoke, his generals treated it as a newfound piece of literature. They hung onto every word.

A young man—only a few years older than Kumiko—bowed his head in respect once again. "You are very wise, my lord." As he lifted his head back up, his eyes gazed at Kumiko for a moment. He was attractive to Kumiko. He was the son of one of her father's generals. His name was Jun.

Kumiko would not smile at Jun, though she wanted to. She would never let another man jeopardize her father's plans.

"For example," her father said, "we have the strange orb that we found." The room was already silent, but it became frightfully so. "No one has found a way to release its power yet?"

Everyone stayed as still as stone.

Kumiko looked up at her father and asked, "What is this orb, Father?"

"It is an orb that releases great power to its wielder."

"How do we know such things if we have not seen its power?" Kumiko turned to face the crowd of men in front of her, but no one spoke a word.

Her father's expression was steady, but his voice raised a tiny fraction. "Someone had better answer my daughter."

One of the generals stood and spoke quickly. "We have spies in other lands that have witnessed its capabilities. Men have become monsters with its power. The orb is a magic unlike any other."

Kumiko could hardly imagine it. Her father had no tolerance for tricks. If he were interested in it, it must have been a sight to see. "What sorts of powers?"

One after another, men began to stand up on their feet and speak of the strange tales. "I've heard that it can give the power to control fire, the air, and the earth."

"There is a pirate who has learned to master the seas."

"The war in Eastern Pearl had ended. Their king was slain by a man who could manipulate lightning as if there were a storm within his grasp!"

Kumiko looked at her father. "All of these reports are true, Father?"

He smiled at his daughter. "There is no doubt that some of the tales of these mysterious orbs are false, but the fall of Eastern Pearl is the truest and the most vital."

It seemed impossible to Kumiko that another human being could have such abilities while her father had none other than his great strength and skill. "You can't have any other man thinking that the world isn't yours. Can you, Father?"

He looked at his daughter pleased. "No. I must obtain this power for myself."

"How so?" she asked.

Right after she asked, one of her father's man servants came into the room holding a box made out of solid gold. He set the box before the feet of Kumiko's father and bowed his head in respect.

"Show her," her father commanded.

The servant did what he was told without a moment's pause. There were two small doors in front of the box. When he opened them up, Kumiko saw a dark blue orb sitting on top of a red velvet pillow.

"That's it?" she asked disappointedly. It looked like nothing more than a glass ball.

"I assure you that this is more than what it appears to be."

Kumiko came closer to see it. As she looked inside—dead in its center—it began to glow. "What is it doing?"

"It hasn't done anything like this before." Her father looked out toward his generals and his advisors, but none of them had any answers. They all marveled at the bright light shining from inside the box.

The more Kumiko watched it, the more entranced she became. She didn't know if her eyes were playing tricks on her. The light inside the orb seemed to be swirling around and calling out to her.

"The time must be upon us, Kumiko." Her father closed the golden doors and patted the back of his dear daughter's head. "Tomorrow, I will ascend. All will be there to witness my great power, and you will be by my side."

Even though Kumiko couldn't see the orb anymore, she still felt it. As soon as she saw it glow, she felt something open up inside her chest. "Then the world will be yours, Father."

He smirked. "Indeed."

Kumiko's father and his men spoke of many other things that night, none of which she paid any attention to. She usually did hang onto every word her father spoke, but she continued to think about that light trapped within that golden box. It was taken away by the servants, but she still thought about it. There was a void inside that she knew the light could fill.

When the meeting was over, everyone bowed in respect to Kumiko and her father. When Jun bowed, he made eye contact with Kumiko when raising his head once again. Kumiko smiled for old time's sake, but she couldn't truly be herself until she saw the light once again.

"May I see it again?"

"See what?" her father asked.

She looked at him even more intrigued. "The orb of power."

He looked at his daughter with a smile. He was usually willing to give the world to her. "No one may see it again until I ascend tomorrow."

"I only want to see it for a moment."

"It acted strange today. Usually, it has only been dark. I assume the time to take its power is drawing near. I don't want anything standing in my way of power."

"I won't do anything to jeopardize that, Father." Kumiko was doing her best not to beg, but she was beginning to run out of options. She desperately wanted to see it.

"Then go to your room and rest, Kumiko." He rubbed her back affectionately. "Tomorrow, we will have a long day."

She couldn't disagree with her father. Disobedience was met with swift punishment.

Of course she couldn't be punished for something he was not aware of.

Kumiko appeared to be the obedient daughter. She bowed her head in respect and smiled in her father's face. It was shocking to her how well she could be devious toward her father. She had never disobeyed him before, but her curiosity was getting the best of her.

When the lights were out, she waited quietly in her bed for a few hours until she knew everyone was asleep. As she lay in the bed, she questioned every instinct she had to defy her father's orders. Emotionally, there was no doubt. There was too much to gain to be bound by fear.

The orb of power was most likely in her father's weapon storage behind the palace. It would be heavily guarded, and it would be impossible for her to get in without using her key that she kept hidden in a box in her closet. There were very few people who had a copy of the key. She was in risk of being an instant suspect, but she couldn't stop herself from going forward.

Kumiko tiptoed out of her bed a few hours before dawn. Her father rose with the sun, and she had to be done while the shade of night was still her ally. She dressed herself in black clothes from head-to-toe and snuck around the halls of the palace. In her training, she was taught to move as if she had never made one step. She was a graceful girl who was light on her feet, so that was never difficult for her. Besides, she knew those floorboards all too well to make a creek. She could hide in the smallest of places and in the shadows.

She snuck out of her home without any sort of difficulty. Her father had a storage room where he kept many weapons. It was usually surrounded by many guards. She hadn't considered how she was going to get around all of them. But that night, there weren't any there at all. Her father had many enemies. It was unlike him to have it unprotected.

She snuck to the front door of the building. The front was the only way in. If all of the guards were inside, she would probably be cut down as soon as she opened the door. She had done well so far, but there was no way to get past everyone unless she cut them down first.

But if they were to kill her, her father would destroy them. For that reason, she took off her mask. All of her father's guards were trained to react, but they were always aware of what they did. She would be safe.

She removed the necklace from around her neck and stuck the key in the keyhole. Surely they wouldn't attack her if she were able to open up the door. As she turned the key, a bright blue light began to appear through the cracks of the door. Her chest began to open up once again, and her heart pounded. When she heard the click of the door's release, she flung the doors open.

Kumiko shielded her eyes from the immense light that poured out toward her. Because she closed her eyes, she couldn't see who had grabbed her. She wouldn't risk screaming and alarming everyone in the house. She kicked, and she punched whoever it was until someone else grabbed her other arm. She still tried to break free, but they were stronger than her.

She opened her eyes when they brought her to a halt. The orb was no longer blinding, but it still shone brightly. Her eyes had not adjusted, but she could still see the men that had grabbed her were five of her father's generals.

"What is the meaning of this?"

One of the men was Jun's father, Yun. Kumiko's father trusted him immensely. She couldn't believe that he would betray them in such a way. "How are you affecting this power?" he asked.

If he had betrayed them, then it was possible that Jun was also a betrayer. Kumiko could barely bear the thought of it. "What do you mean?" she asked.

"It hasn't done this before," said another man. "It has only activated when you have been near."

"Not even your father, Horisho, was capable of making it glow."

That was impossible! No other person in the world could match her father in skill and power. Kumiko was definitely not a match for her father, so she surely could not do something that her father could not. "My father will have your heads for this!"

Yun knelt in front of Kumiko so he could look into her eyes. "You know your father better than anyone, Kumiko. Your father cannot be allowed to have such power."

Her father was always kind and gracious to her. He was stern, but that was because he was great. He needed respect. He deserved it. For them not to understand that was madness. "But you're his most trusted men. You'll live like kings in the new world my father will build!"

"Your father is already too powerful. We cannot allow him to become powerful enough to not need any of us. He'll turn on everyone."

She gazed back fiercely into his eyes. "Not me."

He looked at her questionably but then smirked in her face. "Once he finds out that you were trying to steal his power for yourself, he'll turn on you as well."

Kumiko never had any doubts concerning her father before, but she had never done something that wasn't according to his will before either. If their servants ever looked him in the eye, they would be severely

147

punished. Surely no mercy would be given to his traitorous daughter, who he trusted and loved more than anyone else in the world. He would be heartbroken and forced to take action.

"Let me go now," she commanded them.

One of the men holding her arm squeezed it tight and laughed at her. "What are you going to do if we don't?"

Kumiko might not have been as strong, fast, or as skillful as she would have liked, but there was one thing clear. She was her father's daughter, and she would not be disrespected by anyone. She looked up into the man's eyes. "I will make you."

He reached up his hand to strike her, but he never reached her face. Everyone in the room was suddenly shocked to see the room go dim as the orb ceased glowing and became nothing more than clear, frosted glass.

Kumiko did not take the time to marvel at the glass ball. She instead acted. She shook her arms until she was free and spun in the air to kick her captor in the face. Another man threw a punch, but she dodged it with ease and knocked him out with a quick jab to the face.

She caught them by surprise, but she needed to get away. If she were caught, there was no telling what repercussions her father would provoke. Her eyes caught a glass bottle hanging from a belt belonging to Yun. She grabbed it and broke it against the floor.

A black smoke began to fill the room, but Kumiko was gone before it dissipated. She ran back to her house and snuck in before the first alarm could sound. She stuffed her black clothes under her pillows, climbed under her covers, and tried to force herself asleep.

She had done many things like that in her training, but she had never bested any of her father's trained men before. It was an invigorating experience and perhaps the last great experience before facing her father's judgment.

The day began almost as bright as the night. The light poured in to bathe Kumiko's body and illuminate her pale skin. She whimpered and hid under the sanctity of her covers. It was much better than feeling the bright light of the dawn.

"Lady Kumiko," said a small and humble voice.

Kumiko sighed heavily and graced her servant with her own face, though Kumiko was not pleased. "I did not ask for a wakeup call."

The servant was a young girl who was terribly afraid. Kumiko was probably twice as old as her, and she heard plenty of stories from servants Kumiko disliked. "I apologize for intruding, but your father has an urgent need of you."

Then it all began to come back. Kumiko remembered what she had done and where she had gone. What she didn't understand was the light, and how she was able to accept such power when her own father could not.

Kumiko tried to remain calm, but she was afraid. "Do you know what he wants?"

Her servant spoke almost sternly to her. "I know that he wants you to hurry."

Kumiko knew not to keep her father waiting, but she was stunned in fear for a minute. She sat in her bed knowing that bad things were coming because she disobeyed her father.

She scooted to the edge of her bed slowly and carefully, but something snapped inside of her once her feet hit the ground. She hurried herself to get dressed properly to meet her father. If she could explain everything, then he would see it as a misunderstanding. He loved her. There was no way he would kill her, even if her curiosity got the better of her.

149

Her father was waiting in his war room with his generals and advisors once again. She bowed her head in respect and never raised her head enough to look her father in the eye. She didn't want to take the chance of her eyes giving away all of her secrets.

Her father was silent and still like a rock. Kumiko imagined that a man as stern as he could have yelled at a mountain and laughed as it crumbled from his might. The fact that he was not speaking a word frightened her a bit. Then he spoke her name coldly, "Kumiko."

She bowed her head. "You summoned me?" She slowly looked out into the crowd of her father's advisors. All of the men who were in the storage were gone, but so was Jun.

"There are betrayers among us, Kumiko."

Not even a breath escaped Kumiko's mouth, but her heart made up for the noise. She could hear it pounding in her ears, trying to rip its way through her chest. She tried to think straight. There had to be some sort or lie that he would believe. If there were a way to escape everything unscathed, she had to find it!

"Look at me," he commanded.

She turned her head slowly. As her eyes met his, she knew that there would never be a lie to make her words right. She was her father's betrayer, and he would find out sooner or later. With a shivering voice, she asked, "Who is your betrayer?"

A mischievous smirk began to slowly curve its way around his face. "You needn't worry my daughter." He patted her on the head, but it did not hold its usual affection. It was as if he were mocking her. "I have already sentenced them to death."

Kumiko wasn't sure if that were good news or not. No witnesses meant that there were no men to tell of her minor role in the betrayal, but her father's thirst for vengeance was something she could not ignore. "All of them?" she asked.

He narrowed his eyes at his daughter. "Not quite." Kumiko was being very careful, but there was a bead of sweat on his daughter's brow. "You see, the orb of power wasn't quite stolen last night, but now it seems to be worthless. I interrogated the men myself, but I didn't receive any information as to why the orb no longer holds any power." He reached into his kimono and pulled out a simple, clear glass ball and set it in front of Kumiko. "Do you know how it became this way, Kumiko?"

She looked at the ball for only a second. "Why would I know, Father?"

That wasn't good enough for her father. He was looking for an answer, not an interrogation. It angered and intrigued him. "Bring out the prisoner!"

Through the chamber's door emerged two guards with their arms locking on tight to Jun's. He was gagged, and his arms and legs were shackled together. His face was cut and bruised. His eyes were heavy, and his movements were sluggish. He looked like he hadn't rested for days.

She tried to remain calm when she saw him in such bad shape. She thought of begging for his release only once. That charming smile and confident glimmer consistently began to haunt her, but begging would have made her look weak. "What is his crime?"

"He claims that he knows nothing about his father's treachery, and he swears that his allegiance lies with me alone." Her father stood up on his feet and began to walk toward Jun. "Now, I found that disturbing and that his plea lacked sincerity."

Kumiko hadn't taken her eyes off of Jun ever since he entered the room. They were focused on nothing but her own. "Why so?" she asked.

Her father spoke casually. "I thought he might experience bitterness toward me after he watched me kill his father."

On the inside, Kumiko felt shock and perhaps sympathy for Jun. On the outside, she hoped she didn't show anything but a lack of empathy. "That is odd."

"It is perplexing." Her father's cheeriness was the greatest disturbance to them all. It was all a joke to him. It was all an intriguing game with someone else's life on the line. "So, I asked him. I asked this boy why he would disgrace the memory of his father and fail in his duty as a son to serve me with his last breath. And do you know what he said to me, Kumiko?"

She shook her head slowly, still watching Jun.

Her father grabbed Jun by his hair and yanked his head back. "Tell her," he said threateningly.

Jun swallowed his pride hard like a bitter drink that he could feel sliding down his throat and sitting inside his stomach. He kept his body stiff, and his mouth shut tight until her father jerked his head back again. "I said," he took in a deep breath, "that I love you."

Love. It was something she knew of. She knew that her father loved her. She felt the same way for her father. She always knew that sooner or later, she would have to find love in another way so her father's bloodline and his legacy could live through children of her own. She didn't expect that she would hear those words so soon. Hearing his confession of love did not make her feel sympathy for him. It made her feel burdened, like she had an obligation to save Jun's life.

He didn't expect anything from her. It was clear by the look on his face. He wasn't angry. He was being patient until the final decision was made. He very much expected to die.

"He loves you." Kumiko's father began to laugh, which never bode well for his enemies. "He chooses love over honor, but I know that he does love you, Kumiko." He let go of Jun's hair and began to pace between the two as he spoke. "I see the way that he looks at you. I have seen the way you look at him, though you have hidden it well. I never spoke ill will toward your feelings, because Jun would make a fine husband for you one day."

His smiles turned into a snarl as he became enraged. "However, now it has come to my attention that he could be intending on taking my position, my power, and my daughter."

"That's impossible!" She yelled without meaning to. The room was already silent, but it held an entire new meaning and feeling. The room felt cold and dead.

Her father turned and walked closely to her. "How so?"

She looked at Jun staring at her and felt terrible, but she didn't let any bit of emotion for him manifest on her face. "Because I don't love this boy."

"You don't?" he asked curiously.

She thought of her words carefully. She never thought that disobeying her father would lead down such a path. She didn't want to be so lost that she couldn't find her way again. "I love no one but you, Father. I choose no other life but the one you decide with your great wisdom. Jun and his father's mistakes will not tear us apart. Your will is mine."

"So you care nothing if I kill this boy right here and right now?" As he began to unsheathe his sword, Kumiko's eyes followed the light on the blade travel from the base of the steel to the tip.

"If it be your will, then it is mine," she said.

Her father stared into his daughter's eyes to search for any defiance. "Leave the prisoner here," he said to his men. "Everyone else is to leave."

Kumiko breathed in a quiet sigh. Her father couldn't make a public example out of her if he killed her privately. If he were going to end her life, he would have made her shame and betrayal known.

He waited until all of the spectators had left. He only wanted Kumiko, Jun, and himself there. He was always very stern to his men or very loving to his daughter. He didn't want his men to see him so conflicted. "I know that you would let me kill this boy, but I don't know if it is out of fear of me or love."

"Love, Father," she begged quickly. "I swear to you!"

He regained his rocklike composure and set his sword at her feet. "Then if he is a betrayer, then make our family safe again."

She knew that he was serious, whether he believed she loved Jun or not. She stared steady into his eyes as she picked up his sword and stood on her feet. Then she walked past him to Jun, who was sitting helplessly on his knees because of the mess she and his father got him into. "Jun, did you know of your father's plans? Did you know that he wanted to steal the orb?"

He didn't even pause. "No."

He was still the same boy who had smiled at her yesterday when she came in the room. His betrayal was impractical. "I believe him, Father."

That was not the answer he wanted to hear. He began to raise his voice without even thinking. "Your judgment might be clouded."

She turned to face her father finally ready to defend herself. "Then don't trust my judgment. But you did ask me to kill him if he is a betrayer. If I don't think he is, then I shouldn't do it." As a sign of good faith, she placed her father's sword back into his hands. "However, you are welcome to kill whoever you like."

He looked down at the sword in his hands. He planned not to let traitors or their sons go unscathed from his wrath. Jun should be no different. "Would you hate me if I killed this boy?" He looked back into the eyes of his daughter sincerely.

154

No. Kumiko never had any doubt in her mind that her father loved her. The question was whether or not he loved power more. "I wouldn't think any less of you than I do now, Father."

He smiled and rubbed the back of her head with affection once again. "You may leave."

Kumiko bowed and left the room without looking at Jun. She knew that he was expecting her to say something to save his life, but she would never beg her father for it. She was much like her father in that regard. It was unclear whether love or the love of power ruled her life.

But she was soon to find out the balance in her life and her father's.

Chapter Twelve

An itch. It's something that everyone has. It's not complicated. A brush of the nail against the irritated spot would do the trick. A hard rub against a surface would suffice. It's not a difficult task. But when Diene began to feel that familiar sensation in an unfamiliar area, it became an impossible task.

Something miraculous had happened to Diene. Ever since she was born, she had been ill and couldn't walk. She wanted to more than anything in the world. Then one night, a light came and made her legs strong, and she ran. She ran so fast that it seemed as if she had never left her bedroom to find the light in the ocean's shore.

Her parents were happy, but they were more afraid than anything else. They made Diene promise that she would not tell a single person about her gift to walk. Everything had to remain as it had always been. She had to go to school and be around kids who could run around while she sat in her wheelchair. She couldn't even scratch her leg, because they weren't supposed to feel anything. She had no choice but to sit and wait for the itch to go away.

Diene's best hope was to focus on something else. There was a boy named Dex with dimples and black hair. He was the best looking boy in town, but Diene was always afraid to talk to him. But if she could finally walk, then there was a chance that she could finally get up the courage to speak to him.

"That's all," her instructor said. "Have your books finished for tomorrow. We'll have a test on it."

Diene hadn't realized that she was staring at Dex for several minutes. She couldn't help it. She had been in love with him ever since she was four. When she saw him in town picking out her favorite sweets, she knew that the two of them were meant to be together forever.

When she saw him leaving the classroom, she told herself that she had no choice but to act. She rolled herself outside where he was. He was speaking to Avia, a girl who liked him a lot. Avia spotted Diene first and glared at her. She was intimidated, but she continued to keep going.

Diene was blushing before she even started to speak. "Dex."

He looked around until he realized the voice was coming from below. "Hi Diene." He offered her a kind smile.

She thought she would melt. "Dex..." It was hard for her to continue speaking to him. "I was wondering..." She was blushing and smiling so much that it made her cheeks hurt.

His voice was so soothing. "What is it?"

She swallowed her fears and spoke as clearly as she could manage. "I wanted to know if you would like to go to the dance with me." She looked away from him as soon as she spoke it.

"I'm going to the dance with Dex," said Avia.

Diene figured as much. Avia was tall with such beautiful long legs. Diene couldn't compete with that, not as long as she was in the chair. "Maybe you could save me a dance?"

She got enough courage to look Dex in the face. He smiled as if he was truly flattered by her request, but then he looked uncomfortable. "It's sweet of you to ask Diene, but..." He lowered his voice. "I'm not sure how we could dance with you in your chair and all."

It wasn't right that she could finally dance, yet she wasn't allowed to. It had been her desire for weeks to wear a pretty dress while Dex held her in his arms.

If only she could tell him the truth. Then the two of them would be together. "I understand," she lied bravely. "I can't dance, so we shouldn't."

He knitted his brows together. "I'm sorry."

Diene shook her head. "Don't be." To save herself from further heartbreak, she began to wheel herself away from Dex and Avia as fast as she could.

Jun was shackled to a stone wall in his cell as he had been for days. The palace dungeon was a cold and miserable place for even the greatest of psychopaths and cruelest of men. The smell was rotting and moldy. Plenty of the prisoners were sick and moaned in their sleep. There was a level below him where men were kept in waist high water shackled with their hands at head height until they were executed. It was only a matter of time before his usefulness had run out. He had nothing to tell his lord.

"You have a visitor," said his guard peering into his vision from behind a wall.

Jun sighed and looked up toward the ceiling. It was probably about to end for him.

"Jun."

He looked in front of his prison bars to match the sweet sound he heard with its beautiful face. It was Kumiko, the girl he had been thinking of seeing ever since he was taken away from her glorious face. "You came to see me?"

158

Kumiko held onto the bars as she waited for the guard to open the prison doors. She couldn't help but feel guilty for Jun's misfortune. Jun was thin and covered in dirt from his face to his feet. He smelled like rats, looked horribly pathetic, and it was all her fault. "My father plans on executing you tomorrow. I thought it was only appropriate that I speak with you."

When she entered inside, the guard locked her in as well. For a moment, he thought that she was going to help him escape. He would have been disappointed when he realized that she wasn't if he weren't already so ecstatic to see her. "You risk your father's wrath to come and see me?"

She spoke coldly. "He'll have no wrath once you are dead."

"Don't you mean he'll have no wrath left to be misdirected from you?"

Kumiko turned around to the guard and signaled him to leave. She waited until he was gone before she would speak another word to Jun. "What do you know?" she asked.

He didn't mean to cause her any harm, so he spoke quietly. "I don't know what you did, but it's clear that your father knows something. You might as well tell him the truth."

"So he can have a reason to kill me rather than his suspicions?"

"He feels disrespected. When I'm gone, he'll have no one left to blame but you. I don't want him to hurt you."

"You should be more concerned about your own welfare." Kumiko bent down until she was sitting on her knees. She wanted to be eye level with Jun. He was perfect for her. He was a strong boy, so he was a great addition to her father's empire. When she stroked his cheek with her finger, she felt something.

He imagined what her touch would be like a thousand times. Her gentleness did not disappoint. "What are you doing?"

She leaned in closer until their noses were touching and their lips were just a breath apart. "You love me. The least I can do is give you a kiss goodbye."

She spoke true and kissed the boy. His lips were the only pair to have ever touched her own, and she couldn't imagine someone else's lips taking his place. And if he were to live, he would make sure that no one else ever took his place from her gentle, lovely lips.

He wished that his hands weren't bound together because he wanted to hold her. He wished his feet were free so they could run away to where no one would find them. But he was shackled in his cell, and he would die for her if he had to. "Do you love me?" he asked her.

She really did know that he loved her. She could still feel his kiss throughout her body; his warmth was on her lips. Her heart was calling out to him in rhythm. She even felt a tingling in her toes. "Not in the slightest," she said.

Jun wasn't going to question or beg the truth from her. He was going to die with dignity.

Kumiko felt like she had lost all of her pride, but she would not lose her life for some boy. "Guard!"

When the guard came and let her out, she stopped herself from walking away. If she told her father one sentence of the truth, she could probably save Jun's life—or at least her honor—but she was too afraid to salvage either. "I'll remember you when you're gone," she told him.

He smiled aching. "I'm sure you will."

Dinners had been growing colder in Diene's home. She didn't care what she was eating, and she was beginning not to care for the people she was eating with. Her parents smiled like nothing was wrong, and she hated every second of it. Even the smell of the fresh lilies on the table were sickening. Everything was just a facade of happiness, when she was growing more miserable every single second of her charade of a life.

"How was school?" her father asked with a perky smile.

Usually, she would just tell them what they wanted to hear, but she couldn't take it any longer. "It was terrible."

Her mother reached across the table to touch her hand with concern. "Why?"

Diene looked down at her mother's hand on top of hers. She didn't want to be touched by her. She was the cause of her problems. "Because I'm lying to all of my friends!" she yelled.

Her parents consulted each other with eye contact before her mother attempted to calm her daughter down with her soothing, loving voice. "Diene, we've talked about this."

They had talked. They spoke about it at least one hundred times, but she didn't care. "I want to go to the dance!" she yelled.

Her father lowered his head sadly, knowing what his daughter meant. "For what?"

Diene began to blink, trying to hold in her raging tears. "You've tried to make me have a normal life when I was crippled, and I loved you for it. Now that I can have a normal life, you want to take it away from me as if none of your words ever mattered."

Her parents looked at each other again with even more concern in their eyes. They sympathized with their daughter, but neither of them knew what it was like to be her. But she couldn't possibly know the dangers of revealing the truth. "You have to stay in your chair, Diene."

Diene had defiance in her eyes. "Fine. I'll stay in my chair. Just let me go."

Her father tried to be insistent, but careful of her feelings. "But you can't dance."

"What's the point of being healed if I keep it to myself? What's the point if I can't dance with the boy that I like or play with the friends around me? What's the point?" She wiped her eyes before any tears could fall. "You lied to me every day and told me that I was just like everyone else!"

Her father turned away from her. He couldn't stand to see her cry, but it was even worse that it was him who was making her do it. He reached out across the table to touch her hand. She wasn't a little girl anymore. She had been through a lot with her sickness. She would have to learn what the world was like eventually. "You can go."

She wiped her tears away and smiled. "Really?"

"Yes." He forced a smile on his face, but he was really terrified. "We want you to be happy, Diene."

Kumiko continuously thought of Jun abandoned in prison as she went about her day. She was sure that she didn't love him and that she was merely infatuated with his looks and his potential. However, his words were true. Once he was gone, her father had no one else to take his frustrations out on. Her father would be left to face the truth. Once that were to happen, she would lose her life.

"Kumiko," her sensei said, "are you even listening to me anymore?"

Kumiko blinked a few times until she was able to focus on her sensei and his instruction. "I am listening."

He frowned. It was an honor to teach the heir of his master's empire, but not when it was a girl. He wanted to teach a strong boy and not a struggling girl who could never really bring about any greatness. "Try to hit me."

Kumiko had enough problems to deal with. She didn't want another failure on her shoulders. But nothing was worse than not trying. "Alright."

Her instructor didn't even attempt to get into a defensive stance. Kumiko was slow compared to him and her natural grace kept her from using raw power.

Kumiko took a deep breath and attacked swiftly. She reached out to punch her sensei and a second later, he was on the ground. Kumiko didn't understand it until she heard him grunting on the floor. "Sensei?"

He was coughing and struggling to get up. "I am fine."

Kumiko tried to help him stand, but her sensei refused and tried to smack her in the hand. Kumiko instinctively moved her hands away before he could hit her. She didn't realize how fast she was.

It was interesting. "Can we try again?"

"Of course." He got up and prepared to fight her. "This time, I'll be serious."

He was serious, but when Kumiko came at him again, he failed all the same. He was too slow to hit Kumiko and her grace managed to stay intact along with a remarkably improved force. She had become more than impressive. She was his successor.

Once she had knocked him back down to the ground with a powerful kick to the face, she lost her confidence and traded it with a terrifying revelation. Before experiencing the light, she was unable to defeat her sensei. After being exposed, she beat him without even trying.

"Kumiko..." Her sensei stood to his feet and wiped the blood away from his mouth. He would have felt more shamed if he weren't so amazed. "Who has taught you these things?"

She hadn't learned anything new. She was just better. "I have to go."

She rushed out to retreat from the eyes of the world as she thought. Somehow, someway, she received the ability to fight better. Her sensei would tell her father, and he would realize what had happened. He would know that she stole his power for herself.

The dance was just as Diene had imagined. Her lunch hall had been cleared out of tables and chairs, except for a few tables crowded with food. There was a local band playing drums, flutes, and horns. The candle lighting was dimmed to make the atmosphere romantic, and her dear Dex was in the center of the dance floor looking quite handsome.

Diene was glad to be in her long, green dress. She couldn't believe that her mother and father agreed to let her go. She had no promised dances to cherish her night with, but she was grateful to know that she could really dance if she wanted to. She spent her time in her chair with her hands resting on her legs. Diene occasionally talked to some girls from her classroom, but they were all dancing with boys for most of the night. They smiled and waved, but they were uncomfortable around Diene. It was like they felt guilty for being able to walk. Diene didn't want to be a burden to them, so she sat alone in a corner watching most of the time.

As the night went on, Diene began to clench her fingers tightly. Her dress was beginning to wrinkle where she had it bunched up in her fingers. When she saw Dex, her world ceased turning. All around her was still, and his smile was her entire existence. She should have been held in his arms, not that silly Avia!

Avia spotted Diene watching from the corner of the hall and smirked as she held Dex tighter. Diene knew it was deliberate, and she grumbled under her breath. She wasn't going to let Avia get someone as perfect as Dex while she lied about her life in that chair.

She gripped on tight to her handles and pushed herself up.

The music stopped. Her classmates' voices turned into a whisper and then a sudden hush. Diene felt as if all her clothes had been ripped from off her body. Many people had stared at her before, but they did their best not to see. Now there wasn't a reason to have sympathy or guilt. She was special, and they all needed to know why.

Dex gently nudged Avia behind him to make room for Diene coming closer. She was blushing and walking with her hands clasped tightly together. Her posture was atrocious, her footing was clumsy, but she felt like the most beautiful girl in the world. "I was wondering now…If you would like to dance."

He smiled and took her hand. "I would like that."

Diene began to smile so hard that it became difficult for her to see. She hugged onto Dex's neck as he wrapped his arms around her waist. There were whispers from all around the room as the two of them danced. Everyone's eyes were on her, and it was for the right reasons.

It didn't matter that she didn't know how to dance. She kept her eyes closed and let him lead her. She let him and the music carry her off into a peaceful world that she didn't know she could experience. She was finally getting everything that she ever wanted.

"How did this happen?" he asked amazed.

She didn't want to think about anything else at the moment, so she answered him quickly. "A girl came to me while I was sleeping and told me that I needed to find a light."

He instinctively held her tighter. "While you were sleeping? Did you have a dream?"

She raised her head off of his chest and looked at him puzzled. "What's a dream?"

He looked around the room slowly. The other children had begun to continue dancing, but their eyes found their way back to Diene. Their whispers were probably something most troubling. "It's something that terrible people have." He spoke to her quietly and with great fear. "It's when you see things even though you're asleep."

She laughed. "I was awake." But then her nervousness began to creep in. "...At least I think I was awake." Real people didn't look like that girl. Everything about it was unnatural. "When I found the light she told me about, I could walk. Not only that, but I could..."

"Could what?"

She trusted Dex. She really did. Even though he hadn't showed her any romantic interest until that night, he was always kind with his smiles or occasional few words. "I could..." She smiled. "I could get the chance to dance with you."

He smiled back at her. "Then I'm glad."

She rested her head back on his chest but watched the room. Everyone was amazed. Some were in a good way while others had very frightened expressions. Her parents were afraid of something for a reason. She thought it would be best to keep her dance a secret for the time being.

Diene had everything under control.

"Diene!"

Until her parents came to pick her up from the dance earlier than predicted...

Kumiko watched her father from afar. He was meditating under his favorite cherry blossom tree in his garden with his sword resting in his lap. He often imagined winning battles under that tree. Kumiko would sit by her father's side and try to envision herself as a great leader, but that seemed impossible to her.

The least she could do was be a good daughter to her father. Her mother died giving birth to her, so she had no brother that he could raise to carry on his name. Instead of taking another bride, he dedicated his life to making a daughter who could become someone great, and she had taken advantage of her father's love.

It was time to tell him the truth.

She walked over to her father with stumbling feet. She considered walking away before her father had the chance to notice her.

"Kumiko." But he did.

She gulped. "Yes father?"

"Why have you come to see me?"

It was as if he already knew. Kumiko couldn't take the lies any longer, and she fell before her father's feet and began to cry. "I disobeyed you, Father. I wanted to see the light again, and the men who betrayed you were trying to use it against you. The orb began to glow, and I escaped. I didn't know what happened to me or to the orb until today. When I was training with my sensei, I defeated him with ease. The only explanation is the orb of power. I think I took the power from you, Father, and I apologize!" She collapsed on the floor sobbing and bowing for her father's forgiveness and for his mercy.

He did not speak a word to his daughter for what seemed to be a very long time. He hadn't seen her cry since she was a small girl. He didn't like it, but he knew that she must have hated it more. It only proved what sort of torment she had been going through.

He placed his hand on his daughter's shoulder and smiled. "I knew that you were there, Kumiko."

She slowly lifted her head up in shock. "You did?"

He wiped her tears away. "They told me before I ended their lives."

All of that time she thought she was being wise in her efforts against her father. "Then why haven't you said anything?"

"Because I trusted you, Daughter." He placed his hands on her shoulders and smiled at her. "I knew that you would come to me and tell me the truth."

She felt so guilty. "What about your orb, Father? I took the power for myself."

He laughed at her lightly. Children were such paranoid creatures. "Kumiko, I will ascend. There will be other orbs. However, I am glad that you were able to wield this power on your own."

"You are?" she asked confused.

"Of course. Who else would be more loyal to me than my own beautiful daughter?"

"No one, Father." Kumiko felt her father's obligation heavily on her shoulders. Her father always expected much from her, but she was actually about to deliver. Her father's plans would become reality, and it would be by her doing.

Her father rose to his feet. "I will release Jun immediately," he said. "He's no threat, and I'd rather spend our time perfecting your abilities."

Defeating her sensei so quickly without even thinking was a promising first step. It would be no time at all before she was able to rule lands for her father's glory. "My will is yours, Father."

Dex had enjoyed his day at the dance. It was a night he didn't plan on ever forgetting. He had never seen anyone who was sick instantly get better. It was so remarkable that he couldn't help but tell his father about everything that had happened when he got home.

Dex was shocked when Diene's parents arrived and pulled Diene out in a hurry. He also couldn't understand his father's odd behavior after hearing the news. His father's eyes widened, but then he looked very stern.

"And the girl could walk?" he asked.

Dex was almost afraid to answer. "Yes, Father." He hoped that Diene wasn't a dreamer. His father spoke such terrible things about them, and he wanted to see Diene alive and well again. "What does that mean?"

But Dex wouldn't be able to see her again, not if his father were able to get his way. "It means we have to stop her before her poison spreads."

Chapter Thirteen

Tice woke up with a shiver. She opened her eyes and questioned if she were still dreaming or if it was still dark. She wasn't used to not being able to see yet, but she remembered that she was bundled in many layers of blankets covering her entire body. She wouldn't have slept with so many if Riss didn't tuck her in that way. But still, it felt dark, and it was still too cold.

Something was wrong.

"Riss?" She called out to her brother, but he didn't answer. "Riss?" She pushed through all of the heavy blankets and climbed out of a cave of fabric. Being free from all of the covers didn't make her any colder. It was strange. It was like it wasn't really cold at all, and the chill was just on her skin.

"Evva?" She had never been far from her. Evva took care of Tice in ways she imagined a real mother would. There had been hot meals supplied, a warm bath, and clean clothes. The clothes were too big, but Evva would sew things up or give Tice belts to make everything fit more comfortably. There was never a time that Tice called, and she wasn't there to answer.

Something was definitely wrong.

Tice couldn't shake the chill on her skin or the sinking feeling in her stomach. She had to find her brother. She began to climb on all fours out of the bed as fast as she could. The bed was big, but she overestimated how much space she had and fell off fast and hit the floor hard.

As she laid there on the ground, she swore she heard something strange. It was very faint at first, and then began to grow and surround her. It was a hissing sound of a slithering, terrible snake.

Tice jumped back on her feet and grabbed a hold of the covers on the bed. The covers began to fall off, and she slipped as she struggled to get her legs up. She whimpered as it began to get louder, and the chilling feeling began to choke her lungs. She fell back on the floor and felt something scaly slither against her foot and screamed. She managed to climb on the bed with a second try and pulled the mammoth of blankets so she could hide under its protection.

Instead, she was taken by her shoulder and shoved down on her back.

Tice began to scream and pushed against the hand. It felt cold, and the fingers were long and too thin to belong to a man. She also knew that Evva would never do something like that to her. Tice closed her eyes and pushed her head away as he felt the woman getting closer.

She heard a final hiss loudly in her ear, and it rung throughout Tice's ears and made her insides vibrate until it dimmed into nothing but silence. Then the voice spoke. "Tice."

Tice opened her eyes and lay frozen in the truest terror that she had ever felt and whispered her attacker's name. "Sakai?"

Sakai let go of Tice and placed a long, thin smile on her face. "My dear, Girl! I have a task for you."

Tice was afraid, but she was angry enough to sit up and scold her. "Like the one you had for Mal?"

She chuckled. "Believe me, Girl. You'll want to do this."

"I doubt that."

Sakai reached out and snatched Tice's hand. Tice screamed and struggled to push her away, but she couldn't stop Sakai's great strength. Tice landed on the floor and tried to stop herself by digging her heels, but Sakai continued to drag her through the door, down the hall, and up the stairs to the deck of the ship.

Very soon, Tice began to notice that there wasn't another sound besides her own struggles. She didn't hear the burly crew laughing or yelling. She didn't hear Captain Mayes barking orders. She didn't hear Riss joking around or boasting about how he was doing fine in his chores. When she ceased struggling, there was nothing but the wind blowing through her hair and scraping against her skin.

"Where's my brother?" she asked Sakai demandingly.

"He's right on deck." Tice followed as Sakai led her to Riss's body lying still as the dead on the deck. "Your brother is right here."

Tice wished she could see him to make sure Sakai wasn't lying. Sakai finally let her hand go so she could get on her knees and reach out to touch a small chest. It couldn't have been any of the crewmen. She slid her hand up and felt his neck and then his face. There was no one else who could have been that size, but it didn't feel like Riss. He had an unusual warmth to him, and she couldn't feel that anymore. She could barely tell he was breathing. "Riss?"

Before she began to cry, she stood back up and yelled, "What did you do to him?"

"The same thing that I did to every single other passenger on this ship."

Tice couldn't see, but the deck and the halls had people laid out everywhere. Evva had been lying on Tice's floor the entire time. "I have poisoned everyone on this ship, and if you want to save them, you have to find the antidote."

172

"I have to *find* the antidote?" she asked almost hysterically. "I can't find anything!"

"Oh, but you'll have to. If you want to save everyone, you have to find the antidote on land." Sakai began to laugh. The sound echoed throughout Tice's entire body and chilled her like how it felt when the wind changed when a storm comes from beyond the horizon. And in all of her cruelty, she offered her hand for Tice to take—as if she could ever trust her terrible comfort. "I'll help you off the ship."

Tice looked up sternly and held onto her brother tightly. Sakai was amused that Tice could not see her and snatched the girl's hand. Tice tried to pull away, but Sakai was much stronger than her. Tice's feet recognized the deck. She had walked upon every inch of it in the last few weeks, but she wasn't familiar with the edge or the ramp.

She stopped struggling and began to walk carefully so she wouldn't fall off. It wasn't that many steps after until her feet felt warm gravel. "Where is it?"

"It's hiding in plain sight, my dear girl."

Tice pouted and pulled her hand away. She wasn't going to let someone as vile as Sakai hold her hand and mock her. "There is no such thing as plain sight!"

"Calm down!" Sakai found Tice's struggle so amusing! "This is a test."

"A test?" she asked. "What kind of test?"

"A test to see if you deserve to live or if you need to die," Sakai said very happily.

It extremely unnerved Tice how happy Sakai was. She took a few steps back in case she needed to run. "But I'm not sick. How would I die?"

Sakai chuckled, enjoying Tice's fear. Surely she must have been no threat, but she needed to make sure. "If you find the antidote to save your brother and everyone on that ship, you'll have your answer."

"But how...?" Tice felt the overwhelming chill suddenly dissipate, and she knew that Sakai was gone. Of course she wasn't sad to be liberated from her presence, but Tice didn't know what to do next. She didn't even have on a pair of shoes or anything to guide her way. However, she couldn't let any of that stop her. There was no time for tears or creeping doubts that would nest inside her mind until it grew into a creature of self-pity. If she didn't put her first foot forward, her brother was going to die.

With outstretched arms, she began to walk. She breathed heavily and terribly afraid of her unknown surroundings. There was something incredibly eerie about being at that port. It wasn't until her shaking legs had walked for a few minutes that she realized that there was no sound except for her deep, fearful breaths.

"Hello?" She called out as loud as she could with her tiny, shaky voice. She had never really been alone before. And though her brother had made some mistakes, she knew in her heart that she could always depend on him. She had never been a heroine before.

It wasn't long before she tripped over something and fell flat on her stomach. All of the wind was knocked out of her, and she began to lightly cry. Her hands were burning from being scraped on the way down. She could feel that her palms were bloody. She wanted to curl into a ball and sleep, but what she tripped over felt heavy and wrapped in fabric. When she reached out to touch what she had fallen on, she felt the hairy and burly arms of a plump man. She felt his arms and followed them up to his shoulders, neck, and then his pudgy face. The man was just like her brother and so was probably everyone in that town.

Tice had no choice but to stand up and continue walking. She sped up her pace and was a little less cautious. She fell more often and ran into things more than she wanted to, but those were things that couldn't be helped. If the people needed a hero, it didn't matter if she were small, weak, or even blind. As long as she had the will, somehow—no matter how long it took—she would find a way.

She walked until her feet felt broken and her arms were sore from reaching. She must have searched for hours without any luck of finding the antidote, if there were even one to be found.

Tice collapsed on the ground with her body feeling three times its normal weight. She was sweaty and smelly, and she knew that time was running out. As she closed her eyes to think, it dawned on her the power of her dreams. Her intuition was abnormal when she slept. Perhaps she could somehow find the antidote if she drifted off to sleep.

"That won't work," Sakai's slithering voice said.

Tice opened her eyes and glared. "What are you doing here?" Tice felt Sakai's words fall on her like steaming water to her tender skin.

"You cannot dream. It's against the rules." Sakai was lying next to Tice; their faces were inches apart. She began to stroke Tice's hair with her long, green finger nails while she chuckled to herself.

"I don't believe you." Tice closed her eyes and did her best to ignore Sakai.

Sakai chuckled again, but she was a tad bit irritated. "You cannot fall asleep."

"I don't trust you, so I'll do what I want. Besides, I didn't agree to your rules from the beginning, so I'll make my own." Tice ended her brave speech by sticking out her tongue before closing her eyes and lying limply.

Sakai sneered and slowly stood up on her feet with her mind in a boil. She never expected to be disrespected by such a young, foolish, little girl, and she certainly wasn't about to let Tice get away with it. "I warned you." She raised her hand up in the air and tensed her fingers in preparation to maul Tice's face.

As she stretched out her hand, her arm came to a sudden stop as a burn mark began to appear on her forearm in the shape of a human hand. The pain for Sakai was excruciating, but she could not force her arm away. She looked up and hissed as a man began to appear in front of her. "This isn't any of your business!" she yelled.

Tice lifted up her head on instinct toward the voice of the man who suddenly appeared. She blinked once, and then again, and then she squint her eyes. There was something far away, but she was sure she could see it. It was just like the snake in the water. It was coming into vision, except it wasn't terrible. The man she could see was gorgeous, and he glowed with a light as beautiful as the sunshine.

"You are not allowed to touch this girl." He threw Sakai's hand back and forced her to step away from Tice.

It had been too long since Tice had seen anything. There was nothing but darkness around her, but she trusted the man and stood behind him as he talked to the dark emptiness that must have been Sakai.

Sakai glared at the man once more before she disappeared. Tice could feel everything change once Sakai had gone. The chill that had been on her skin was replaced by the man's warmth. When she tugged on his pants leg, she knew that she was going to be alright. "Who are you?"

He bent down and looked at Tice amazed. She reached out to touch his face and looked into his eyes. "What do you see?" he asked.

"I see you." He was the most beautiful man that she had ever seen. He reminded her of the boy in her dream who rescued her, except she knew they weren't the same. The man before her had such intriguing eyes. It was like the sun was trapped inside them.

"And how do I look to you?"

176

There was something about him that was powerful, yet very gentle. If she could keep him by her side forever, she would. But it was strange to say all those things to a man who appeared out of darkness, but apparently, he was looking for something strange. "You're glowing."

"Glowing?" he asked intrigued.

"Are you..." She frowned nervously. "...Not really glowing?"

"Not to normal eyes. No." But he knew staring into Tice's eyes that they were not normal. She was evolving without even realizing it.

"Who are you?" she asked.

"I cannot say, Little One. The time is not yet right for proper introductions." He smiled and tapped her nose playfully. "But know that I will always be here to protect you."

She knew that she could hold him true to that, but she wasn't concerned about her life. "Can you help me save my brother?"

He sighed and stood up straight up. "As cruel as Sakai may be, she was right about one thing. This is a test."

Tice knew that she had been going through many changes, and a test would have been fine, but not at the risk of losing her brother. "But what if I can't save them?"

"You fail as soon as you begin doubting yourself." There was a load too big to fit upon Tice's tiny shoulders, but she would have to somehow manage the weight without it pulling her down. He had no way to help her until she had proven herself except for a kind, confident smile. "Listen within yourself, Tice. It's simpler than what you think."

And then with a blink of her eye, he was gone. She couldn't see him, but she knew he was still watching her from afar. She wasn't even afraid. "It's simpler than what I think," she said to herself.

Tice closed her eyes and remained quiet and still. If she could find it, then she didn't need to see with her eyes. Somehow, she knew things, and she didn't question them. It was probably no different. It was as easy as taking a first step.

She began to walk with her hands at her side. She was sure that she would find it, but her hands were shaking from the fear of running into something that could hurt her. She was still afraid of the dark and terrified of the unknown, but she was fine as long as she knew that she could save her brother. She pushed through it all and continued to step out.

She stepped to the side when she felt she needed to, though she had no real reason for it. She turned and lifted her foot a little higher or ducked her head without thought. There was something compelling her to move in what she believed was the correct direction, and then she finally stopped.

She opened her eyes, and there was still nothing but darkness. The glowing man was not near, and she didn't feel Sakai's terrible presence either. She just knew she was where she needed to be. She got on her hands and knees and began to pat the dirt for what she came for. Within a few seconds, her hands touched a small glass vial with a tiny cork.

She could barely believe it, but she had found it. She laughed and shook it to hear the liquid tossing around. Her brother would be safe!

But there was only enough for her brother.

Tice stared at the bottle in her hand and thought about her brother lying on the deck. The entire crew was sick and probably that entire town as well. She didn't know how she would go on without her brother, but how was she to choose his life over so many others?

What sort of test was she involved in? There was no way to pass it. There was no way to justify so many lives lost. Sakai was truly evil.

Tice began to cry lightly until all of those lives that were depending on her became burdensome stones against her shoulders. She fell forward to the ground and sobbed until a sudden breeze fell upon her and made her drift off to sleep.

178

Tice opened her eyes and stared upward. She still wasn't used to being blind, and she felt broken. "Riss..." she spoke quietly with a tear coming out of her eye. She whimpered and cursed herself for failing.

"I'm right here."

She opened her eyes as she felt his warm hand touch her. It was as she remembered. "Riss!" She sat up and followed his hand to his chest to hug him tightly. "I was so worried about you!"

"It was the weirdest thing," he said. "Everyone just began falling and couldn't move. I was ill—barely able to breathe—and I thought I was going to die. I was stuck for hours wondering if this was the end and then suddenly," he snapped his fingers, "we were all fine."

"Everyone?" she yelled surprised.

"Everyone who was sick." He kissed Tice's forehead happy to see that she was alright. "When I woke up, I couldn't find you on the ship. How did you even get off of it?"

"It's a long story." It must have been the stranger who helped her. She knew that his eyes were never off of her while she searched for the antidote. He also said that he would protect her. Whatever the test was, it was very important to her and her brother. "But I should explain everything to you."

"Before you do that, I need to know something." Riss became very serious and even worried. It was difficult for him to even bring up what he wanted to. "When we found you, you were asleep on a picture that the town residents didn't know about."

She thought about where she had fallen asleep. It was dry and dusty. "Painted on the dirt?" she asked confused.

He shook his head, even more puzzled than before. "No. It was on a slab of stone, like marble, but there was something painted on it. There was a picture of the orbs—seven of them—all a different color."

179

Tice was sure that there was no such thing! "It wasn't there before I feel asleep." The stranger must have moved her. It was the only explanation. "There was a man who saved me from Sakai. Maybe he made it. Maybe he's trying to tell us something."

He shook his head again, reaching the height of his perplexity. "I think you were right, Tice."

Riss didn't know what man Tice was speaking of, but he remembered clearly what it was like finding her. The slab of stone was in a perfect circle. It was a very beautiful painting with the seven orbs circling Tice's body, with their colors swirling around the orbs themselves. But when he lifted her up and carried her in his arms, he saw her image drawn in the center, completely identical. She was in the center of it all, but on the edge of the slab was black encircling everything. Riss of course thought that Tice couldn't have made such a detailed drawing, even if she had her sight. But then he saw that where her finger's once laid were indentations in the marble that she must have left behind. "You have an ability."

Tice thought about the picture carefully. "Seven of them…" She had been dreaming of other people she had never seen before. Thinking about the picture and the orbs, it was all beginning to make sense. There was herself, her brother, the boy she knew she should find, the girl that was now able to walk, and the brother and sister who were in danger. "I think there's one more."

"One more what?" he asked.

"One of us."

Chapter Fourteen

The sun is such a cruel and beautiful thing. There is nothing more powerful on land or in sea to equate to its beauty. A flame can bring warmth, but does not breed such life in the way the sun does. The day rises and falls when the sun decides.

The only contender for the sun's vast greatness is water. Every creature needs it to survive. Without it, plants would shrivel up and die. The ground would crack and split and would never produce food to eat. And people would thirst until they grew weak and died.

But as long as the sun stayed so steady and stubborn in the sky, there would not be a drop of water that would fall to replenish the land and the people who lived there.

Yes, the sun was certainly a cruel thing to let its people sweat through their skin and leave their mouths thirsty for just a drop of water.

"What are we going to do?"

Nilliana was only thirteen, but she had to watch many terrible things, such as her parents discuss what they were going to do for food and water for not only their family, but for a village full of orphans.

There was a time when Nilliana and her family never worried about anything. They used to live far away in a big home where there was always a hot meal and a cold drink of water. Nilliana never had to worry about dust in her shoes or smelling nice or feeling clean. She took her perfect life for granted, and her parents did as well. They were giving people and left everything they had behind to help those who were not as fortunate. Now they were not so fortunate as well.

"There's nothing we can do," her father said.

Her mother sighed and began to look desperate. "Maybe we should go ask Dib'lo and his men to—"

"No!" he spoke firmly. "Their help never comes free."

Nilliana sighed and left her family's tent. She couldn't stand to listen to another conversation about desperate times. She wasn't naive, and that was the problem. So many children were sick and weak in that village. She hated being there because she hated seeing everyone—including herself—suffer.

It was an unusually hot day, and it was best to stay inside, but Nilliana needed to get away. She did her best to ignore the sun's constant pressing on her skin and walked throughout the village. Some of the girls were fanning themselves with leaves or fans made from cloth and sticks. Some of the younger boys managed to run around and play while others sat on the ground and conserved their energy. Some of the smallest girls were playing with dolls that Nilliana gave away. They were tattered and dirty now, just like she was.

Nilliana bent down to a girl named Maala, who was combing Nilliana's old favorite doll with her fingers. Even though Nilliana had grown out of the age to love dolls, she hated seeing it in such poor condition. Still, she knew that Maala loved that doll. "Are you doing alright today?"

Maala nodded her head, but her lips were pouted and her eyes hung heavy.

"You're hungry?" Nilliana asked.

"And thirsty," she replied sadly.

Nilliana sighed and sat on the hot dirt next to Maala. Nilliana remembered eating sweets and being chubby when she was Maala's age. She wished Maala could know what it felt like to have more than enough. Nilliana's parents still had some food for the orphans until their next shipment came. They would all be fed their rations in a half hour or so. Until then, Nilliana wanted to do something for Maala. "Do you want me to cheer you up? How about a story?"

She shrugged her shoulders and replied lazily. "Sure."

Nilliana smiled, flung her long hair back behind her, and hugged her knees to her chest. She loved telling stories—mostly daring ones. But every so often, she would think of a good romance or two. "There once was a man of a royal bloodline who left his cousin's kingdom to travel the world. In his travels, he met a woman unlike any other woman he had known. You see, he was very fair skinned. His skin was the color of clouds; his eyes were the color of the sky, and his hair the color of the sun. She had very dark colored skin as if she were birthed from ground; her hair was the color of bark, and her eyes were the color of ash. He was the sky, and she was the earth, and the two of them fell in love."

Maala had become entranced with the story as soon as she heard the word "love". It wasn't something they heard too often in that village, but it was precious when it came genuinely. "What happened next?"

Nilliana thought carefully about how she should word her story to Maala. Children may understand what it's like to be different, but they seldom understand why. "It was very strange for other people to see them together, and they were very strange for each other. It was as if they were from two different worlds. She couldn't live in the sky with him, and he couldn't live on the earth with her."

"That's very sad!"

"But it gets better," Nilliana promised quickly. "The two of them decided that it didn't matter what the world was like. They decided to make their own. He built her a kingdom just for the two of them, and they had a beautiful baby boy." Nilliana smiled from ear to ear, ending her happy story on a high.

Maala was still intrigued and barely waited for Nilliana to catch a breath before spouting out questions. "And what was he? Was he the sky or the earth?" she asked curiously.

Nilliana rested her chin on her knee as she thought about it. "He was better. He was both. He was love—their love."

"And where does he live now?"

Nilliana laughed at Maala's anxiousness. She didn't know that her story was quite so interesting. "He returned to his mother's roots and found a woman of the earth. She was kind and beautiful and loved him for everything that he was. They were happy in their kingdom, but he was a hero. He gave up everything he had to help the people of the earth."

Maala's eyes were big and bright from hearing the romances and heroics. It was everything she wanted to hear in a story, but then she began to slump her shoulders sadly as she thought about it. "But he abandoned the sky?"

"No." Nilliana stuck her neck out proudly toward Maala and pointed to her eyes. "I'll always have these blue eye—a gift from the sky." She smiled and hugged herself tightly.

Maala gasped and began to widen her eyes very slowly. She thought she understood Nilliana's connection to the story, but then she wasn't sure herself. "So you're a princess and a hero?"

"I'm not sure if I'm either, but I'll save whoever I can."

Nilliana heard the sound of footsteps behind, so she quickly rose to her feet and turned around. There were three boys behind her; one of them was a year older than her. His name was Ky, and he was known for being an ungrateful brat in Nilliana's home. "Which is better?" he asked. "Is it the earth or the sky?"

Nilliana crossed her arms, recognizing Ky's rude posture and tone and mimicked it herself. "I don't think either is better. I think they are what they are."

"But you think together they're better?" Perhaps a young child like Maala wasn't completely aware of what Nilliana had just explained, but Ky was old enough to understand, and he remembered and resented the day Nilliana and her parents arrived to the village. Nilliana's parents gave so much to the village, but her father was not easily accepted by her people, and neither was she.

Nilliana understood the mistrust, but her father and mother had been good to the people, just as she was sure her grandfather before her would have been. "Tolerance is beautiful, and I think it's the only way we'll learn how to grow."

Maala stood to her feet and took Nilliana's hand. She didn't know why some of the older children treated Nilliana nastily. When Nilliana looked down into Maala's brown eyes, she was grateful for her innocence. "Think about water. All life needs it. It lives on the earth and in the sky. Whether we realize it or not, we're all connected."

"I think it's a cute story, but it's all wrong." Ky lowered his hands to his side and clenched his fists angrily. "The sky people—or rather the pale skins—came and destroyed our village." He glared at Nilliana with a hatred too true to belong to such young eyes, yet it was powerful and without compromise. "We can't trust them, and we can't trust your mud father or you!"

Many years before Nilliana arrived, the village was attacked by an army of men from across the waters. They were from somewhere not too far from where Nilliana's grandfather lived, but the village was a land not ignorant of the ways of fear and death before the pale skinned visitors. There were many gangs not far from the village who had taken much from its neighbors, despite being children born from the same land.

185

Nilliana refused to let someone as despicable as Ky make her cry. He was ignorant, terribly ignorant. Too many people remembered the faces of evil, and too many failed to realize that the same evil is a mask that any man can wear, despite the color of their skin. "Well, our people haven't done anything but hurt each other since then."

He laughed at her with a burst of disbelief. "Our people?" But then there was no laughter and no smiles—not even to mock her. He stepped closer to her to stand above her and make her feel less than what she was. "You're not one of us. You're not one of anybody."

Nilliana could feel tears welling up in the back of her eyes, but she refused to cry! He was scum, and she might not have been like her mother or like her father, but she was their child all the same.

She knew Ky wouldn't listen our understand, so she addressed the two boys behind him, Maala, and the other children who were pretending not to watch. "We're here now. Why can't we help each other? What does it matter whose hand is reaching?" Then she directed her question right back to Ky. "You take my father's food. Why is he good enough to take from but not to accept?"

He glared at her harder and stepped just an inch closer. Any closer than that and he would have had to touch her, and he found that to be revolting. "You don't belong here," he seethed.

Nilliana stood steady. She didn't have anything else intelligent to say. There were no witty remarks or proud and brave justifications. There was just a tiny wound on the inside of her that would eventually turn into a scar.

As Ky walked away with his friends following behind, Maala took Nilliana's hand and shook it until she would look at her. "He didn't mean that, Nilliana."

"It doesn't matter." She smiled small and spoke weakly. "I like who I am."

Maala smiled happily. "I do too."

Nilliana's mother came out of her tent and saw Nilliana playing with Maala. The little children were the only ones who made Nilliana feel welcome. She was always so grateful to see her interact with them. "Nilliana," she yelled to her daughter, "can you please round up the rest of the children? It's time to eat."

"Yes, Mother."

But that didn't take much effort on Nilliana's part. Every child was waiting for those words and found strength where they thought they had none to run toward the hut they used for food storage. Nilliana walked around the tents to make sure no one was lagging behind. She took special notice of Ky walking by. They both had glares reserved for each other.

The hut served as their kitchen. Nilliana's mother prepared all of the food for the children. Nilliana would help prepare the food sometimes, but she would always help serve it. She grabbed an apron and wiped her dirty hands on it. She couldn't spare a drop of water, and she promised to be careful with the ladle as she gathered up the children's stew. Nilliana's parents had outdone themselves to make up for the lack of water with a hardy stew. There was even meat in it, but Nilliana wasn't sure what it was, nor did she care to ask. It did smell delicious.

Everyone had smiles toward Nilliana when they came by with their wooden bowl. There was no point in pretending that they liked her then. She wasn't spiteful. Even when Ky came by with his readable frown, she still served him the same as everyone else.

He was the last child served, so Nilliana began getting bowls for herself, her mother, and father. "He hates us," she told her mother. "You know that, right? He thinks you're a traitor, and I and father are abominations."

Her mother didn't even have to ask to know that Nilliana was speaking about Ky. "I know that."

187

"Then why take care of him so much?" she asked quietly. "He'd probably join Dib'lo and take from us if he got the chance."

Her mother sighed and stroked her daughter's cheek. "Sometimes doing the right thing is hard."

She moved her head away from her mother frustrated. "Giving someone something that they don't deserve is not right, and it's certainly not fair."

"Life seldom is, Nilly. That's why we're here. We're here because it's not fair. We're here because these kids had people that they loved taken away from them. That's not fair."

Nilliana frowned guiltily. She knew well what some of the children had been through. Even with all she had lost, at least she still had her parents.

Her mother lifted her daughter's chin up. "You're here because your father and I wanted to play hero without your consult. That wasn't very fair either. But one day, these kids are going to have to stand on their own two feet. They're going to have to make their own choices, but they can never say that they weren't given an opportunity. They can never say that they didn't know any better. They'll have to live with the consequences of their actions, whether they are good or bad. But for right now, they're just children."

Nilliana knew that was true, but Ky was already much too cruel. "He's a little tyrant. The things he says and does now hurts people. It doesn't matter how old someone is. Everyone makes an impact."

Her mother looked up and pointed behind Nilliana. "The same goes for you, Nilly."

Nilliana turned around to see that Ky was standing right behind her. She wasn't sure how much he had heard, but he must have definitely caught onto "little tyrant". He didn't say anything. He just grabbed a spoon from the serving table and walked away.

Nilliana's mother looked at her with disapproving eyes, and then left out of the hut with her husband's bowl. Nilliana didn't want to follow after her mother, because she thought she was justified in what she said. Nilliana walked to a canopy to sit at the wooden table they had for the children to eat off of while they could be protected in the shade. Ky seemed to be upset and refused to sit down. He ate quickly and rushed off. There was a space reserved for Nilliana next to Maala on the bench, but no one spoke to her. Nilliana didn't usually eat with the kids. They didn't stare at her, but it was more unnerving how they all refused to look at her. She wondered if it were because what she had said to Ky. She didn't want things to be even worse, so she finished her meal and followed after him.

But she was not going to apologize!

Ky had returned to the tents and was looking through one after the other frantically. Nilliana was angry to see him violating everyone's privacy, but she bit her tongue and approached him calmly. Once she saw his face, she realized that he was afraid. "What's the matter?" she asked him.

He stopped and looked at her frustrated, but his disgust for her broke for something more important. "I'm looking for my brother, Pabou. He was with his friends earlier. I haven't really seen him since this morning." Ky was different from what she thought. Of course nothing could take away from how he always treated her, but Nilliana realized that he could at least love something.

"Follow me." She ran to her own tent where her parents were eating together. They didn't get much time to themselves, so Nilliana was sad to interrupt them. "We can't find Ky's brother."

Nilliana's parents got up quickly and ran out. Ky was waiting outside looking more vulnerable than he ever had before. Nilliana's father walked over to him and placed his hand on his shoulder—like he would often do to his daughter—and spoke familiar words to Nilliana's ears. "Don't worry," he told Ky. "We'll make this right."

Together, they all ran to the canopy where all the other children were still eating. They had become rowdy without any real supervision, but they all quieted down to a silence when Nilliana's father began to speak. "Does anyone know where Pabou is?"

They all looked at each other worriedly without any knowledge in their eyes.

Nilliana's father sighed heavily. "I'll start searching for him," he said to his wife.

"I'm coming too!" Ky announced desperately.

Nilliana's father nodded to Ky, then kissed his wife affectionately on the forehead. "Navia, I'll be back soon. Take care of the kids while I'm gone."

She held his hand tight and kissed it. "Be careful, Nulin."

As Nilliana watched her father and Ky run off, she felt helpless. Pabou could have been anywhere, and if he had stumbled into hostile territory, such as where Dib'lo and his men lived, there was a good chance that Ky might not have ever seen his little brother again.

Her mother stayed calm though. She gathered the children and sent them off into their tents. She counted them all and everyone was accounted for except for Pabou and Ky. Thinking about how Pabou was alone in such a dangerous place made Nilliana feel lonelier than ever. She wanted to stay in her mother's arms until her father returned, but Maala begged for Nilliana to stay in her tent. Knowing what it was like to be afraid, she agreed.

The tents were small, but there were about five girls sleeping in one. All of the girls in Maala's tent were tiny, so they made room for Nilliana on their mats and thin blankets. The temperature dropped tremendously when the sun went down, so they huddled together restlessly as they waited for word on Pabou.

After waiting a long time in silence, Maala rolled over to face Nilliana. "Do you think Pabou is alright?"

"I'm sure my father will find him." She smiled confidently, remembering all of the terrific adventures they used to go on together. "He can do anything."

Maala rolled away, but her worries began to overcome her until she rolled back over to face Nilliana again. "What about the light that fell from the sky?"

Nilliana cocked her eyebrow confused. "What about it?"

"Do you think it was a gift from the sky?"

Nilliana chuckled. "It's not from the people in the story, Maala." She wasn't surprised that Maala took the story so literal. She was only a child.

Still, it was something to wonder about. She remembered the day the light fell. There were so many beautiful colors streaming across the sky, and she had never seen anything like that, despite having so many travels with her parents. The light seemed to reach on forever, but some of it must have landed somewhere close. She remembered feeling the ground shake and seeing a dust cloud in the distance. "I don't know if it came from the sky. It wasn't like anything I had ever seen before. I think it might have come from somewhere else."

"Past the sky?" Maala asked amazed.

"I'm not sure. I've never touched the sky or anything like that. I just think there might be something else beyond. It's kind of lonely looking up at the sky and thinking that all we have is what's before us. Do you understand?"

She shrugged. "I'm not sure."

"Neither am I, Maala." Nilliana sighed and turned to the side so she could see Maala's face. It was dark, but she could tell that Maala was distressed. Everyone was worried, but she was worse. "Maala, do you know where Pabou is?"

She sunk into her mat and covered half her face with her blanket. "Am I in trouble?"

Nilliana took the blanket and pulled it down so she could see her face. "Only if you don't tell."

She sat up and sighed. Maala didn't believe that she wouldn't get in trouble, but it was too late to hide the truth. "He said he found where the light had fallen, and he went to bring it back to us."

"Why?" Nilliana asked confused.

"He thought it might bring rain, or more food, or stop Dib'lo and his men from stealing from us."

It was not only foolish but dangerous! Nilliana was upset, but she couldn't wait for her father to get home. Pabou might have been hurt, and though she wasn't fond of Ky, she didn't want to see him lose someone important to him. "You have to show me where he is."

Nilliana decided not to tell her mother what Maala had told her. Her mother would have them wait for her father to return, and Nilliana didn't want to leave any more time for Pabou to be out alone.

She grabbed a lantern and snuck out with Maala. All of the other girls in the tent were sworn to secrecy until a half hour had passed. Nilliana really shouldn't have taken Maala with her, but Nilliana would do her best to protect her. Maala squeezed Nilliana's hand the entire time. There barely seemed to be anything but barren land during the day, but the night had a way of making things come alive. Even the poor vegetable garden seemed like a monster out to get Maala. Nilliana remained brave for Maala, but she was beginning to get nervous from the sound of the howling wind and its force blowing through her clothes. The only thought that kept her from running back to camp was the haunting feeling that Pabou was alone somewhere wishing that he wasn't.

Nilliana didn't completely trust Maala's sense of direction, especially in the dark, but she didn't have anything else to go on. When they were walking for about an hour, they came to a ravine. Nilliana was familiar with it, but her parents often warned her not to explore around in that area. The rocks were very unstable, and Nilliana had a bad habit of climbing trees and whatever else she saw as a challenge.

Nilliana stretched out the lantern. "Pabou?"

"Nilliana?" he yelled.

Nilliana moved the lantern upward and saw Pabou on a small, rocky balcony hanging out of the stone wall. "Help me!" he shrieked in fear.

A purple light began to glow from something Pabou was holding in his hands. A crack of thunder roared across the sky, and rain began to pour down across the land and hard on their heads. Nilliana and Maala looked at each other astounded. Surely it had to be a coincidence that Pabou found the light and shortly after it began to rain. Surely!

"Hold on!" Nilliana could see much clearer with the light beginning to glow brighter. The ravine was very narrow. If she climbed down a little bit, she was sure she could reach over to the opposite side where Pabou was and scale the wall until she could get to him. But though there was light, it certainly wasn't enough. And though she was also glad that the drought was over, she also had to take into consideration that pouring rain would make the rocks slippery. "I'm coming for you. Just stay put."

Nilliana gulped and let go of Maala's hand. She handed the lantern off to Maala, and then proceeded to climb down her side of the mountain. It wasn't a terribly long way down, but it was certainly long enough of a fall for Nilliana to severely injure herself. It also would have been very unpleasant if she knocked out some loose rocks as she went down.

"I'm scared!" Pabou said.

Nilliana was afraid as well, but she had to get to Pabou somehow and help him. If she couldn't help him down safely, she could at least be with him until morning. Anything was better than letting him stay there alone. "Don't be. I'll be right there."

Nilliana was afraid herself, but she pretended that she was on an adventure with her father. She had rock climbed before. It was simple. He would be there to catch her if she would fall, and her mother would clean and bandage her cuts if she hurt herself. She was just a girl exploring and being a hero, as always.

When she got to the closest spot to the opposite wall, she reached out to touch it. It was a lot further than what she thought. When she first reached out, she missed and was overcome with anxiety. She drew back onto her wall tightly and thought about waiting for her parents.

"This is too dangerous!" Maala yelled.

"Please don't leave me!" Pabou said with tears welling in his eyes and his voice beginning to break up. "I want to go home!"

Nilliana closed her eyes. "You can do this. You can do this!" she thought. Somehow, she reached out with her hand and touched his wall with her fingertips. That wasn't enough. She had to do something quickly, or she was going to lose her grip and fall. She took a deep breath, and then stretched out her legs to move until her hands and feet were on both walls. With a final breath of courage, she let go of her side and joined the boy's.

That was the simplest part in getting to him, but there were obstacles to watch for as she slowly moved her fingers against the wall. One of her first few steps, she stepped on a loose rock and began to slip. She thought she was going to fall and hurt herself, but she gripped onto the wall as tight as she could. It was frightening watching a few loose rocks fall into the bottom of the ravine. That very well could have been her.

She still pulled it together and continued moving. It was more dangerous than anything she had ever done before. She thought she was stronger, but her arms were sore, and her fingers ached. If there weren't some foolishness mixed in with her bravery, she probably would have started climbing down and away from Pabou.

"Hold on," she told him. "I'm almost there." She was right under Pabou, so she began to climb upward. But when she touched the platform that he was sitting on, the rock underneath her feet began to crumble and slid away from her in a thunderous escape.

She screamed and held on as tight as she could. Pabou reached out to grab her with his free hand, but he wouldn't let go of the orb. Nilliana looked below her, and the ground seemed to stretch away from her. Her eyes widened as she realized how dangerous her task was. She turned her head and closed her eyes and screamed to herself. She was going to die, and she wasn't going to be calm about it!

"Maala," Pabou yelled, "go get help!"

Maala didn't think twice about running back toward camp to go fetch Nilliana's parents. She ran as fast as her little legs would carry her.

Nilliana knew that she had enough strength in her to get up, but she didn't think she could do it at that moment. Pabou watched Nilliana's struggle and her fearful expression. His brother told him some very treacherous things about her, yet she came to rescue him. He dropped the orb, and it bounced on the rock and fell down into the ravine. Pabou used his other hand to try and pull up Nilliana, but he was too small. Nilliana knew with her footing gone and her arms about to completely give out, she didn't have much time.

She closed her eyes tight and imagined she was home. She pictured being with her parents in the comfort of their simplicities and their over prioritized belongings. She left a lot behind, and she feared leaving life unfulfilled. But the greatest tragedy was going to be separation from her mother and father.

Her hands slipped right through Pabou's, and she fell. She remembered screaming and a bright light before everything went black.

"Nilliana!"

Nilliana opened her eyes slowly. She couldn't move, and she could barely breathe. She didn't hear a voice too well, but she knew someone was calling. It was dark all around her, except for a light that shone through a crack of blackness. She leaned her head back to see what was out there. What she saw was a little girl whiter than any pale skinned she had ever met. She was so entranced that she was no longer afraid or questioned what had happened. She couldn't do anything but stare at the little girl.

"Nilliana!" The voice grew louder, and she realized that the voice belonged to her mother.

"Mom?" She tried to move again. Something was on top of her body. She could only move her head, but as time went by, she could move with more ease. "Mom! I'm right here!"

"Hold on!" She felt a tugging on her skin as the weight began to lighten. She heard other voices panicking. Nilliana did her best to move her shoulder and legs to press whatever was on top of her off. She gritted her teeth and pushed as hard as she could until she was finally free.

She became disorientated as the sun poured down on her face, and she was swept up into her father's arms. He was crying and shaking, and so was her mother. She no longer saw the mysterious pale skinned girl, but

Pabou, Ky, his friends, two older girls, Maala, and her parents were also there with stunned faces.

Nilliana looked at the rocks piled up, and she began to realize that she had fallen and was buried alive. But the boulder that had held her down was bigger than her father's entire body. The other children were amazed that Nilliana was alive.

"Father!"

Nilliana's father held her so he could look into his daughter's eyes, and then he shook her frightfully. "Don't ever do something so reckless like that again!"

Her mother hugged her crying hysterically, but then stepped back to look at her carefully while rubbing her arms. "Are you alright? Does anything hurt?"

Nilliana was so frightened; she didn't know what to think. She was sure she had seen a girl, but that was impossible. But what was even more impossible was her body. She didn't see any cuts or bruises. She wasn't even sore anymore. It was the oddest thing. "No," she said dumbfounded. "I'm fine."

Chapter Fifteen

Tice sat still on her cabin floor with her hands in her laps, concentrating on trying to see anything in front of her. She didn't feel the presence of the man that protected her, but she knew deep inside that something was there. She was trying to find whatever it was that pulled her to the antidote without fault. She wasn't sure exactly what the light had done to her, but she felt a power deep inside guiding her. If only she could concentrate...

"Tice!" Riss entered into the cabin and sat in front of her. He had finished his bit of chores and was waiting until they landed at their destination. Eastern Pearl was so close that he could barely stand waiting around!

Tice ignored her brother and tried to feel out whatever it was inside of her.

"Tice!" He waved his hand in front of her. It escaped his thoughts that she couldn't see it, but then he sat in front of her and leaned in closer to her face. "Do you hear me?"

"What do you want?" she snapped at him angrily.

He blinked wide and confused. "What's your problem?"

"I'm trying to figure out my ability from the light!" She sighed and calmed down. "It would do you some good to try working on your powers as well."

He leaned back coolly. "I've got my powers all figured out." He stretched out his fingers and created a small flame on his pinky finger. Then, he lowered his fingers one at a time, switching the flame from his pinky until the flame traveled to his thumb. Then he opened his hand back up and repeated the process in reverse. When the flame was once again on his pinky, he closed his hand up, and the flame disappeared. "I'm very good at this."

Tice could feel the heat from his fire, so she knew he was making it, but she glared at him for thinking that she should be impressed when she clearly couldn't see what he had done. "I don't find your tricks impressive."

"You don't find them impressive?" He laughed in disbelief and jumped onto his feet. "The crew loves this one." He created a fire ball in the palms of his hands and began to juggle them both in a circular motion.

Tice was beginning to become very frustrated. "I can't see any of these tricks that you're doing!"

"I know you can't, but..."

"But nothing!" she yelled. "You're such a showoff and you crave attention."

Riss was so surprised by Tice's outburst that he lost his concentration and dropped the fire on the floor. He yelled in horror and began patting down the fire with his foot until he put it out. It was a close call, and he burned the floor, but he smiled innocently anyway. Riss didn't really like that Tice was glaring at him, especially since she wasn't directly staring at him. "No harm done."

"Riss," she said seriously, "when we land on Eastern Pearl, you have to promise me that you're not going to be so reckless."

He sat down in front of her with a smile still on his face. "I promise."

She pointed her finger in his face. "I'm serious, Riss. It's really, really important."

He took her hand and placed it back in her lap. "I promise, Tice. I really do promise."

She didn't really believe him, but there was nothing more she could say.

"What's that smell?" Evva asked behind the cabin door. Riss sat still as a statue when she came in and gasped at the scorch marks on her floor. "Riss! What did we tell you about your fire?"

He looked up at her with a dashing smile, hoping that it would be enough to get out of a punishment. "Only when it's needed?"

She glared down at him. She really did love those two, but Riss was a young boy, and it could be difficult dealing with the immature behavior of a child. "Dishes. Now!" she yelled.

He sighed and stood to his feet lazily. "Fine. Fine. I'm going."

Tice shook her head knowing that her hotheaded brother was going to get her into a lot of trouble.

Kumiko sat by her father's side with her head held a little higher than usual. She loved being at his side, and she wasn't only sitting there because he loved his daughter. She was sitting there because she was worthy. She was above all of her father's generals, and if they ever crossed her the wrong way, she wouldn't need to take up her case with her father. She had the tools to teach respect herself.

Her father affectionately touched his daughter's shoulder and smiled with great pride. "The orb of power has given Kumiko a great ability," he said to his men. "Her skills only match my own greatness, but I am still ready to ascend."

"What can we do to make my father's wish come true?" Kumiko asked them.

"We have heard rumors of the whereabouts of more orbs, my lord," said one of his men.

"Rumors?" Jun asked. He was sitting on the other side of Kumiko. She secretly enjoyed the fact that he was next to her. He did miss his father, but he was no fool. Horisho was power, and Kumiko was beauty in its finest form. It would be insane for his allegiance to lie anywhere else. "Truly there should be some word from our spies by now."

One of the advisors spoke up meekly. "It would appear that the orbs of power are destined for certain people. Kumiko's found its way to her, my lord. I'm sure that if you have one, it will find its way here."

Horisho glared at him.

"Of course," he said quickly, "I am not implying that you are incapable of receiving the power. I am sure you will have it, my lord. You will have the greatest power of them all."

"Where was mine found?" Kumiko asked her father.

"My men took it from a merchant from across the sea."

"I saw the light fall with my own eyes, Father." Kumiko remembered watching the shower from under her father's tree, but as brilliant as it looked, she didn't think any landed within her father's lands. "I know there must be thousands of them spread across the world. You should control more than one. Hundreds!"

"If not them all," Jun said.

Horisho was pleased with the words from his future successors, but it was not enough to bring his spirits up. "But it would appear that finding them is proving more difficult than what I would have hoped for."

Kumiko looked ahead and saw the double doors at the back of the room. They were made out of solid gold, but they seemed to be melting before her very eyes. However, she didn't feel any heat. She saw no one in the room was sweating besides from sheer nervousness. "Something is wrong."

Everyone's eyes followed to the back of the room. There were men who walked closer to observe the door, but others wisely stepped away from it. There wasn't a fire, but there certainly was something making the doors melt.

When one man felt the urge to touch the door, he yelled, and the doors exploded into liquid gold and darkness began to spread inside. It was a fire, but Kumiko had never seen a black fire, nor had she ever experienced any fire that didn't have heat or give off light.

Some of Horisho's advisors and generals were yelling from their burn marks. Horisho smirked and welcomed whatever challenge was coming through the door, because it would take him one step closer to finding his own power.

The fire began to die down all on its own. It was clear that it was alive and acted according to a will of a master. And when the fire was gone, the master emerged into the room with a vile smirk on his face.

"What is the meaning of this?" Jun yelled.

The master of the flame was only a boy probably no older than Kumiko. He was dressed in black, his hair was also the same shade, and so were his eyes. He was like a creature in tales that old men would whisper about in the dark. He looked like a normal person, but there was something dark about him. His skin was tan, so he was a foreigner, but Kumiko recognized that cocky smirk on his face. He was someone treacherous indeed. "I have come here seeking Horisho, the great and powerful ruler. Instead, I find a man who controls nothing but weaklings."

"How dare you!" said Jun just before he lunged out to fight the boy.

The boy dodged the first few hits. He was fast and might have been strong for a young man, but he wasn't as skilled as Jun in fighting. Kumiko could tell simply by the way he moved.

He couldn't avoid Jun forever. Jun punched him in the chest and then kicked him in the face, but that was all he got in. The boy knocked Jun's hand away, and Jun felt it burn. He stepped back just in time to avoid a black flame extending from the boy's hand.

Kumiko looked toward her father who was carefully watching silently. "I wish to fight with him, Father."

Horisho smirked amused and spoke with his eyes still transfixed on the boy. "Do as you please."

Kumiko rose to her feet and drew her sword. There was a time that she would have been afraid to approach someone so formidable, but she was different now. She had tested herself many times and had proven to be unbeatable. No boy with a black flame was going to prove anything different.

"I still wish to fight him," Jun told her defensively.

"Don't be foolish, Jun." Kumiko continued to walk until she stood by his side. "This isn't about your pride." Then she smiled. "This is about my fun."

"Step aside," Horisho commanded.

Jun was defiant, but would not dare speak a word against Horisho's will. He bowed in respect and then stepped aside.

Kumiko made quick eye contact with the boy. She found something about him completely unnerving. She attacked him without much of a warning, but he moved out of the way quickly. Her second strike was a kick to his face, and then her third was a kick to his chest, and the next in his gut. He bent over to hold himself, but she jumped in the air, spun, and kicked him in the head. He lost his footing easily and fell to the ground.

Kumiko stood over him with a smirk. "Who's weak now?" She lifted up her sword with every intention of finishing him off, but before she could, he looked up at her with such a fury. The darkness in his eyes began to expand beyond the pupil and iris and extended until the entire eyeball was black.

Kumiko began to step back. She wasn't afraid. She was merely bracing herself. He looked like a rabid dog about to attack her.

His skin began to catch on black fire until it covered his entire body, yet he seemed to feel no pain or discomfort. He still had that smirk on his face, and as he began to laugh, his black eyes turned a bright red.

Kumiko was so disturbed that she was nearly struck by his first fireball thrown. He flung them at her effortlessly. She was agile enough to run, jump, and flip out of the way if needed. Horisho's advisors and generals had already made room for a duel, but they began to become concerned for their own safety. Some had already left with the wounded so they might be attended to, but the other men didn't want to leave and look like cowards. They did their best not to be hit with the mysterious black flame while they watched Horisho's daughter make them look inferior.

Horisho watched the battle intently. He thought his daughter could not be defeated by anyone but him, but she very well couldn't fight what she couldn't touch. It was brilliant, but he personally wanted something a bit more hands-on. He wanted to crush his enemies. "Enough!" he yelled.

Kumiko had slipped and fallen. She hated that she had failed in her father's eyes. She wouldn't let the fire boy get away with that.

The boy did as instructed and ceased the fight. Within an instant, his flames faded, and he became his normal self. He slowly began to walk toward Horisho. All of Horisho's men were willing and ready to charge the boy if he raised a hand against Horisho, but the two of them looked completely calm. They stared at each other until the boy bowed.

Everyone stood silently and watched until it was all over.

"This power can be yours, Horisho. I have come to help you." The boy stood back up with the same wickedness all over his face.

"Why?" Horisho asked.

"Because you were destined to have this power. It's my duty to help you."

Horisho knew that every man had his own intentions with every task, but the boy's words were true. He was destined to have that power. "What do you call yourself, Boy?"

The boy had to think about it until he was ready with a smirk. "Ash."

Horisho chuckled amused. "Kumiko, show Ash to his room."

Kumiko stood and glared at Ash angrily. She wanted to strangle the life out of him. "Rather me than a servant, Father?" she yelled disgusted.

Horisho narrowed his eyes in on his daughter to strike fear into her. It mattered not that she was powerful. He would not allow her to defy him with any request. "This is a special occasion, and he is a special guest."

Ash turned to her. "I would be honored to have such a beautiful woman escort me to my room."

Jun was instantly enraged. He was going to die for Kumiko a short while ago. If any man deserved her, it was him, and he would not let a stranger get in the way of that. But for the meantime, he kept all of his emotions tucked away inside.

Kumiko made no attempt to keep her emotions away from her face. She headed for the side door, lacking her usual grace. "Follow me."

The skies and seas had been very kind to Tice and Riss. Tice spent most of her days in her cabin, but her brother would take her up top to the deck during his breaks if the sun weren't too bright. She didn't like the smell of the salty water, but she did love how the breeze felt on her face. It was nice taking a break.

Riss didn't really like being up on the deck. It was a spectacular experience being on the ship, traveling, and seeing things he wouldn't have seen otherwise, but he just preferred to be on land. The only small consolation was that he knew he was safe from his former friend. "Do you think we'll see him again?"

Tice outstretched her arms and let the wind blow through her hair. "I'm not sure."

"And you know who I'm talking about?" he asked oddly.

"Mal." She lowered her arms and sighed. She knew that her brother was upset, but there wasn't a whole lot she could do. "I don't know if we'll ever see him again. I think it's safe to assume that we will."

"I don't think there's anything safe about him anymore." Riss did his best not to think about how Mal set himself on fire and laughed terribly. If he could dream like Tice, he was sure it would be about that day. The worst part about it all was that he felt it was his own fault. "Do you think he can go back to normal?"

"Anything is possible."

"Since when?" he asked sadly.

She smiled. "Since I started to believe."

Riss wished it was that simple. The world was terrible, and terrible things happened because of it. Even if the world was changing and powers were given to good people, there were bad people with resources and abilities.

Captain Mayes was watching the two of them from across the deck. He didn't know how to break the important news, but he marched over to them stern and steady as always. "Boy."

Riss straightened up and turned around. "Sir?" He was sure he was about to be in trouble for scorching the floor.

"How good are you with your abilities?"

Riss looked surprised at first but then recovered with a slick smirk. "Well—"

"Not very good," Tice pointed out quickly.

Riss dropped his mouth and looked at her with unbelief. "I am too!"

Tice rolled her eyes. "Why ask, Captain?"

"There has been word about pirates around these waters. Usually I wouldn't mind that much seeing as I have a crew full of men who know how to fight and take care of themselves." He began to speak irritable as if he could already see what trouble Riss and Tice were going to cause. "Now I have two children on my vessel, and these pirates are rumored to have strange powers."

Tice latched onto Riss to get his attention. She really didn't need to though. He picked up on the trouble just fine. "What sort of powers?" he asked.

"I'm not sure, but many ships have been destroyed."

Things couldn't have gotten any worse for Riss. He hid from the land to be free from Mal, and then a monster of the sea was born. He held Tice close to show that he could protect her, but it was really him who was afraid. "I can take care of Tice. Don't worry about us."

"Good." Captain Mayes didn't know how to treat children, but he tried to be affectionate. He rubbed his hand on top of Riss's head and messed up his hair. He jerked his head around very hard, but Riss didn't say anything. "We'll be arriving on land soon."

Riss frowned and fixed his hair as soon as Mayes started walking away. He looked down at Tice, who seemed very worried. "Tice, I'm going to protect you."

She could read right through her brother by the sound of his shaky voice. She trusted him fine, but there were some promises he couldn't keep. Not always. Besides, there was more than just the two of them on that ship. "We're probably going to be in a lot of danger for a long while, Riss. I think we should stay at the next stop. Sakai is after us, and she'll be after us until one of us is gone. I don't think we should endanger Captain Mayes and his crew."

Despite being a little bit shaken from the talk of monster pirates, Riss did like adventuring with Captain Mayes. Sure he treated him like a child and yelled a lot, but he practically did that to his entire crew. Riss felt like he was a real adult while he worked for his fair share. It was much more satisfying than theft.

For that, he would always be appreciative. "Well, we wanted to go to Eastern Pearl," he said melancholy. "We're almost there."

✧

Kumiko was so angry walking with Ash behind her. She knew that he was looking upon her in ways that he shouldn't, and she already despised him. She thought she was invincible. Reality isn't a very satisfying meal for anyone, but it especially didn't settle well in her stomach. She led him to the plainest room that she possibly could and slid open the door. Hopefully he would accidentally burn the paper and wooden doors down while he was doing something embarrassing. She would make sure to laugh the loudest. "This is your room."

Ash stepped inside. There was a bed for him to sleep in and only one for only him. "I've never stayed in place this nice before."

Kumiko was upset that her plan backfired. "Then where did you stay before? Who were you before this power was given to you?"

Ash chuckled to himself, thinking about the pathetic life he used to have. "I was a silly boy named Mal." Every memory he had before the black fire was like a ghost. The people he used to care for, he detested. The person he used to be disgusted him. "Now he's dead, and I have a much bigger destiny than you could ever imagine."

He turned and looked at Kumiko with another unsettling smile. "You have one too."

She crossed her arms and asked sarcastically, "I do, huh?"

"Of course."

She narrowed her eyes in on him hard, but he wouldn't stop smiling at her. How could someone be so comfortable with hatred? He finally annoyed her enough for her to step closer and point her finger in his face. "Let's get one thing straight. I don't trust you."

He shrugged. "You'd be a fool if you did."

"You think my father is a fool?" she asked offended.

"Your father doesn't trust me. If he didn't think I could deliver, he would have me killed." He raised his head up cocky. "Or rather, he would *try* to have me killed."

"Are you saying you're immortal?"

He smirked. "No."

She quickly drew her sword and held it under his chin. "My father can kill you, and so can I."

Though she could have applied a little bit of pressure and killed him, he was not afraid. "I'm not your enemy, Kumiko. I'm going to show you how to raise an army."

"An army for what?"

209

"To rule this world." He slowly touched her hand and guided her sword away from his neck. He knew that talk of power intrigued her. It wouldn't be long before they were great allies and perhaps even friends.

"Why me?" she asked. "Why was this ability given to me?"

"Because," he stepped closer to her, so their lips were only a few inches apart. "You were born to rule."

Though she loathed him, he brought a full smile to her face. She did love power, and she did want her father to control the world. "I'm listening."

He stepped backward to give himself a little more space, and then reached out his arms as if the whole world belonged to them. "There are people with powers who will rise to stand in your way. I know who they are, and you—only you—can destroy them." Then he lowered his arms and began to walk around her. "The greatest challenge will be a boy with abilities similar to your own, yet they do surpass."

"No one fights better than me."

He spoke from behind her, and his words fell right on the back of her neck. "But he does." Then he placed his fingers on her shoulders and gently slid them down the side of her arms. "He's guided by the light, but you will learn to be guided by the darkness like I am." He ended with his fingers intertwining with her own. "This boy will become great, and the people will call his name Legend."

"Legend?" It was so comical that she resisted the urge to laugh.

"Yes." Ash spun Kumiko around to face him again. "But for now, he is only beginning to know himself and his magnificent powers. You have to work quickly if you want to catch up with young Davin."

"Davin?" She was certainly intrigued.

"Yes. That's his name."

There was something wrong with Ash, no matter what he or her father told her. But no matter what his true intentions might have been, she was going to have ultimate power. For that reason, she held his hands tighter and pulled him into her for a kiss.

Jun was a resilient and very loyal boy with a kiss that ignited a flame within her, but Kumiko wanted to be set on fire so she could watch the world burn under her feet, and she only knew one boy who could wield that fire.

When she pulled away from him, she breathed out a small breath of his black fire and smiled. She felt his power and desired it. There was something more beyond what she already had. If light guided Davin, then she would settle for the darkness. "Teach me."

✦

Captain Saxon stood at the bow of his ship with his arms outstretched, feeling the power of the wind rushing throughout his body. There had never been such a man who could travel with the waters high and fast like him. He loved it.

"That's quite impressive," said a woman's voice from behind.

He slowed down the waters and brought them to a calm as gently as he could without causing harm to his ship or his crewmen inside. He did not know the voice, but he knew good and well that no women were on his ship before their last encounter. He drew his sword before turning around and pointed the tip of the blade to her throat before he could clearly see her face.

She was a strange looking woman indeed, and she did not cower in fear like he knew other women would. She laughed and touched the blade. "These little toys cannot harm me."

The sword in his hand began to move on its own accord and felt like scales of a creature. He dropped the sword on the ground, and it slithered away in the form of a snake.

211

He was mystified at the woman's strange power, but he would not be made a fool. He grabbed her by her black cloak and yelled in her face. "What sort of trickery is this?"

"You have your power, and I have mine."

He blinked, and she was gone. He clasped his fingers tight to make sure she was out of his grasp.

"Turn around."

He looked behind him, and there she was standing on the bowsprit. He was amazed, and a little angry, but he managed to laugh. "You're quite impressive."

"And you're quite deadly." She disappeared and reappeared behind him. She tapped his shoulder, and he faced her again a bit more frustrated. "I need you to do something for me," she said.

"And why exactly would I help you?"

She smiled wide until her eyes closed shut like a child, but there was no innocence behind it. "Because I can help you gain more power."

He narrowed his eyes in on her. He already had tremendous power, but it would seem like she had much more to offer him. "And what will it cost me?"

"Only a few more innocent lives to weigh on your black soul."

It only took him one second to consider her offer. "Then we have a deal."

Chapter Sixteen

Dex woke up the same as he did every single day—miserable. He ate and dressed well, but nothing really satisfied him. When he looked in his mirror, he knew that he was an attractive boy, and it would only take one step outside of his house and into the public for a girl to confirm his suspicions. But everything he had was all too superficial, and he didn't know what to do to make himself more.

When he came downstairs, his father wasn't there to greet him off to school. He was a teenager. He really didn't need for his father to see him off, but Dex lived by tradition, like his father, and his father before him. He wasn't really the type to break it.

He opened the basement door and began to walk down the stairs quietly. There wasn't a speck of daylight down there. The way was lit by candles, but it was still dim and dark in some places. The stairs wrapped around, but he didn't want to go all the way down. He hid on the stairs out of sight so he could listen to the voices he heard speaking.

"Thank you all for coming," his father said. It was one of his father's very important meetings. Dex didn't understand, though his father explained it at least a dozen times. The secrecy and the wickedness didn't interest him at all. There were four men, one woman, and all of them were dressed in black robes. Everyone had their hood up, so he couldn't see their faces.

Another man answered. "If you don't mind, we'll dispense with the pleasantries. Some of us are quite busy."

"Yes," his father replied smartly, "I've heard that there has been a little bit of trouble on your end with your camps."

The man raised his hand and swatted the problem away as if it were a fly. "It's a small scuffle."

"It's all because of this mysterious light that's fallen from the sky," spoke another man. "It's doing unspeakable things to people."

"For example," his father said, "I called you all here today to discuss a girl who lives in this village."

Dex began to feel nervous when he heard his father mention Diene. She was the only person who he liked seeing in school or in the entire town. She was no threat to anyone, only a joy.

"My son tells me that she was unable to walk, and now she does all because of this light."

"We have to stop this!" said the man who owned the camps.

Then another man spoke. His voice was very sly, and he had an accent, so he must have been from far away. "Not everyone who uses the light is our enemy. Some of it can and has been used in our favor. A young man in our care has become very powerful because of it."

"And he's loyal to our cause?" asked the man with the camps.

The foreigner smirked cruelly. "He turned in one of his blood relatives. He outed his brother as a dreamer, and now he works for us."

"Then the question is how do we get those who have the ability to wield the power to work for us?" asked the woman.

"It's no use with the girl though," Dex's father said. "She can't be one of us."

Dex was becoming more worried by the minute. He considered going to school and warning her, but he didn't want to ever do anything against his father or his legacy.

214

His father spoke again. "What about our contacts from The Dark Realm? Has anyone received orders recently?"

"It would seem like they are taking matters into their own hands," the foreigner said.

The man with the camps stroked his beard and thought carefully. "Then we had best act on our own. What should we do with the girl?"

The woman spoke again. "She's just a child. She poses no threat."

"The camps will be a fine place for her," the man with the camps assured.

Dex couldn't take it anymore! He didn't understand what was going on, and he wanted some answers! He got off of the stairs and walked over to their table. "Father!"

He pulled his hood off and addressed his son like the loving father he was. "Yes, Dex?"

Dex knew that his father cared about him. He knew that he did well for the town. If he knew something about Diene, then he was probably acting in everyone's best interest. He wouldn't go against him. "I'm off to school now."

"Yes, Son." He got out of his chair so he could hug him. "Have a good day."

Davin kept looking on ahead. He knew his people behind him were tired, but they couldn't afford to lose any more time. He had set a few traps for the guards that sought after them. He led fake trails and created hazards for them, but he knew it was only a matter of time before they were found and a confrontation was forced.

"Davin!" Alm struggled to get to his leader. He knew that if he was having a difficult time keeping up the pace, then so was everyone else. "Davin!" He finally touched Davin's shoulder and grabbed it tight so he would stop.

"What?" Davin turned around a little frustrated, and then saw the expressions on everyone's face. He was pushing them all too hard.

"We're not all like you, Davin."

Davin sighed. "Let's rest."

Everyone seemed to breathe a sigh of relief, and most of everyone sat down wherever they were. They had escaped the barren lands of their captors and had found forests filled with plants, wildlife, and even fresh springs of water to drink from. With stones and wood at their disposal, they were even able to make weapons for themselves. Ever since they became free, a way had been provided for them somehow.

They could have traveled to villages. There were a few they decided to pass. Davin was sure that the people couldn't be trusted. It seemed like a lifetime ago, but he remembered, and so did many of the others. The only way to be safe was to take out the guards and the camp. That way, there wouldn't be anywhere to turn them in.

Davin took a seat on a tree stump. He didn't really bother trying to relax. He knew they didn't have much time. "They're going to find us soon."

Alm looked surprised and took a seat next to Davin. "How do you know?"

"I just..." He raised his arms and shrugged. "I just know it somehow."

Alm looked out to the people. They were scrappy looking, but he had to have some hope. "Do you think we're ready?" he asked.

Davin knew that they were walking up an incline. "We have the higher ground." He knew that he had a couple hundred people, but the

216

guards probably only had a shy of one hundred. But even though that was a positive, they had lost a lot of their men during the escape. Most of their ranks were women and children. The small children couldn't fight, and he would want some of the women to look after the children and keep them safe during the battle. "We outnumber them unless they gained reinforcements from somewhere else."

"Somewhere else?" Alm shrieked. "You think there might be other camps?"

"I think our guards received orders from someone. No one is without some kind of higher authority."

"What about us?" Alm asked seriously. "Who's on our side? Who decides when we're really free and where we should go?"

"We do. We decide whatever we want for ourselves. No one has to follow me, but I guarantee I'll fight with my last breath to protect us."

He thought about what he had spoken. There had to be a reason beyond freedom for what he was doing. After all, he was free and strong. He could leave and never be bothered again. "But as far as what I'm following..."

The image of the little girl dressed in white came to mind. He thought of her often, when he had the time to think of something other than battle. She never reappeared, but she was out there somewhere in the world. It was something else that he just knew. "I'm certain that I have to find the little girl."

"The one who told you to find the light?" Alm thought Davin was crazy at first, but he soon learned better.

"I know she'll tell me what I'm supposed to do next!" Davin wondered why he hadn't even seen her again in his dreams. But he did know that he would see her when the time was right. "You all won't need protecting forever. You won't even need it after we make our last stand. I

217

don't think I'm going to lose my abilities after the final battle." He put on a sad smile. "I don't think there is a final battle, at least not for me."

Alm could see how troubled Davin was about finding the girl. There was no sense in worrying about it since they didn't even know where to begin looking. He just knew that if anyone in the world could find her, it would be Davin. "We'll find her." He patted Davin on the shoulder and smiled.

Davin smiled a little bit more, but he wasn't really any happier. Something was troubling him, but he wasn't sure what it was. "Make sure everyone eats and gathers whatever they think they need to survive." He stood up. "If they're tired, they can sleep. We might need their dreams."

"What are you going to do?"

Davin couldn't put his finger on it. He just knew it would soon be time to fight. "I'm going to go look around."

When Dex entered his classroom, Diene was standing in a corner surrounded by people. Plenty of those kids had never spoken more than a few words to Diene while she was crippled, but they treated her like royalty ever since they learned she could walk. Everyday someone asked her to tell the story, and then someone told her about their problems and asked Diene whether or not she believed that something spectacular and impossible could happen to them as well.

Diene always said the same thing. "Anything is possible. If it happened for me, it can happen for you."

Dex couldn't take it anymore and marched up to her. "Diene, may I speak with you?"

Diene was flattered by all of the attention, but what she enjoyed the most were how people's faces lit up when she gave them a reason to believe in impossibilities. It was also a plus when her favorite boy would thrive for her attention. "Sure."

He took her hand and led her away from the group of kids so they could speak privately out in the hallway. Diene began to blush as soon as his hand touched hers. He didn't notice it until right before he spoke, and then he blushed himself. "Diene—"

"I'm sorry that I've been so busy since the dance," she said nervously. "I do still really like you." She smiled so hard that it became hard for her to speak. "I just wanted to tell other people about what happened."

Dex thought she was a lovely girl, and she was kind. That's why he didn't want anything to happen to her. "You have to stop talking about the light."

"What?" she asked horrified. "Why?"

"Because it's making other people upset, and you're going to attract the wrong kind of attention."

"I don't understand. When I tell my story, it makes people happy. It gives them hope. Why wouldn't you want me to give them that?" If she knew that one day she could have walked, it would have made her life so much more bearable. If she knew that somehow, someway she could be free, she would have smiled because she meant it and not to make her parents feel better. "I wish someone gave it to me!"

"It's a very nice story, and I care about you. I care a lot about you." Dex could see how much he was upsetting her, but he really was trying to help. He knew what kind of man his father was, but he couldn't tell her that. He couldn't tell anyone what really happened in his home. "That's why I'm trying to protect you."

She had tears in the back of her eyes. She thought Dex was so perfect for her, but he couldn't be anything if he didn't understand. "I'm sorry Dex." She let go of his hand. "You're not who I thought you were."

"Diene!" He reached out for her, but she stepped away and went back into the classroom. He didn't know what else to do.

Davin walked around the forest, and it brought back memories. He was so young the last time he climbed a tree or played hiding games with his parents. He used to spend a lot of his time out in his yard at his home. He could barely remember what it looked like. His life seemed like someone else's. It was filled with such a great darkness that he never spoke a word of it to anyone. He always remained positive to hide all of the grief, until he became that positive person full of hope.

As he explored further, he noticed a few trees knocked over. The breaks were jagged and splintered, not the precise work of an axe or saw.

He kept searching for any clue to find out what could have done such a thing. When he looked up in the trees, they looked disturbed, like something big had knocked loose branches like a sloppy child. The more he saw, the more he wished he hadn't.

He stepped back while looking up until he tripped in a shallow hole. It was wide enough for his entire body to fall in, but it was a strange shape. When he stood back up to observe it, it resembled a footprint. It was a giant footprint!

Davin wasted no time returning to his tree stump overlooking his people. Most of the children were sleeping. Alm had fallen asleep with Mina sitting on his lap. He really wished he had better news to disturb them with, but it couldn't wait.

"Everyone!" He yelled loud enough to get all of their attention. Those who were awake began to wake up those that weren't. Everyone was to listen to Davin when he spoke.

"What's going on?" Alm asked while yawning and wiping his eyes.

"We can't travel ahead." Everyone began to talk amongst themselves and shout out questions, but Davin didn't give them much time to speak. "If we double back, we waste too much time and risk running into other towns and villages. We can't go forward because there's a big threat ahead of us, and we can't risk fighting a war on two fronts."

"What sort of threat?" asked Mina frightened.

He didn't want to scare her any further, but he wasn't sure what it was himself. "Something big that I think we should stay clear of for now."

"So what do we do?" asked a man.

So many eyes were looking toward Davin. He had never felt nervous before. Something about all of their fearful eyes looking at him made him anxious. "They'll be here soon. I'm sure of it. We have to prepare ourselves to fight."

They all knew it would happen eventually, but some of the women whispered in fear to each other. One of them asked, "Is there no other way?"

"There was never another way." Davin honestly didn't think they were ready. They needed more time and more weapons. They needed more men, or at least not so many little children. He could usually see clearly what they had to do to ensure a victory, but it wasn't clear at all.

He couldn't let that stop him though. He stood tall, and brave, with his chest out like a man, and with an unshakable determination in his eyes. "They made this decision for us. We're not going to let them end this the way they want it to. We will stand, and we will fight, and we will be free!"

He could see the fire—that craving for life within them all rising up. That was all they really needed. They needed the will and something worth fighting for.

"I will fight to my last breath if I have to, but we will be free!"

Diene took her time walking home. She was very upset about Dex trying to silence her, but she felt even worse about what she had said to him. During class, she felt his eyes on her the entire time. She didn't want to look at him because she was so upset, but he did really care about her.

Oh, what a terrible mistake she had made! She imagined her parents would make her feel better with a nice meal and stories of their long day. She enjoyed spending time with them now that they didn't have to spend just about every single second tacked onto her.

As she came closer to the house, she saw a large carriage outside with big black horses. She had never ridden on a horse before and hadn't traveled much in a carriage either. She rushed to her door to ask her parents' guests for a ride. "Mother! Father!"

When she arrived at the door, a large, odd looking man came out. Diene was afraid and stepped away from him. "H-hello?"

She looked behind him and saw other men inside her home. Her mother was on the floor with her hands and feet tied and her mouth gagged. She gasped as she saw the men grab her father and wrestle him to the ground. "Father?"

He looked terrified for his daughter's life. "Diene, run!" Then they gagged him and began to tie him up as well.

Diene tried to run away, but the man in front of her grabbed her. "No!" She began screaming as loud as her voice would allow, but the man quickly covered her mouth. She scratched his arm and kicked him. It wasn't until she bit him that he let go of her for a brief second. That brief second was all that Diene needed. As soon as her foot hit the ground, she was gone.

She ran as fast as she could, and everything stood still to her. The birds were frozen in the sky, the people passing by, and even the leaves flying in the wind. She was too afraid to stop and figure out why.

She ran to the only person that she knew cared about her, besides her parents. She ran to Dex's home. Everyone in town knew where it was. It was the biggest home. Five families could have lived in there very comfortably. She didn't know exactly what Dex's family did to merit such wealth. She only knew that his father was involved with a little bit of everything in town.

She didn't stop running until she got to the door, and then the world snapped back to normal—continuing on as if nothing strange had happened at all. She didn't care either. She only wanted to be safe again.

"Dex!" She banged her fists on his door, crying and screaming to the top of her lungs. "Dex! Please!" She didn't want him to hate her, and she wanted him to hold her in his arms while they thought carefully about what to do.

When the door opened, she smiled and began crying hysterically. Dex was standing right in front of her, and she basically fell on top of him. "Dex!"

"What are you doing here?" He looked around frantically for his father that he knew was in the next room over. "You have to leave!"

She quivered her lip. "You're still mad at me?"

"No! I'm not mad. You just have to go!"

"I can't." She was crying so hard; it was difficult to speak or to breathe. "My parents were taken by some men in black. If I go home, they'll find me. I don't know what they want with my parents, but they'll do something bad to them!"

"Very bad," Dex's father said as he came into the foyer.

Diene let go of Dex and ran to his father. He had many friends and much influence. If anyone in the world had the power to set them free, it

223

was him. "Please! Sir, you've got to help my parents. I know you can save them." She held onto his clothes, begging him with all the desperation she had.

He smiled at her evilly. "Now why would I do that, when I'm the one who issued the order?"

She stood still, completely shocked by what he had said and the weight of his words. She believed that she was in the safest place in the world, and it was her greatest threat. She let go of him and backed away. Surely it was some kind of joke. Surely they were all about to laugh.

But no one was laughing.

She turned to run away, but Dex caught her. Diene never would have believed that Dex would be so cruel. "Why?"

Dex closed his eyes. He didn't want to see her suffer.

His father, however, enjoyed the fear in her face. "Because people like you can't be spatting out your gibberish. All this talk of hope and change and miracles..." His nostrils flared and he glared at her. "It's sickening!"

She just couldn't understand. "Why?"

"Because we like the world the way it is, and you and your little allies aren't going to change that."

"I don't know what you're talking about!"

"It's well that you don't know, but you'll never find out."

She closed her eyes and screamed as he reached out to grab her. "Dex!" She hoped that he would let her go so she could run away and be free. She wished it so hard until she felt his hands loosen. She opened her eyes surprised and then she was gone.

Diene didn't know where she would go. She didn't know who to turn to or who she could trust. She didn't know what they were going to do with her parents or if she would ever see them again. All she knew to do was to run.

Chapter Seventeen

Riss and Tice were the first two to make it off of the ship and onto the shores of Eastern Pearl. For so long they had been waiting to arrive to the only destination they knew they needed to be at. They had heard the crew speak of its beauties from its landscapes to the women. They had heard of the delicious foods and fine drinks. But the most appeasing thing to Tice and Riss were the great tales of King Raymon and his lineage. Riss knew that his sister and her unique gift would be accepted on their shores. They would be safe.

But when they arrived on the docks, they realized that there were no merchants waiting to greet them, or women strolling down the streets to buy groceries for their families. The entire place seemed empty.

There were only two people within sight. There was a young blond boy and a beautiful teenaged girl with long black hair sitting on a chest, kicking her feet impatiently.

Riss breathed in and out heavily and spoke in awe. "She's gorgeous." At least the tales of pretty women were true, but he never thought he would find someone so crafted for him.

Tice could recognize the look on her brother's face without even being able to see it. She squeezed his hand as tight as she could. "Do not show off your powers," she warned.

"I know." He knew better alright, but he also knew that girls wanted to be impressed and he planned on making quite the impression. "I'll just be myself."

She hung her head down low, feeling like it was already a lost cause. "That's what I'm worried about."

He marched right up to her with a dazzling smile on his face. He planned on fulfilling every single desire that she had by becoming her one and only desire. "My name is Riss."

She stared at him emotionless for a while until she became bored. "I didn't ask."

The little boy tugged on her arm with disapproval. "Samara, we weren't raised that way."

Riss smirked. "Samara, huh?" It was a lovely name indeed.

She crossed her arms and waited for someone with hair on their face to come out. "I assume you aren't in charge of this vessel."

He stuck his chest out. "Of course I am—"

"Not!" Tice corrected quickly. She shook her head at him. "You'll have to excuse my brother, but he can be quite—"

"A liar?" Samara asked smartly.

Riss laughed at the comment, though rejection stung. He wasn't a quitter though. He hadn't seen a pretty teenage girl since he left the orphanage. He was going all out. "I think we've gotten off on the wrong foot."

"It would seem that you're the only one trying to go anywhere, and no, pulling my arm won't work." She smiled hard at him, but it wasn't very nice. She was highly annoyed.

Obviously, things weren't going anywhere with the girl. "Who is your brother?" Tice asked.

"I'm Raymon." He reached out his hand so he could greet her properly like a real gentlemen, but she didn't take his hand.

226

"You're blind?" Samara asked Tice.

She nodded and rested her head on Riss's side. She felt vulnerable and shy when people asked about her blindness. She felt so silly not being able to see them.

Raymon felt like a complete idiot for not noticing, but he had never really met a blind person before, and he certainly hadn't seen anyone with eyes like Tice. He had never seen anyone like her at all. She was so strange, but he liked it. "If you don't mind, I'd like to introduce myself." He bowed and kissed her hand. "My name is Raymon, heir to—"

"That's enough." Samara jumped off of the chest and gently nudged her brother behind her. "We need to speak to your captain."

Tice was blushing. She never had a feeling like the one she was experiencing. She wished she could see Raymon, the boy who made her heart race. She knew that Samara was irritated by Riss, but she still thought it was only polite to give a response. "I'm Tice."

Riss didn't like the way Tice was looking. He didn't like it one bit! He quickly stretched out his hand to break their hold. Then he made sure to glare at little Raymon with a deathly stare. "Highly inappropriate."

Samara looked at Tice and Raymon dumbfounded. They were much too young to be making googly expressions at each other, and it was idiotic to be done so quickly. "Excuse me." She pushed past Riss and began walking down the dock toward the ship.

Captain Mayes came on deck looking around befuddled. He just couldn't imagine Eastern Pearl so lifeless. "Girl, where is everyone?"

Samara glared at the captain's lack of respect toward her, but they didn't know any better. She let it go. "Everyone is gone."

"Gone?" he barked. "Gone where?"

"I don't know," Samara said annoyed. "They could be dead. They could be captured. Maybe they all moved away to a safer place. I'm not sure. However, I am willing to purchase some of whatever you've brought. Is there food?"

"I have grains, spices, and material for garments…" Captain Mayes was completely stupefied. "You mean to tell me that you and that boy are the only people here?"

"Eastern Pearl was completely abandoned when we got here." Samara brushed it off quickly. She really had no interest in dwelling on the sad things in her past. "Are you going to sell me what I want or not?"

He nearly laughed at her. "I'm not doing any business with a small child."

Samara tensed up her face, and she glared even harder. She really didn't like being disrespected, and she wouldn't stand for it any further. "Fine." She turned around and marched back over to her chest and lifted it open with a big smirk. "But know what you just missed out on."

Riss's mouth dropped, and his eyes bucked. He had never seen so much gold in his life. Even when he wasn't living at the orphanage, he never had money like that. She must have been the richest person that he had ever met. He either wanted to marry her or let the thief that laid dormant inside of him rise again.

"Where did you get this?" Captain Mayes asked her with a bit of anger in his voice. He was sure that she had stolen it.

"It's ours."

Captain Mayes didn't even understand how they could have gotten such a heavy load of gold out to the dock all by themselves. He was just a little boy, and she was only a woman. "If you took it from someone's home, then it's not yours."

"She took it from our home," Raymon said.

Everyone looked over at Raymon. Samara was glaring at her brother. She warned him a dozen times not to give out a lot of information to strangers. The wielder of fire who was responsible for her father's death was supposed to come to them, and he very well could have been on that ship.

"Who are you, Boy?" Mayes asked.

Raymon knew better that time and looked to his sister.

Samara thought that the people on the ship would leave as soon as they learned that their buyers were gone. If she bought something, she figured it would buy her some time to figure out exactly who her enemy was. Perhaps there was another way though.

Samara wanted to be cautious about giving up too much information, but she honestly didn't like people not knowing who she was. "My father is—or rather was—King of Eastern Pearl. His name is the same as my brother, Raymon."

"You're a princess?" Riss was so amazed that his voice screeched. It was truly embarrassing, but he had every intention of pestering her until he was right in her eyes.

Samara didn't care though. She thought very little of everyone who couldn't get her to her enemy. "He won the war with Lord Rovin, but something happened."

Tice began to squeeze her brother's arm as she realized who Samara and Raymon were. She didn't have any dreams about them, but she knew that a brother and sister would be placed in great danger because of Mal and the light he had corrupted—thanks to Sakai. They were the people she was supposed to connect with.

"How did your father die?" Tice felt wrong for asking, but she wanted to make sure.

Samara didn't want to talk or even think about it. It hurt too much. "You probably won't believe me."

"Try us," Riss said.

Samara turned to watch Captain Mayes's face. If anyone knew of any men with strange powers on his ship, he would. "Lord Rovin received a strange ability and was able to shoot lightning bolts out of his hands."

Captain Mayes usually kept a steady expression, and he held together well, but his eyes gave it away. When Samara followed the captain's eyes behind her to Riss and Tice, it was very clear that the two of them knew something vital.

She couldn't imagine what an idiot like Riss knew, but she was going to pry the answers she wanted right out of him. "Captain, I hope you don't mind, but I'd like to enjoy Riss's company alone for a little while."

Riss slowly smiled from ear to ear. Time alone was perfect! He continued to think that until Tice squeezed his hand again even tighter. "I'm not going anywhere without my little sister," he said unconvincingly.

Samara innocently walked behind her brother and placed her hands on his shoulders. "Raymon will keep her company then."

Captain Mayes didn't fear anything from children, but he was suspicious of Samara. There was trouble in her eyes. "Why only them?"

"I haven't seen a child my own age for months." She smiled at him, though it wasn't very convincing. "Feel free to help yourself to some of my gold while I'm gone. I have no need of it."

Captain Mayes nodded slowly. He wasn't going to pass up gold! "And the supplies?" he asked.

"I'm not sure I'll have need of it. Do me a favor and wait on your ship with your crew for an hour. We'll be back by then, and I'll have a decision."

He was still concerned about Riss and Tice. Riss should have been able to take care of himself against a girl and a little boy, but Samara very well might have been lying. There could have been men waiting in houses or down alleyways to kidnap the children. Of course, he saw no purpose in that.

"It's alright, Captain Mayes," Tice said. "We'll be fine."

Captain Mayes didn't know all what Tice could do, but he did know that she held something special within her. He would trust her word, because they were bound to do whatever she felt she needed to do anyway. "One hour," he said sternly.

Samara quickly took Riss by the hand and pulled until he followed. She was making him drag Tice along, but he wasn't about to speak out loud about a beautiful princess holding his hand. He wasn't crazy.

Raymon grabbed Tice's other hand, and she began to blush again. She knew that her brother wouldn't like it, but she slipped her hand away from Riss so she could walk at a normal pace. "We are following them?" she asked Raymon.

"Yes. I promise." Raymon continuously kept staring at Tice. Even though she looked younger than him, she seemed older. She was special somehow. He wondered if something was wrong with her though. The longer he held her hand, the more extremely red she became. "Are you alright?" he asked.

Riss overheard and looked behind him to see Tice so red in the face. It was a cloudy day, so he didn't know how the sun could have burned her. He had never seen her look like that. "What's the matter?"

"Nothing!" She pouted embarrassed. There was no way for her to see what she looked like, and she was making a fool out of herself.

Raymon chuckled at Tice. He liked her and wanted to be her friend. He loved Samara, but she wasn't good company in her condition.

Samara eventually let go of Riss's hand once they were far away from the dock. She kept quiet as they followed her into town. As Riss looked around at all the empty houses, he felt something terrible in the pit of his stomach. It was all such a terrible waste, and it was because of greed.

He didn't want to travel too far from the ship. Riss wanted to sweep Samara off her feet, but she wasn't saying anything to him. She wouldn't even look at him. "You are very beautiful." He sped up his pace so he could see her expression, but it didn't change from its former cold and stony appearance. He kept trying though. "What's it like being a princess?"

She glared at him quickly, but that was all.

He was beginning to lose his patience. "Do you ever smile at all?"

She stopped walking and exploded. "Can you be quiet for two seconds?"

Tice and Raymon were both afraid about Samara's outburst. Riss, however, felt challenged. He never backed down to anyone, and he certainly wasn't going to back down to a pretty face. He stood up straight to hover over her and pointed in her face. "Now you listen here, Princess—"

She grabbed Riss and pushed him through a door right in front of them into a house. "No, you listen!"

"What's your problem?" Riss wasn't scared of her. He was just extremely caught off-guard.

She pushed him until his back hit a kitchen table. "I want to know whatever it is you know about what happened to my father!"

"What are you talking about?" Riss really didn't know, but he didn't sound very convincing either.

Raymon ran inside the house while still holding onto Tice's hand. Tice knew whatever was going on must have been bad by the way Raymon gasped.

"Don't play stupid with me!" Samara yelled. "You know something."

Tice had a feeling that if she didn't step in, her brother was going to mess up everything. "We know what it's like to lose parents," she said

232

sincerely to Samara. "Our parents are dead and there's no way of getting them back. We're sorry that someone else has to know what that is like. Right, Riss?"

Riss shifted his eyes away from Tice because of his guilt. He was such a liar, but Tice didn't need to know that their parents were really alive somewhere and didn't want them. "Yeah. I'm sorry."

Samara reluctantly let him go and crossed her arms. "I still think you're hiding something."

"Please." Riss stood up and fixed his clothes a little bit, trying to look sly again. "Let's stop pointing fingers at each other and let's try and learn a little bit more about each other." He grabbed her hand and gently kissed it. He didn't know any girl who had skin that soft.

She thought about socking him in the face, but she let him kiss her and smiled. "Fine." She did retrieve her hand when he was finished and scrubbed it on her side. "As you know, my brother and I are heirs to this kingdom. We were sent away when we were young for protection during the war. We received word from our father that the war was over, and we could come home. When we arrived, everyone was gone, and our father was dead."

"So why are you staying here?" Riss asked. "Why don't you leave and move on?"

Tice spoke up. "She's been waiting for someone."

Samara looked at her astonished. "How do you know that?"

Riss crossed arms and tried to tighten his muscles to make them look bigger for her. "My sister has a gift. She just knows stuff sometimes."

Samara didn't doubt that piece of information could be true. But if she had a power, it was possible that the fire wielder was there as well. "What about you?" She pretended to be sweet and tapped Riss on the nose playfully. "Do you have a gift?"

233

He smirked. "Of course I do."

Tice panicked and began walking toward his voice until she found his foot and stepped on it as hard as she could.

"Ouch!" he hollered and glared at her, but she was glaring toward his general direction.

It wasn't very subtle, but she didn't have much of a choice. Riss might as well have shouted out all their secrets!

Samara placed her hands on his shoulders and smiled. "What is it?"

Riss wanted to tell her. What girl wouldn't be all over him once they saw all the cool tricks he could do with his fire? He smirked at her. "I'm terribly handsome." His stinging foot was the only reason why he didn't blab everything to his future wife.

She frowned and backed away as she once again crossed her arms. "You're terrible alright."

Raymon spoke up, wanting to change the subject. "What about you guys? You can't be part of the crew."

"I am!" Riss beat on his chest, offended by Raymon's tone. "I work my way to pay my fare."

"To go where?" Samara asked laughingly.

"Here."

"Why?"

"Because Tice knew that I was supposed to come here." He tried staring at her with his boyish eyes. It worked when he begged for food with older women. Perhaps little women were just as gullible.

"Do tell." Samara wanted to trick him and be flirtatious, but it was becoming very difficult to stand Riss's presence.

Riss took her hand again and spoke as sweetly as possible. "She knew about a beautiful young girl that would be here and something else…Something very important." He stepped in closer and kissed her hand. "Destiny."

She stared into his eyes with an evil glare for about five seconds. "Remove your hand before I break it."

He let go quickly. "This is going too fast? I understand."

Tice wanted to take her brother aside to speak to him in private about his big mouth, but she swore she heard something before she took the first step. "Do you hear that?"

Samara tried to listen, but she didn't notice anything. "Hear what?"

Tice's ears had gotten better. She recognized the sound of a man's foot grinding against dirt when they took a step. "Someone's coming."

The doors and windows burst open, and men came exploding in. Tice screamed, but Raymon pushed her behind him and held her hand tight. It all began to happen so fast that he couldn't count how many men had come. He clearly did remember a bald man as big as a monster standing over him and growling. Raymon's legs were shaking, but he wasn't going to move out of the way.

The man snatched up Raymon as if he were a paper doll. Tice refused to let go of Raymon and was lifted up in the air until Raymon's coat ripped and she fell. Her heart was racing, and she was terrified. "Run!" Raymon yelled.

She got up and began to run, but she ran right into a chair and hit the ground again. Before she could regain the wind in her, she was taken up into the arms of the man who had Raymon. "Riss! Help me!"

Riss was also having his own problems. He couldn't overpower the man he was struggling with, and he knew Samara couldn't. He had to do something brave and heroic to save the princess and his sister! He began to concentrate in his hands, and he burned the arms of the man who had him gripped so tight.

Samara was struggling, but she was watching Riss. She found it hard to believe that he could overpower a man twice his size. She didn't see Riss do anything to merit arrest, but he must have done something spectacular to make his attacker let him go and yell out in pain.

And she wouldn't be outdone. "Unhand me!" She concentrated and remembered that power within her. Then the man was forced to let go and flew into the wall until he was pushed straight through it.

She began doing the same thing to the other men who didn't have Tice and Riss in arms. Riss was very confused when his attacker flew through the wall, but he felt small on the inside once he realized that Samara was somehow doing it.

The man who had Raymon and Tice ran outside and began to make a run for it. Samara didn't even attempt to run after him. She stretched out her hand and imagined a wall, and then *bam*! The man fell backward as if he had run full speed into something.

Tice was hurt from the landing. Raymon was knocked out. She climbed over the big man with shaky hands until she felt Raymon's face and chest to know that he was still breathing. "Raymon…" She was so confused and afraid that she just fell on top of him crying.

Now that they were all free, Samara needed answers. She set her sights on the man who Riss was fighting. He was still conscious and was getting up to start running away. She stretched out her hand and imagined her shield as a bubble floating above the man, and then she slammed it on top of him and swatted him like a fly.

Riss was openly a little afraid of Samara. He didn't know what she was doing, but it was brutal and something he really couldn't compare with. "W-what are you doing?" He ran over to her side as she walked up to her prisoner.

She stood over the man looking down at him in the crater that she made. She placed her hands on her hips, feeling very powerful. "Who sent you?"

He was barely conscious, but he answered weakly. "Lord Rovin…"

Samara narrowed her eyes in on him and smirked. "Rovin, huh?"

Riss was horrified and reached out to stop her. "What are you doing?"

She slapped his hand away and slid down the crater. She walked to the dead center where the man was laid out and pressed down on his chest with her dainty foot. "I'm not weak anymore." Then she kicked him in the face as hard as she could, which knocked him out.

Riss would have never imagined that a girl that beautiful would be that deadly. She looked like she had never been in a fight at all! He didn't even piece together that she had special abilities. He was too concerned with looking like the weakling in their relationship! He looked around for the bad guys for any chance to redeem himself. The only one left was the other man she had somehow knocked through the wall. Just his luck, he was starting to get up and make a run for it!

Samara heard the man beginning to run and climbed out of the crater to catch him. Riss cleared his throat and casually rubbed his knuckles on his chest. "Don't worry, Princess." He extended his hand out toward the man escaping. "I'll handle this for you."

Tice felt something inside of her terribly wrong. It was a feeling similar to right before Mal touched the light. "Riss, don't!"

He didn't listen to her and shot out a stream of fire until it hit the man's backside. Riss didn't burn him too badly. He only started a little fire on his butt to make him scream and panic as he ran away. He was impressed at his skill and restraint. He also thought it was hilarious, so he had to laugh. "What do you think of that, P—?"

Suddenly, all of the wind was knocked out of Riss as he was knocked up into the air and fell on the ground several feet away. He was hurt, but he managed to lift his head to see Samara walking toward him with fury built up in her face. "What are you doing?"

"You killed my father!" She held her arms in close to her body and imagined her power until she felt it around her. Then she reached out her arms and legs as it exploded from around her.

Riss couldn't see anything, but she created another crater underneath her that extended at least twenty feet around, and stopped a foot away from his feet.

He could then admit that she terrified him. "Stop! I didn't kill anyone!" He backed away on his arms and scouted away with his legs. He was still in a lot of pain, but he had to move.

Samara was fighting off tears. "You're the reason why he's dead!" She extended out her hand and pulled it down, making another shield to the right of Riss that only missed him by a couple of inches. "I'll make you pay! Someone has to pay!"

"Stop it!" Tice screamed. She couldn't see what was happening, and she didn't know how to stop Samara in time. "Please!" She shook Raymon as hard as she could. "Please, you have to wake up!"

Riss rolled over and pushed himself off the ground, but he was only able to walk a few steps before falling. His ankle was killing him, but he didn't have time to stop and nurse his wounds. He knew when he looked into Samara's eyes how much she wanted to hurt him. "Don't do this!" He began limping away as fast as he could.

"You can't get away from me!" She pushed him over with her powers and knocked him to the ground again hard enough to keep him down long enough for her to walk over to him.

Tice hoped for the man who had protected her from Sakai to come and save her brother. He had to be watching from somewhere. "Please!"

Samara heard Tice's voice echoing through her ears. From what she knew, Riss was all she had. She wouldn't survive without him. She probably wouldn't want to. Samara knew what it was like to lose someone that she loved. She didn't want anyone else to feel that way...

But she was so angry!

She placed her foot on his chest and looked into his weary eyes. He was just a boy. She should have let him go, but then who would pay? Who could she hurt for hurting her so badly? Why should she have to suffer alone?

She was shaking and crying hard about her decision, but she didn't know what else to do. "I'm sorry..."

Before she could raise her hand against Riss, she felt a force tackle her, and it was powerful enough to knock her over. Desperate and afraid, she wrestled with the mystery force until it was off of her. Then she realized that Tice was looking straight into her eyes. "How...?" She was so puzzled when she saw Tice's eyes. They looked just like crystals. "How can you attack me when you can't see?"

"Because, I can see you." Samara suddenly came to her vision, and she ran. Tice didn't know how or what she was actually seeing. "You're broken," she said sadly.

To Tice, Samara was her beautiful self, but she looked like she was made out of glass, and she was cracked and chipped. Tice slowly touched one of the cracks on her face to see if what she felt was real, and it wasn't. She felt such soft and smooth skin.

But slowly, the cracks began to spread until everything fell apart. The sight forced Tice to let out a fearful gasp as she saw Samara crumble before her, but what she felt was Samara falling into her arms and her tears.

Samara sobbed heavily. She knew her father was dead, but she couldn't let herself feel all the pain she knew she truly had before. Now, she could finally let go. "I'm sorry," she told Tice. "I'm so sorry!"

Tice was still startled, but she rubbed Samara's back and rocked her gently. "It's okay. It'll all be okay. I promise."

Chapter Eighteen

It had been a hard last three days preparing for battle. Davin worked tirelessly with the men preparing axes and clubs made from stones and wood. Most of the women that Davin felt were old enough to fight were hidden up in trees with bow and arrows. The children that were too small were hidden away in a small burrow covered with leaves somewhere near the top of the hill.

Davin had to scout the land while he left his people with directions. He feared that too much time would be lost, but some of the men had dreams about what sort of traps and weapons they could make to protect themselves. When he returned, he was surprised to see how much they had done.

Davin knew that the guards would find them sometime during nightfall. They would probably seek to camp in their location. The advantage would belong to Davin. His people were used to the darkness.

Davin was covered in mud and leaves and was hiding on the ground along with other men. Alm was right next to him shaking. It was either because he was cold or because he was afraid. Davin could understand both. "Do you think we can win?" Alm asked.

"I don't think we should speak." Davin could hear the sound of horses treading from a distance. It wouldn't be very long.

"Please, just answer me," he said.

Davin sighed. They prepared for the battle as much as they could. Davin really couldn't see the outcome before a battle. Everything began to become clear once it was all happening. "I'm not sure yet."

Alm wasn't the only person who was troubled. "Then why are we fighting?" Alm asked.

"Because, it's a battle that needs to be fought." Davin thought about all of his people. They weren't really scared to die, but rather scared to lose their freedom. It was something that he was also terrified of. "All battles are fought with the goal of winning, but that's not always the reality. Sometimes we fight because losing is better than surrender. At least we tried. At least we have our pride, and if by some miracle we are able to overcome and take the day, then that's what we wanted, and it's what we earned.

"We can keep running, but we can't outrun them forever. We'll either be prisoners or there won't be anything left of us. It's better to fight now that we're prepared. We have a chance. It's not great, but we do have one. It all depends on how bad we want it."

The sound of the horses treading became louder and the ground began to shake. Everyone was struck with a bolt of fear in their chests, and their hearts began to beat with the sound of thunder in their ears. "They're coming!" an archer whispered.

The guards had always looked like a mad pack of dogs. For many of the archers who could see them clearly, they were just as fearsome as ever. But for some of the others, they could see through their own fear and see the guards clearly. The guards were completely unaware and spooked about something. They began to slow up their horses as they entered into the forest.

Everyone stayed silent and tried not to even breathe. Everyone was well hidden, but they were frightened that they would be discovered and lose the element of surprise, or they were afraid that the guards would travel too far up the hill and gain the advantage of higher ground. Then there were also the children to consider. It would be terrible if they discovered them first. Everyone was anxious to begin. They were only waiting on Davin to give the word to attack.

Davin closed his eyes and took in his moment of being free. It might have been his last, but at least it was his to have.

"Now!"

People began to rise from the dirt, screaming and clanging rocks together and sent the horses on their heels in a fright. Some of the guards fell off of their horses while others barely hung on. One of the guards in front stayed steady with their horse and spotted Davin and recognized him from the escape. He narrowed his eyes and clicked his heels against his horse to force it forward toward Davin.

Davin began to run forward, completely clear on what he had to do. "Fire!"

Arrows began to pour from the trees above. Some aim was good; some was surprisingly impeccable while others were unable to hit much of anything. There was a mother of four up in the trees. She was so much better when she practiced, but she hadn't hit anything but a man's ankle. She was running out of arrows fast, and one of the guards was beginning to draw out his bow toward her. In a desperate attempt, she threw her quiver to her closest ally and jumped out of the tree with a battle cry and onto the man before he could attack. She knocked him off his horse, and he hit his head—knocking him out. She rejoiced with a quick, hysterical burst of laughter before stealing his horse.

The arrows weren't the only things being flung from above. Teenagers were armed with stones and muck. If they were lucky, they could knock the guards out, but at the very least, they could hinder their vision.

Davin began to lose speed on purpose, so the man chasing him would think he had a chance. He aimed himself right for a tree, and just before the guard could catch him, Davin ran up it and flipped into the air. He landed behind the guard and on his horse. The guard was so confused that he really couldn't stop Davin from throwing him into another guard, knocking them both off the second guard's horse. But he didn't send the guard on his way before stealing his sword from his sheath.

Alm had managed to steal a frightened horse, but he had caught the attention of quite a few guards. He was riding fast, but he had never ridden on a horse before. He didn't know if he could make it to his trap in time.

Davin came up from behind to aid Alm, but he wouldn't get to him in time, and Alm wasn't going to get to the trap either. "Move out of the way!" he warned.

Alm maneuvered to the left, and Davin threw his sword into a net that was holding up boulders. They didn't have much material when they made it, so it was barely hanging on at all. When the sword snapped one side of the rope, the rest of the net collapsed and flung out the rocks toward the unlucky guards.

Davin didn't look at his wounded enemies or even his fallen friends. He had to keep moving. He always had to keep moving until the very end!

And so, there were many other traps that were beginning to be set off. The guards would chase women, only to fall into deep and narrow pits, and if it weren't the pits, there were nets that would sweep them up.

But not everything could be done with traps. Davin's people had axes, clubs, and staffs. For those who were fortunate to steal a sword, they used them. They weren't as advanced as the guards were, but Davin was there to fight for his people. He was stronger and faster than any man there, and he would never give up until he was dead—but he was difficult to kill. He could catch any arrow, could outrun the horses, and no man could survive toe-to-toe with him. But more important than all of that, he inspired his people and gave them courage.

The night wouldn't be without loss. The guards had goals of bringing them back, but they weren't well prepared to bring back an angry lot of that size. They were armed for a reason, and they were more experienced.

Davin needed to find a way to end the battle before anyone else was lost, and then he heard a terrible scream. He ran toward the voice before he could even think. He knew it was Mina, and he wasn't going to let anything happen to her.

The guards had been trying to gain higher ground, but they were spooked about something. Davin figured that they must have known about the giant footprints and had a better idea than him about what they belonged to. However, there was a guard who had slipped past everyone. The children heard him treading closer on his horse and began to whimper. He could have ridden right past them, but he heard their cries.

He uncovered their hideaway and laughed at them all huddled together like little piglets. He drew his sword and smiled at Mina, recalling that Davin had a fondness for her.

Davin came flying through the air before the guard could even get off of his horse. He kicked him in the chest, and they both took a hard landing on the ground. Davin wasn't fazed at all and dug his knees into the guard's chest and drew his sword from his sheath.

"Wait, wait, wait!" the guard yelled frightened.

Davin was so angry when he thought about the guard's cowardice and all of the cruel things they had done. Davin held the sword up to his throat determined to set things right and to make them free.

"Davin!" Mina was watching terrified. She was holding onto another girl with tearful, big eyes. "Please don't…"

There were many things that Davin did that day that Mina wouldn't be proud of. She was too young to understand something like war. He was too young. But nevertheless, he did, and he would do her a kindness and spare her the loss of her innocence.

"Do you surrender?" he asked the guard while still holding the tip of the blade on his throat.

"Yes!" he yelled.

It surprised Davin how brave a man could be while with a weapon, and how worthless they could be without it. It surprised him even the more how his ability to see the next step toward victory had ceased with that man. Surely, he couldn't have been anyone important. "Can you give the word to make them all surrender?"

The man closed his eyes and swallowed hard. "Yes."

Davin didn't recognize the guard at all. They all worked and took shifts except for the ones higher up. He must have been in charge of them all. "Then do it." Davin sneered at the guard and got him on his feet. Davin wrapped his arm around the guard's chest and held the sword across his throat as he led him down toward the rest of the battle. "Order them to stop!"

He was the guard in charge of the facility that lost Davin and his people. If it were up to him, he wouldn't have tried to take any prisoners. He hated Davin and people like him, and he didn't know why. It was something that he had held onto before he even knew how to think for himself. He despised Davin most of all. Davin's power and influence was something that could not be tolerated. One day, an example would have to be made. He knew that it wouldn't be by himself, but there were people much crueler than him watching, waiting, and biding their time.

"Stand down," he told his men. "Everyone, stand down!"

The guards did as they were told. They dropped their weapons and fell on their knees with their hands in the air. Alm and the others were so stunned that they didn't know what to do. They all looked around at each other with smiles slowly starting to form on their faces until one by one, they laughed and cheered.

Davin was excited himself, but he couldn't let his ranks fall apart. "Raid their equipment." Davin pulled the sword away from his prisoner's neck and forced him onto his knees. "I'm sure they have lots of things for prisoners."

The remaining men did as instructed and went through some of the carts that the guards had brought. They had food and water for themselves and plenty of chains. Near the dawn, Davin ordered them to be tied up and or chained to the trees high in the forest where they were afraid to be.

One of the guards had even begun to cry and shake while Alm was chaining him up. "Please, don't leave us here. I beg of you!"

Alm looked away wide-eyed and embarrassed. "Is it really that dangerous here?" Alm asked Davin.

"Apparently." Davin was enjoying tightening the grip around the leader's body.

He gritted his teeth from the pain, but then he laughed at Davin. "You know nothing of this world, Boy."

Davin took offense every time he opened his mouth. "We're a part of this world."

"How long have you been underground, Davin? Seven years?"

Davin was surprised but covered it well with a smirk. "How do you know so much about me? I'm not anyone important to you all, and I wasn't a threat until the light fell."

"Yes, but the light did fall, and it did choose you." He laughed again. "But you're not the only one chosen, Davin, and the light isn't the only power in this world." Then he leaned in as close to Davin as his tight rope would allow, so he could speak most sinisterly to him. "Most importantly, you'll learn that you aren't that special after all."

There was a deep meaning behind everything that he spoke. They were answers that Davin would never receive—not when all of the guards knew that they were going to be left to fend for themselves in the forests where giants dwelled. It was meant to pester Davin and keep him up in the night thinking about what it all meant. Maybe it would. But for the meantime, there was too much victory for questions.

"I'm special enough." Davin playfully slapped the guard in his face and smiled triumphantly.

"Are you ready?" Alm asked.

Davin nodded and began to walk downhill with his men. The dawn had come, and their bodies were tired, but their spirits had never been stronger. Not long ago, Davin had been a prisoner seeing the sun for the first time in seven years. Now, he was free.

"Davin!" Mina had been waiting for him at the edge of the forest with the rest of their people. She ran into his arms, and he scooped her up for a hug. "You did it!"

Davin held her tight as he looked around. There were injured people and those he would miss that would never return. "You're free now," he whispered in her ear.

That would have to be enough.

"What are we going to do now?" someone asked.

Davin laughed bittersweet and sat Mina down. "You all can do as you like."

"What are you saying?" Alm asked sadly. "Are you saying that you're leaving us?"

Davin was incredibly sad, but he forced himself to grin. "I'm saying that I want you all to look after each other and live happy lives. Me," he shook his head, "I can't do that."

"Why?" someone else asked. "You deserve it just as much as the rest of us!"

"Even more!" Mina chirped.

"Maybe..." He really did want to be free and live with them. He could finally have a normal life. He remembered what that was like. He used to live with his mother, father, and brother. They lived comfortably and happily. If he could only find his family, perhaps he could salvage what he had lost. Maybe there was some good left within in the bad.

He was determined to find out one day. "But I've got to do something with this. There are other evil people and people who are oppressed just like us. If I have the power to do something about it, then I should. I have to!"

Alm remembered hating Davin so vividly. He was just a naive, skinny kid who got him into too much trouble. Alm never thought the day would come when he would hate to see Davin go. "Why?" he asked near tears.

"Because someone should," Davin said.

Alm wiped his eyes, and then crossed his arms stubbornly. He couldn't doubt Davin after all they had been through. "Then I'm coming with you."

"No." Davin spoke sternly. It was a command coming from a superior officer. Every single one of them would slow him down. He just didn't have the time to accommodate them.

But then, he spoke as a friend. "Stay with everyone. Take care of Mina and the other kids." Davin trusted Alm enough to do that. "Make sure they grow up happy."

Alm sighed and shook his head with a chuckle. Davin was just too unbelievable to be real. Yet, there he was. "Take care of yourself, Davin."

"You too." Davin smiled and patted Mina on the head. She pouted and hung her head down low, trying to hide her tearing eyes. "I'll see you again."

Mina sniffed and rubbed her eyes, but it didn't do anything to stop the overflow of emotion she felt. She felt like she didn't have a choice but to hold onto Davin and hug him as tightly as she could. Many of the other children began to follow her lead, and they hugged him. The remaining adults also expressed their gratitude by patting him on the shoulder or shaking his hands.

It was an unbelievable feeling for Davin. There was a time when he was singled out by everyone because of his faith in his dreams. He would have never imagined light falling from the sky and giving him an ability to save lives, yet that's what happened. As long as Davin continued to help those in need, he knew he'd be fulfilling his calling.

Davin finished his goodbyes and left with nothing back toward the place where they kept him and taught him how to be a slave, only he wasn't a slave or a prisoner. He was a young man on the path to a destiny bigger than what he could imagine. He only had one clear goal in mind.

To save people.

Chapter Nineteen

"It's been two weeks," Evva said to Riss in front of her cabin door. When she met Riss and Tice, she did her best to take care of them. She was a little hesitant to take in two more children, but she couldn't turn them away, especially not after she heard why they were alone. "She doesn't speak. She barely eats. She does nothing but lie in bed and cry all day. It's unhealthy."

"I'm not really sure what I'm supposed to do." Riss had to explain everything to Samara. They started from the beginning of when and why they left the orphanage; they explained the light, Sakai, Mal, and how they had been trying to get to Eastern Pearl ever since. Riss wasn't sure if Samara understood or forgave him for how Mal was turned into a monster. She didn't say much. She only cried.

Raymon wanted to return to his previous caretaker, King Valdor. Samara didn't have the heart to refuse him. Tice knew that it was possible that Sakai would come after them again, but she couldn't afford to be separated from Samara and Raymon. Riss also kept in mind Tice's mural. Samara had a power, and so did he and Tice. If they stayed together, then maybe they could solve the mystery.

As far as Samara's wellbeing, Riss figured that she had to be away from the grief. After all, the only way he felt better about his own parents was to not think of them at all. "Maybe everything will be better once we get her home."

"She was home, Riss," Evva said sadly. "That's what makes it so terrible."

Riss could relate. He did still like her, despite how she tried to kill him. Maybe he would open up to her one day about his parents if he really thought it would help. "I think she still needs some time."

Evva didn't know her uncle to be one for changing his plans, but Samara paid him a chest full of gold to take her to Cavastinova. Besides, it would do her uncle well to make some new business there. "What about you, Riss? What will you decide to do?"

It was something that Riss had been thinking about a lot, but he couldn't make a decision. "I have to talk to Tice about that."

Evva looked at him oddly. "You would just follow her like that? You would listen to these dreams?"

At the beginning of their journey, he didn't even really want Tice to speak of having dreams. He didn't take her serious most of the time, and times when he was selfish caused the most damage. He left her alone in the cave so he could be the hero, and he revealed his powers to Samara so he could impress her. "I'm the one who's been messing up everything."

He had made a lot of mistakes, and maybe he couldn't take back some of them, but it wasn't too late to learn and be better than what he was. "I owe it to her to listen. She's earned that right."

Samara lay on the bed while Tice brushed her hair. Tice tried speaking encouraging things about how life would get better, but Samara didn't respond. For that reason, Tice was going to try something different.

She was going to pretend like nothing was wrong. "You'll be back at your palace soon."

"It's not my palace." Samara wouldn't move when she spoke, and it would be with barely any strength, but at least it was something!

"Still. It must be nice to be a princess. I couldn't imagine all of the nice things you must have and all the wonderful dresses! It must be nice to look pretty."

Samara wiped her eyes and rolled around so she could look at Tice amazed. "Do you not think you're pretty?"

She shrugged her shoulders, but she knew the answer. "I don't think so."

Samara sat up and folded her legs. She wiped her eyes some more and fixed her hair. She knew she must have looked like a mess. "You haven't been blind forever."

She shook her head. "I know what I look like, unless I've changed." She had grown and become stronger, but she could still remember what she saw in her reflection. "I don't look like my brother. I don't look like anybody."

Samara smiled, trying to cheer her up. "You do look like your brother." She took Tice's hands and locked their fingers together. Then she pressed her forehead down and looked into Tice's eyes. "Even though you're the innocent one, I can see that schemer within you."

Tice giggled, feeling tickled from Samara's nose.

Samara began to play with Tice's long, white hair. She was interesting. Even her eyebrows and eyelashes were white. Her eyes didn't always look like crystals, but they were such a pretty color all on their own. "You're so beautiful, and you're a very sweet girl."

Samara struggled to keep her tears down on the inside of her. "I know I haven't been talking a whole lot, but I've been listening." She grabbed Tice's shoulders. "Thank you for being here with me, and thank you for stopping me from hurting your brother."

Tice chuckled. "You did hurt him."

Samara wiped her eyes again and sniffed. "You know what I mean."

Tice wished that she could have still seen Samara. She was very pretty when she saw her broken, but she wanted to see her for what she really looked like. "I don't think you would have done it."

"I'm not sure." When she thought about herself standing over Riss and trying to hurt him, she was disgusted with herself. "I was so angry because I didn't know if I could let myself be sad. If I grieve, then I have to move on eventually, and I don't know how to let go of my father."

Tice heard Samara's voice beginning to break up, so she reached out and rubbed her arm. "Maybe you don't have to. Maybe you can take him with you. You can remember him, and he can make you stronger." Tice didn't know why so many terrible things had to happen to her and her brother, but they learned to watch out for one another. She learned how to fight and the importance of believing in something more than herself. "Maybe everything happens for a reason—for better or worse."

Samara couldn't really be optimistic, but she didn't want to bring Tice down. Not everyone had to be sad just because she was. "I think the same thing goes with your eyes," Samara told her. "Everything happens for a reason. Maybe you need to love yourself on the inside until you realize that outside isn't so important."

Tice smiled hard as she heard the washroom door open. Raymon came in fully clean and ready for the day. She knew from the gentle footsteps that it was him, and she began to wonder if he thought she was beautiful. Raymon was happy to see his sister smiling, and he knew that Tice was to thank for it. When Samara saw Raymon looking at Tice and

Tice beginning to turn beet red, she quickly realized the way the two of them felt.

She spoke to Tice. "You are wrong though." Then she looked at Raymon. "Raymon, don't you think Tice is pretty?"

Raymon himself began to blush as he climbed up on the bed to sit next to his sister. "I think Tice is wonderful."

Tice hid her face in Samara's stomach. She felt so silly.

Samara thought they were both adorable and hugged them and kissed their foreheads. "I feel like you two are the only people I have in this entire world."

Riss overheard Samara as he opened the door to come in. "What about me?" he asked.

She smirked at him and held her head up a little higher. "What about you?"

He laughed to himself and walked over to her with a little swagger in his steps. "You could stop being so mean and apologize to me."

"Apologize for what?"

"For trying to kill me!" he yelled in disbelief.

She rolled her eyes. "Boys are such babies."

He plopped on the bed in front of her, and she gaffed at his rudeness. He thought her appall was humorous. "And princesses are apparently snobs."

Samara let go of Tice and Raymon and leaned in closer to Riss. There was something annoying and immature about him, but she didn't detest him anymore. She almost found him tolerable. "Well, since I actually paid my fare in gold, I only think it's fair that I'm treated with a bit more decency."

"Than me?" he harped.

She shrugged. "Sure."

Riss really did like Samara. She was beautiful, and she liked to joke around like he did. In a few short years, he could see himself married and living in a palace with many babies. If he only had the time to spend with her, he knew he could make her his. "Seriously, what are we doing when we get you to King Valdor?" he asked.

Samara was actually beginning to feel good, and he had to bring that up! She still wanted to avenge her father, but she didn't know where to start. They were getting farther away from Lord Rovin by the minute, and there was no way for her to find Sakai. To top off everything, the fire wielder who was truly responsible was Riss's friend, and he wasn't really himself.

Raymon looked at his sister lost in thought and couldn't stand it. He grabbed her and shook her lightly. "I want to stay."

"But we can't stay," Tice said sadly. "We have to find the boy from my dreams."

Raymon heard Tice tell him of the strong and handsome boy. He was intimidated just trying to imagine him. Raymon knew that he was a bit of a baby sometimes, but he was a prince. "Cavastinova is a beautiful place, Tice. You could live in the palace with us. You would like it."

Tice smiled at the thought of it. "I'm sure that I would, but we really can't!"

"We need to stay together," Riss insisted.

"Because of an image that just appeared one day?" Samara asked, mocking Riss. She believed in Tice, but there wasn't enough evidence to set her whole life on a wild journey!

Riss glared at Samara and returned the tone back to her. "No. It's because of the image that the blind girl made while she was unconscious."

Even Samara was speechless after that comment, and he smiled when he got to see the dumbfounded look on her face! Riss didn't care if no one else believed in Tice's dreams or the confirmations. He knew that they were real. "What color was the light that you saw?" he asked Samara.

She thought back to the day that Captain Saxson attacked her and her brother. She remembered hitting the water and thinking that her life would soon end. She also remembered the darkness of the water that surrounded her, and then there was a light. "I think it was kind of blue." She shook her head. "I can't really remember."

Riss could remember his light just fine. "Mine was red." Out of all of them, he probably liked his power the best. "What about you, Tice?"

Tice tried to think back, but the only thing she could remember was the brightness, and then she couldn't see at all. "I don't remember."

Riss sighed a little frustrated. "We fit into it." He was so convinced! There were seven colors, and all of them were the colors that would appear on a rainbow: red, orange, yellow, green, blue, indigo, and violet. "I'm not sure what we fit inside of, but we do. We just have to find the others."

The more they talked, the more Raymon's head began to sink into his shoulders. His sister was so powerful, Riss's fire was spectacular, and Tice...She was unique in a way he could never be. He was so inferior to all of them. How was he ever going to be king over his father's legacy? "I just want to go home." He held his sister and begged her. All he was good for were false hopes like lying at his mother's side and wishing for her to wake up. At least he could never disappoint her.

Samara had been harsh to her brother ever since their father's death. It was time for her to be a big sister and his friend. "I can't promise anything," she told Riss. "I need to take care of my brother, and he needs a place he can be safe."

That wasn't good enough for Riss! He pouted, glared, and pointed in her face. "Now listen up, Princess—"

Before he could speak, the ship began to toss and rumble. Samara held on tight to Raymon and Tice, but Riss fell backward off of the bed and on a trunk that sat in front of it.

"What is that?" Raymon asked afraid.

The ship continued to rumble, and they held themselves tighter as the room continued to shake. Picture frames and trinkets began to fall on the floors. The trunk that Riss was on began to slide as the ship began to tilt to the right. The slow tilt finished fast, and Samara, Tice, and Raymon were flung off of the bed and to the side wall. Samara took the brunt of it, but they were all hurt. Samara blinked and opened her eyes just in time to see their bed about to crash into them. She stretched out her hand on instinct, and the bed ceased to move. She breathed a sigh of relief once she remembered that she controlled great power.

"What do you think is happening?" Riss asked as he hit the wall while still on the trunk.

Tice felt a terrible chill on her skin and an aching inside of her stomach. "We're in trouble."

"It's got to be Captain Saxson," Samara said under her breath.

Raymon heard her, and his eyes grew wide with fear. "Captain Saxson?"

Tice shook her head. "It's much worse than that." She knew it had to be Sakai, but she wasn't afraid for herself. Tice knew that she was protected. Now all she had to do was protect her friends. "Go up on deck, Riss! They need your help. Samara, you need to go too."

Riss wasn't going to refuse her intuition, but he didn't want to leave her alone. "What about you?"

She reached out her hand. "Raymon will stay with me."

Raymon hesitated. He wanted to protect her, but he was afraid that he wasn't good enough. "You sure?"

"Raymon," Tice smiled with certainty, "take my hand."

He did as she instructed and held her hand. "I promise I'll protect you."

Riss turned to Samara. "We had better go up there." Riss took her hand and helped her on her feet. It was a bit difficult to keep their footing with the ship tossing back and forth, but they struggled through the door.

Once the door opened, it was all panic from there. Men were running everywhere to get up to the top of the deck. There was a bell that was sounding off and barking that everyone recognized as Captain Mayes. It was a madhouse. Riss could actually see fear in the eyes of all of those burly men.

As they came up on deck, one of the crewmen came running past them with Evva unconscious in his arms.

"Hurry up! Get her help!" Captain Mayes shouted.

Samara ran to his side. "What happened to Evva?"

"She slipped." Captain Mayes was distraught, but he continued to push through it the best way he knew how. "You go attend to her! The deck is no place for little women during a situation like this."

Samara narrowed her eyes at him. "This little woman is about to save your life." She pushed past him and walked to the front of the ship to get a better look. Everything was odd. She couldn't see the seas in front of her, and the wind blew too fiercely for such a cloudless sky. When she got to the front and peered over the edge, she realized they were being suspended far up into the air on a pillar of water while the rest of the sea lay far below them. The culprits were on their ship down below.

Many of the crewmen were on the sides of the ship marveling at their unique situation. There were plenty of men that were afraid, but Riss stayed steady when he came to stand next to Samara. "I can't let these people die because of me."

"Because of you?" she asked confused. "Captain Saxson is after me."

"Get back!" Captain Mayes grabbed Samara and Riss and pulled them away from the edge of the ship. Water rose like a powerful geyser and overflowed onto the deck to carry Captain Saxson on board. He wasn't nearly as big as Samara remembered. She wasn't afraid, but Captain Mayes pushed her and Riss behind him. Captain Mayes had fought many pirates in his day, and he wouldn't be intimidated by trickery. "What is the meaning of this?" he howled.

"You are Captain Mayes?" he asked with a smug smirk. "I assume you know who I am."

"It would seem that my reputation precedes me, but only your arrogance precedes you."

Captain Saxson snarled at Captain Mayes. The only reason why he didn't draw his sword was because he saw Samara hiding behind Mayes. He smiled pleasantly when he recalled what he had done to her. "She knows who I am."

Samara stepped away from her protection and approached him with absolutely no fear. "Captain Saxson, a wretched scum and The Pirate King of Cowards!"

Captain Saxson lost his good mood with her insult. "I never suspected that you would be alive."

"I'm not as weak as you thought."

"So I've heard." He really did think that she would have been an interesting addition to his crew. He recognized the killer instinct within her that wasn't quite there before.

"What do you want?" Captain Mayes asked.

Captain Saxson looked around at the crew prepared and ready to fight with their swords pointed in his direction. They were rattled by the waterworks, but they didn't fear just a man. He was still confident though. "Four children and I think you know which four."

"Out of the question!"

He smirked. He was so looking forward to that response! "Then I'll destroy your entire crew and ship."

"You didn't spare my crew, did you?" Samara asked. "Where are they now?"

He nodded to her in respect of her lack of naivety. "Clever girl." He never had any intention on sparing anyone that he took as his prisoner. "I suppose I'll dispense with the false hopes and get right to the killing."

Captain Saxson lifted his hands and the water that had brought him on deck jumped up and began to surround everyone's face except for his own. They all forgot that they were fighters for a brief moment while they all panicked from the lack of air. Some of the men did begin to charge at Captain Saxson in a desperate attempt to stop him, but he fought well while they quickly exasperated themselves. Captain Mayes tried to push the water away from his face, but it swished around continuously and still deprived him of any air. Samara was afraid and couldn't concentrate. She didn't want to die! However, Riss's first instinct was to fight and to burn. The water bubbled around his face and boiled until it evaporated.

Captain Saxson questioned Riss's astonishing escape, but he didn't have to wonder for long though. Riss outstretched his hand toward Saxon and flames shot out at him. "Stop it!" Riss yelled.

Captain Saxson dodged Riss's flame just enough to miss his face. The flames hit his chest, but he was always calm and in control of his water manipulation. He put the fire out in seconds.

Samara saw Riss and remembered what she could do. She concentrated and created a shield around her face and expanded it until the water exploded away. She dropped to her knees coughing but relieved. "You can't fight us like a normal pirate? You've only got your tricks?"

Riss concentrated fire in his hands. He had never tried to do something that big, but he needed to try. With everything that he had, he stretched his hands forward and pushed all the fire he could muster out in a stream of powerful flames. "Real men have pride!"

"What would a boy like you know of pride?" Captain Saxson called upon the water to aid him. He was of the sea. He sailed upon its graceful wonders since he was a lad. No one understood its power as much as he. Riss was boiling his water where they met each other. It was steaming, and the heat was almost too much for Captain Saxson or the surrounding crewman to stand. He would only have to hold his ground for a little longer. Riss's flames were dying out fast.

Samara wanted to help the other crewmen, but she didn't have full control over her powers. She might have hurt someone if she freed them the same way she did for herself. She had to defeat Captain Saxson somehow! She took her time and caught her breath as she concentrated. When she was ready, she yelled before she pushed him with her shield as hard as she could. "He's twice the man you'll ever be!"

Captain Saxson flew up into the air and was far away from the ship before he had much time to think. The water fell from the crewmen's faces, and they all caught their breath. Samara was highly satisfied to see Captain Saxson flung up into the air, but she expected consequences for her actions. But if the pillar of water could still hold them up while Captain Saxon fell into the water, then that meant he had more control over the water than what she thought.

"Riss!" she yelled. "Get up!" He was on his hands and knees looking flushed, but Samara didn't have time for his weakness. "Get up now!" She grabbed him and forced him to run with her.

"What are you doing?" he asked worriedly.

"Use your abilities."

His eyes bucked as he realized they were heading toward the front of the ship at top speed. "For what?"

"Just do it!" She used her power and forced her shield under their feet. The two of them went flying into the air, and Riss began to scream from being flung out to the mercy of the sea by a crazy woman. She was irritated by the sudden ache in her ear, but she couldn't be concerned with that. "Now!"

Riss stretched out his hand and closed his eyes. He created as much fire he could muster up, but he was certain he was going to die.

"Open your eyes and aim for the boat!"

He was much too afraid to argue. He opened his eyes and saw the ship under him. Why she wanted to land on Captain Saxson's ship was beyond him, but he sure didn't want to land in the water. He pushed out his fire harder until it pushed them over toward the ship. The feeling was so insane—spectacular! For a second, it almost felt like he was flying.

But for the second after, he was overcome with the fear of breaking every bone in his body from landing on the deck of the ship and then having pirates eating the rest of him for lunch. "Ahhhh!"

Samara stretched her hand out in front of her and concentrated. She had been using such brute force, but her shields were mainly to protect her. She could control them, and she knew everything would be alright.

Riss closed his eyes when he realized which spot of wood he was going to crack his skull open on. When he landed he yelled again, bounced, and then fell on the deck.

Samara had let go of Riss, and she bounced gently and landed on her feet. Her shield had acted like a soft, rubber ball.

Riss was grateful to be alive, but they had a new problem. Captain Saxson's crew was on deck with their swords pointed at them. "Any bright ideas?"

She smiled. "Always." The men came at them with their swords, but they couldn't get close to the children. Their swords snapped against the might of Samara's invisible shield.

263

The men kicked, punched, and pushed on the shield to break through. The more they failed, the more frustrated they became. They beat with their fists and with whatever weapons they could find. Samara was cocky at first, but it slowly began to give her a headache.

"How long can you keep this up?" Riss asked.

She grunted as she felt it in her head each time they pounded. "Not all day." She didn't realize how tired she was before.

Riss prepared flames in the palms of his hand just in case she failed. "We're a team. We'll make it out of this alright."

"I know we will because I've got a plan."

The water began to shake and bubble something fierce, and everyone stopped pounding on the shield. All of the men began to laugh cruelly, imagining what sort of terrible things their commander would do. Captain Saxson burst through the waters like a great whale. He truly was the master of water. He took out the water from his hair and clothes until he was dry, and then he walked on a path of water to his own ship. He was furious in his eyes, yet his face looked so calm. His men stepped aside for him to walk toward the children. They knew better than to stand in the way of his wrath.

"You..." he was seething mad. "You dare raise your hand against me knowing that I hold your ship in my hands?"

Riss's eyes bucked as he remembered Tice and Raymon aboard the ship. If Captain Saxson willed it so, they would drown, and he was too far away to make a difference.

"And you dare speak to me with no respect when I hold your ship in mine!" Samara said.

There was a silence that overcame them all. Captain Saxson looked into her serious little eyes, and he knew she believed every word that she said. But the silence didn't last long, because he and his men busted out into roaring laughter.

264

Samara ate it all up, because her victory was going to taste absolutely delicious. "I meant what I said."

"Please!" He couldn't even glare at the children anymore. "Your friend's pathetic fire can't do anything to me."

Little did they know, Samara had lowered her shield. She wasn't sure how to make more than one, and she needed it to be powerful. "He's not the threat."

The crew ducked at the sound of the sudden explosion and splinters flying everywhere. Captain Saxson didn't know where it was coming from until his mainmast fell and crashed into the foremast, destroying them both. There were men who did not move out of the way fast enough and fell to the ground injured, and some were even trapped. Captain Saxson didn't even care about them though. He was angry about his ship. "How did you...?" He moved to grab her, but his body ran into a force that stopped him.

Samara smirked. She wanted Captain Saxson to know that she had done it. "Lower my ship safely or suffer the consequences."

He was so furious that his head felt like it was bound to explode. "I would rather die!"

"Than not have a ship?" she chuckled. "That doesn't make you much of a pirate, now does it? And it certainly would disqualify you as a captain."

"I can survive on these waters on my own!" He was more than confident about that.

"Then I suppose you plan on making your men fend for themselves. Even if you carry them around in the water and you attack whomever you wish, it'll be your power and not theirs." She looked around at the crew looking at her and Captain Saxson. They were thinking very carefully. "Then you'll realize that you don't need each other. Then they'll have to rebel because if there's no need for them, they can't expect

265

that you would be loyal to them. They either leave, or you destroy each other."

She smirked mischievously. "Admit it, Captain. The only thing that holds you all together is this ship. It's your home. You don't want to see it destroyed."

Captain Saxson despised her. He knew that she was mocking and provoking him while keeping herself untouchable. The only thing that would appease him was crushing her friends in that ship, but he couldn't! "Fine," he said quietly. "You have a deal."

Riss watched amazed as their ship was slowly being lowered back to sea level. Captain Saxson had so much control that he barely looked at it. The boat waved in the water when it landed, but Riss had been through rougher waters in storms. "Oh boy…" He really couldn't compare to his power, and he doubted that Samara could either.

She smiled full and triumphantly. "We'll be leaving now in your long boat."

She didn't wait for Captain Saxson to give the order. She grabbed Riss's arms and began walking over toward the boat, and that infuriated him all the more. "Are you mad?" he screamed.

She stopped and turned around—never losing her composure. "No. I'm in control."

Captain Saxson was red in the face from all of his rage. He would destroy them if it was the last thing he did. "Get them off my ship!" he yelled to his crew.

His men stared at their captain with disbelief. He had never bent to the will of any man in authority, and now he answered to the will of a little girl? That wasn't the man they all swore to follow. However, they all moved quickly to aid Samara and Riss into the boat and lowered them down safely into the water.

Captain Saxson took his position at the helm and waited anxiously for Samara and Riss to arrive safely on their ship. He was tapping himself and gritting his teeth from holding in all of his rage.

Riss was the only one rowing while they both were on their way back to the ship. Samara was leaning back with a prideful smile smothering her face. It was obvious that she had no regret, but Riss was still shaken. "That was real bold of you, Princess. I've got to say, I find you a little insane."

She laughed. "Why?"

"Testing Captain Saxson's patience like that...? He could have killed everyone on our ship!" The more he thought about it, the angrier he became. He would have never jeopardized Tice's life like that!

Samara rolled her eyes. "Don't be such a simpleton. What I said was true. He'd lose everything if he lost that ship." Samara turned around and looked at the men watching them. They were waiting for them to arrive back on their ship. Even though Samara could destroy their ship, she suspected threats wouldn't rest Captain Saxson's hatred. She didn't understand evil men like him that would want to hurt for no reason, but she did understand hate. It could be a powerful weapon and highly seductive. She knew it well because she hated someone. And until she could release that hatred on who rightly deserved it, she was going to settle for the next best thing.

Samara closed her eyes and concentrated. It wasn't really that hard.

Riss knew something bad was about to happen, but he couldn't predict what he saw. Captain Saxson's ship exploded, and it was without fire or storm. It was fine, and then within the time it took for him to blink, men were flying into the sky and sea. Wood was splattering everywhere. It was terrible, and so was Samara's power. "What did you do that for?" he yelled.

She opened her eyes and looked at Riss like he was a fool. "He tried to drown my brother and me for no good reason!"

"He's going to get us!"

She actually laughed loud and hard while shaking her head and pointing at Riss. "Wow. Cute and stupid." She calmed down and spoke with sarcasm. "You're quite the catch."

"This isn't funny!" he yelled.

She knew that it really wasn't, but he had it coming! "He was always going to get us, Riss. He was probably waiting for us to get back on the ship." Captain Saxson acknowledged that Samara wasn't naive. He should have predicted that she would figure him out.

Riss hadn't even realized that, but he was beginning to think there was no way for him to protect his sister. "And what will he do now that you've taken the one thing in the world that he loves?"

The answer she knew for Captain Saxson was the same she held for Lord Rovin. "He won't stop until he destroys us."

Riss hesitated before asking, "And what will we do to stop him?"

She looked into Riss's eyes and answered truly. "Destroy him first."

Chapter Twenty

Tice was still holding on tight to Raymon. She wasn't nearly as frightened as she was appearing to be, but she didn't want him to be the only one afraid. She knew what it felt like to be like him—thinking that he had no value. Tice found out differently, and so would he. In the meantime, it was good for him to play hero.

Raymon had moved Tice into the bathroom. The tub was bolted down to the floor, so it was one of the safest places. He wasn't sure what he would do if he saw a pirate, but he wasn't going to let Tice go. "I'm sure everything will be fine soon."

Tice held Raymon tighter and rested her head on his chest. She closed her eyes and listened to the rhythm. She knew that Raymon's voice shook when he meant to say something profound and that he couldn't articulate well. He had faults, but she knew that he would be a good leader one day. She wasn't sure if she was having one of her feelings about him, but his heart was so strong. That had to count for something.

Even though her world was dangerous, and it was very possible that she could die, Tice was at such peace with Raymon. Maybe she was too small for such a thing as love, but she was wise enough to know that it was something.

She opened her eyes to stare at him. Unfortunately, she still couldn't see anything. But there was something unusual that did begin to bother Tice. The familiar chill began to whirl through her body as a terrible hiss began to slither inside her ear.

"Samara!" Tice jumped on her feet startled.

"Is something wrong?" Raymon asked her worriedly.

Tice knew she hadn't fallen asleep, but she swore that she saw Samara. She was sweating, pale, and she looked like she was about to collapse. "You have to go to her! If you don't, she'll die."

Raymon stood to his feet and grabbed Tice panicked. "How do you know that?"

"I just do, and you have to trust me!"

He couldn't doubt her after getting to know her. But he swore he wouldn't leave her side. "What about you?" he asked.

Tice knew that she would be in terrible danger, but she couldn't breathe a word of that to him or else he would never leave her alone. "I'll be fine. I promise."

He hurried out of the tub and headed for the door. But before he placed his hand on the knob, he slowly turned around to ask meekly, "What can I do to save her?"

Tice shrugged her shoulders. "Try."

Captain Mayes himself aided Samara and Riss back onto the ship. He didn't know what sort of trouble he had taken on for having those children there, but after what he saw, they might have had a fighting chance to survive. "You destroyed their boat?" he asked Samara.

Samara had a smug smile on her face. "I did."

She was so demanding when he first met her, but she had been a mess ever since she arrived on his ship. It was unbelievable to Captain Mayes that Samara could be that powerful. "And now he's gone?"

"Stalled at best," she said.

Riss sighed, feeling like the only sane person left in the world. "What are your orders, Captain?"

Captain Mayes had never before felt helpless, but how were men supposed to compete with monsters? "How am I supposed to fight a man who can control the seas themselves?"

"You're not fighting a man," she said bitterly. "You're fighting an immature, spoiled, brat! He'll challenge me for making him look like a fool."

He laughed and asked her mockingly, "And will you win?"

She held her head up high. "As long as my body can hold up with my will."

"And what if it can't?" he asked.

Samara tried not to think about what that would mean. However, she reached out her hand toward the Captain. "Then it's been a pleasure."

Captain Mayes didn't want it to be the end, especially not for an odd group of kids. But he had no regrets. "It's been my honor, Princess Samara." He took her hand and shook it as if she were a proud member of his crew, instead of a little girl.

Riss shook his head while he watched the two of them give their goodbyes like it was all over. He couldn't accept that. "You can't fight him!" He grabbed onto Samara's shoulders desperately. "We have to run."

Samara put on a brave smile. "Run where? Even if we found land, he might be able to create a hurricane." But the smile began to fade. She was overcome with a fear of death. "There's nothing we can do."

"Maybe I can distract him while you guys escape."

Samara frowned when she heard his noble plea. All of her guilt overcame her, and she rushed toward him for a hug. "I'm sorry for trying to kill you, Riss." She was near tears, but she held them back. "You're a good guy."

Riss was too stunned to move at first. After all, she did detest him not too long ago. But even though she was tricked, she wasn't completely misled. "I'm sorry about Mal." He wrapped his arms around her. He really just wanted to protect her, but she was the most powerful one of them all. There wasn't much he could do.

Riss pulled away and looked into her fearful and tearing eyes, but he managed to smile small. "It's better to die with a smile," he told her. "At least people will know you lived a good life."

"Or died a brave fool." She didn't feel like smiling, but she did for him.

"No one's going to die today." Riss and Samara turned around to see Raymon coming up on deck, and the two of them became angry and frightened.

Riss even began to yell at him. "What are you doing here? Why aren't you with Tice?"

Raymon was timid as he continued to approach them. "She said I had to be here…To save Samara."

"Save me?" Samara was confused. She knew Raymon better than anyone, and he was a bit of a coward and weak. She didn't blame him. He was only a boy. "Please, go stay with Tice."

He pouted with his mouth full of defeat, but he shook his head. He didn't believe he was anything special, but he wasn't going to let Samara get hurt.

When he refused to budge, she pointed her finger in his face and yelled. "I mean it!"

Riss got in between the two of them and pushed her away. "If Tice says something, it's usually true."

She glared at him and prepared to yell, but the waters began to shake and rock the ship. Raymon lost his balance and fell off of his feet. The waters were dangerous, but how could he save her? "We'll find out soon enough," she told Riss.

Out of the waters, Captain Saxson rose. He stood upon a giant wave clenching his fingers so tight that he didn't know if he'd be able to ever outstretch them again. The rage was evident on his face—like a dog gone rabid. The seas were his alone to control. He would not be mocked by a child! "Girl! You think you can defeat me? You're at my mercy!"

Samara had never been so afraid before. Her body was sore. Her mind felt strained. She had never pushed herself that hard before, and her brother was right in harm's way. His might surrounded them all. Even if she could protect them from above, the water below could shred the ship into splinters. Even if she created a shield around the entire ship, he could toss the entire sea on top of them and roll them around like a bag full of marbles. Everyone must have seen how they were doomed.

Riss stepped in front of Samara and yelled out at the Captain in a cocky voice. "You're just jealous because you can't break through her shield!"

Samara bucked her eyes. She thought that surely he had gone mad! But then, she saw the look of mischief in his eyes. He was being a scoundrel alright! "Of course you're jealous!" she yelled. "You may destroy me, but it will only be because we're out here in the water. But you could never win in a fair fight. I may be a little girl, but you're nothing but a coward!"

"Real captains have pride!" Captain Mayes yelled. His crew cheered in a roar of agreement. They all knew what Samara and Riss were doing.

Everyone caught on except for Captain Saxson. "We'll see about that!"

Samara raised her arms as Captain Saxson raised his. In a mighty clash, his wave began to create powerful streams of water that shot out at Samara like a cannon. They were fast and strong, but Samara had already placed her shield up. She could feel pressure in her head. She knew that she couldn't last for very long.

The crew gazed above them in wonder. It was as if they were in a glass dome being drenched in rain. They knew that their very lives depended on nothing they could see, and it was surprisingly spectacular!

Samara dropped to her knees, and her arms began to shake. She yelled out in pain as her headache became stronger. She could barely look up at Captain Saxson, who was laughing malevolently. The pressure was far too much!

"Samara!" Raymon ran behind his sister and hugged her back. He might not have been anything special, but no one knew how strong Samara really was. Samara was the only one who took care of him. If not for her strength, he wouldn't be anyone. "You can do this!" he yelled.

Samara opened her eyes and felt a burst inside of her. The pressure began to lift off of her head, and she felt her shield increase without even trying. She slowly stood up on her feet with her brother holding onto her. She could barely make out Captain Saxson because of the water disrupting her vision, but she could visualize him being gone. She knew that she could somehow defeat him!

"What is this?" Captain Saxon felt her shield was becoming stronger by the second. He could not afford to lose to a child. His pride and his sanity were on the line. "You will not win, Girl!"

Riss and the rest of the crew had begun to shout out cheers for Samara. It was all they could do, and it seemed to be helping. "I believe in you!" Riss shouted. He encouraged her faithfully until he looked out into the sea at the waters rising up in a swirling cyclone.

Tice was spread out in the tub. The boat was rocking so much that she was at risk of flying across the tub and hitting her head if she weren't careful. The fight did not seem to be in their favor, but Tice had a terrible feeling that was much more powerful than her fear of drowning.

"Ticesssssssssssssssss!"

She could hear Sakai's familiar slick tongue faintly in her ear. She would arrive soon, if she weren't there already. Tice couldn't feel the presence of the mysterious man who had saved her. Samara and Riss were busy fighting with Captain Saxson. There was no one left to fight except for her.

Yet she was not afraid.

"Ticessssssssssssssssss!"

She got on her feet and climbed out of the tub. If she was going to die, she wasn't going to do it in there. The ship rocked as soon as she got out, and Tice nearly fell. But she had to keep moving.

She tried to be careful as she walked, but she slipped around the wet floor that continuously swayed back from side to side. But still, she managed to find the door leading back into her cabin and the door leading out into the hall. She didn't have much of a plan. She just needed to move.

She recognized the number of steps she would have to take to get to the stairs leading up to the deck, but that's not where she went. She felt the same thing that led her to the antidote to save her brother. She didn't think anything about where she was going or why she was even moving. She just continued to move until she entered through a door.

The room reeked of rum, and the floors were covered with soggy grain. Tice hated the feeling of it squishing between her toes, but she felt comfortable in that room. She deduced that it was the storage room, and she knew there was no point in running any further.

One at a time, the cheers began to dim, and their enthusiastic flying arms lowered to their sides. Riss didn't want to lose faith in Samara, but staring death in the face was powerful enough to make him lose faith in everything.

Samara saw the cyclone, but she found it impossible to be afraid. She knew she could somehow win. It was as if Raymon were making her more confident. Even though he was shaking, she felt stronger with him simply being by her side.

"Say goodbye!" Captain Saxson sent the whipping cyclone for the boat. It pounded away at Samara's shield. The waters tossed the ship about from side-to-side. Many of the crewmen fell and flew from the force. Raymon fell on his feet, and Samara fell back to her knees.

"Samara!" Raymon got on his feet as quickly as he could to hold his sister. Her eyelids were flickering, and her arms were shaking. She couldn't withstand another attack, not even if they could both still believe.

Tice must have been wrong! There was nothing that he could do to change his sister's terrible fate that would be the same as his and everyone else on that ship. He held on tight to his sister and screamed. "Please! Just go away!"

Then, the waters swayed the ship back and forth until they were calm. The constant screams of men and elements were transformed into complete silence. Everything was still.

Raymon slowly opened his eyes. Captain Saxson was still on his wave of water, but he was looking at them all oddly.

It was just like when Lord Rovin had attacked him and Samara. She was going to lose, until he yelled for Lord Rovin to leave them alone. He immediately stopped his attack and left without any sort of explanation.

Riss couldn't believe it. Raymon also had an ability! "What are you doing?" he yelled. "Tell him something else!"

Raymon was still stunned. It was so difficult to think at all! Samara would probably want him to say something that would keep Captain Saxson from ever bothering them again.

He stuck his head up and puffed his chest out, just as he did the first day when he faced Captain Saxson. He was still afraid, he was still small, and it would take some more time before he would be strong, but he could do anything because everyone was depending on him. "I order you to leave! Never sail the seas again and never seek us out. Ever!"

Captain Saxson glared at Raymon. He appeared to be fighting it. Every part of his being didn't want to do what Raymon was commanding, but he couldn't stop himself! He was quickly losing his desire to destroy Samara and her friends. He was losing his passion for the sea, yet he knew that he loved it. It didn't make any sense, yet the command rang within him until it was his own.

He fell within the water, and he and his wave rejoined the rest of the sea. The crew ran to the edge to see Captain Saxson, but he was deep within the waters and did not return.

Samara lowered her arms and collapsed. Her eyes were so heavy, and her head was throbbing.

"Samara!" Riss ran to her side held her in his arms. She was an insane mess alright, but he couldn't imagine what tomorrow would be like without her.

"I'm fine!" She flinched from the extra noise coming from her mouth and held onto Riss. When she realized how close she was to him, she slowly looked up into his eyes.

He had begun to smirk the moment she grabbed him. "You did well, Princess."

She smiled herself. "And you follow my instructions well."

Raymon laughed at the two of them. He was very tired and wanted to sleep, but he was too excited to do it. He had actually done something to save everyone! He was honestly a hero.

Captain Mayes and the crew came to surround the three of them. They were all amazed, but all of them were most amazed with young Raymon. "Prince Raymon," Captain Mayes said, "what did you do?"

They all knew what he had done. They simply didn't know how he ever managed to accomplish such a thing. "I'm not sure."

But Riss could. "That would make four of us."

"Ticessssssssssssssss!"

Tice could feel her voice on the back of her neck. Tice was a little startled, but she maintained focused. Tice slowly turned around, but she didn't sense that Sakai was still behind her.

Sakai had indeed entered the room. She was beginning to bite her nail out of excitement. Tice was finally alone. Her friends, family, or the strange man who had saved her from Sakai's last attack was finally out of the way. "I'm right here," she mocked as she circled Tice from a distance. "You're all alone and no one can save you."

Sakai enjoyed stalking her prey. Tice was so small and meek like a little, white mouse. Tice had zipped about and hid in corners long enough. She couldn't outrun Sakai forever. The chase had made Sakai quite hungry. She licked her lips at the thought of ending her insignificant life. "Poor, poor girl."

Tice tried to follow her voice, but she moved around so much that Sakai's laughter was everywhere. "I will defend myself!" She opened her eyes, still holding onto a dream of seeing.

Sakai laughed louder as she leaned in closer to Tice. "Such a foolish girl!" Her light footsteps never made a sound. Tice probably felt surrounded and desperate. It was so delicious when Sakai thought of all Tice's fear. "It must be so terrible to be in this much danger, and you can't even see me."

Sakai reached out to stroke Tice's white hair before she ripped it out. But before she could touch a single hair on Tice's head, Tice reached up and grabbed her hand. Sakai looked at the girl shocked. They were staring directly into each other's eyes.

"I can see you," Tice said, "and I see you for what you truly are."

Sakai was furious. She was a far bigger problem than she ever could have anticipated. But it was no matter. "Really?" Sakai smirked and backed away confidently swaggering until she had enough space. "Then I suppose there's no point in hiding it any longer."

Sakai's smirk began to grow into a full, wide smile. Her tongue slithered out long and thin. Her skin began to change from smooth and pale to green scales. Then, her eyes grew large as her body did as well.

But Tice could see it all very clearly before the transformation. She could see Sakai great, huge, and vicious. She stepped away on instinct, but she was not afraid. Sakai hissed, but Tice was not going to run. She stood there bravely as Sakai leaped forward, prepared to swallow her whole.

About the Author

Christina L. Barr has been a serious composer as far back as twelve years old. As a daughter of an evangelist, Christina has had the opportunity to sing her songs around the world to thousands of people.

Christina graduated from Holly High School number nine in her class and attended College for Creative Studies. Her talents as a film maker increased and she used her skills for television production, started a popular website called *The Gorgeous Geeks* with her sisters, and was even featured on *Times Magazine*'s website for some of her work.

Christina's true passion for writing emerged when she was eighteen and she started on her first novel. *Almost Alive* was the eighth book that Christina completed, but the third to be published. Her other published titles are *Superkid*, *Sunrise Sunset*, and *The Light Book: The Awakening*.

Some of her personal goals are to complete thirty novels by the time she herself is that age, to see her books translated into film, to one day win *The Celebrity Apprentice*, and to be like one of her idols—Stan Lee—and create many iconic characters that span generation after generation through multiple franchises.

Enjoy these other titles from

Made in the USA
San Bernardino, CA
11 March 2014